D0467337

BROKEN PIECES

Also by Carla Cassidy

Promise Him Anything
The Perfect Family
Are You Afraid?
Without a Sound
Paint It Red
Every Move You Make

BROKEN PIECES

Carla Cassidy

A SIGNET ECLIPSE BOOK

SIGNET ECLIPSE
Published by New American Library, a division of
Penguin Group (USA) Inc., 375 Hudson Street,
New York, New York 10014, USA
Penguin Group (Canada), 90 Eglinton Avenue East, Suite 700, Toronto,
Ontario M4P 2Y3, Canada (a division of Pearson Penguin Canada Inc.)
Penguin Books Ltd., 80 Strand, London WC2R 0RL, England
Penguin Ireland, 25 St. Stephen's Green, Dublin 2,
Ireland (a division of Penguin Books Ltd.)
Penguin Group (Australia), 250 Camberwell Road, Camberwell, Victoria 3124,
Australia (a division of Pearson Australia Group Pty. Ltd.)
Penguin Books India Pvt. Ltd., 11 Community Centre, Panchsheel Park,
New Delhi - 110 017, India
Penguin Group (NZ), 67 Apollo Drive, Rosedale, North Shore 0632,
New Zealand (a division of Pearson New Zealand Ltd.)
Penguin Books (South Africa) (Pty.) Ltd., 24 Sturdee Avenue,
Rosebank, Johannesburg 2196, South Africa

Penguin Books Ltd., Registered Offices:
80 Strand, London WC2R 0RL, England

First published by Signet Eclipse, an imprint of New American Library,
a division of Penguin Group (USA) Inc.

ISBN-13: 978-1-60751-086-4

Prologue

He loved her. Mariah Sayers hugged the knowledge close to her heart as she hurried home through the darkness of the night.

She'd taken a big chance sneaking out of her bedroom window to meet Clay, but that afternoon at school he'd told her it was important, so she'd agreed to meet him in the gazebo in the town square.

She'd been secretly dating Clay Matheson for the last three months, and tonight he'd told her he was in love with her and that as soon as they both turned eighteen, they'd get married.

Dancing through the dewy grass, she felt her heart was so full it might explode. She'd never known this kind of happiness before. Never in her whole miserable life.

Some of her euphoria waned as the Sayers house came into view. A two-story farmhouse, it sat on four wooded acres. Even through the trees, Mariah could see that the light in her father's study was lit.

If he knew she'd sneaked out, he'd be waiting to deliver his brand of punishment. The backs of her thighs burned at the thought of the thick willow switch he kept in an umbrella stand next to the front door.

"Spare the rod and spoil the child," Reverend Jed Sayers would shout as the willow switch whistled through the air with enough force to draw blood.

Maybe he's just working on Sunday's sermon, she thought as she slowed her pace. Please don't let him be waiting for me.

If he caught her coming back in through the window, he'd just assume she'd been up to no good. He wouldn't believe she was still a virgin, that she and Clay had agreed to wait until their wedding night. Her father always thought the worst of her, expected her to be sinful and bad.

She paused beneath an old oak tree, waiting just another minute or two so she could savor the feeling of loving and being loved. In the distance lightning flashed, followed by a low rumble of thunder. The air smelled of the approaching spring storm and she hoped her father went to bed before it started to rain.

An unexpected gust of wind rustled through the trees and sent a shiver dancing along her bare arms. She hated storms. A sigh of relief escaped her as she saw her father's light go off. He would never have turned it off if he knew she wasn't in the house.

She'd give it a couple of minutes; then she'd crawl back up the tree and into the window she'd left by, and nobody would be the wiser.

Thunder crashed again and a rustling noise sounded from behind her, but before she could turn to see what it was, something dark was yanked over her head and she was shoved off her feet.

She hit the ground on her back, the air whooshing out of her lungs. "If you scream, I'll kill you," a deep guttural voice whispered through the bag that covered her head.

Her breath returned with a sob of terror. "Don't move," the voice whispered as her assailant grabbed her wrists and bound them together.

Oh God, what was happening? What did he want? She didn't want to die. A scream clawed up the back of her throat, but she clamped her mouth closed, afraid to release it.

If she screamed, her father might hear. If she screamed, the man who lay on top of her would kill her. Someplace in the back of her mind beyond the terror, she wasn't sure which would be worse.

She heard the faint whisper of a zipper and then she knew. Her blood chilled as he shoved his hand up beneath her skirt and touched her on her panties, where nobody had ever touched her before.

He growled like an animal and ripped down her panties. The scream she'd swallowed seconds before rose up once again and released itself, a muffled cry that nobody could hear above the booming thunder and screeching wind.

He took her then, savagely, brutally, and as he did, she found a place in her mind to hide, a place she'd been before when the switch whistled in the air above her father's head.

It wasn't until he was finished with her that her terror returned. She heard the zip of his pants and waited for death.

"I broke you," he whispered, "and now I have a piece of you that belongs to me forever."

And then he was gone.

Chapter 1

She'd expected ghosts. She'd anticipated dark memories and the faint stir of remembered terror. What Mariah Sayers didn't expect was the odd sense of homecoming that swept over her when she saw the sign that read PLAINS POINT, MISSOURI—10 MILES.

She'd sworn she'd never come back here. When she'd left sixteen years before, she'd made herself that promise. But, as in all things, *never* was never for certain.

"Hey." She reached out and nudged the sleeping teenager in the passenger seat. "Better sit up and wipe the sleep from your eyes. We're almost there."

Kelsey uttered a groan without opening her eyes. She was never particularly pleasant when first waking. "I can't believe you dragged me out here," she complained. "This is probably going to be the worst summer of my life." She finally opened her eyes and stretched her arms overhead, her T-shirt riding up to expose her slim, tanned stomach.

"I'm sure you're right," Mariah replied. "This will be the worst summer of your life and it will forever scar you. After this, whenever you approach a small town, you'll break out into hives and have horrible nightmares."

Kelsey gave an unladylike snort. "Nightmares are your deal, Mom, not mine."

Mariah didn't reply. Her daughter was right. Mariah had suffered from nightmares for far too many years of her life. She hoped this trip would offer some closure with a past that had haunted her for too long.

Kelsey reached out and punched on the radio, hitting the button to seek a station. Another groan escaped her as the first two that tuned in offered rousing country-and-western music.

"And hell is waiting for the sinners of this earth," a deep voice boomed from the radio.

"Turn it off," Mariah said, an icy chill washing through her.

There must have been something in her voice that made her daughter instantly comply. She hit the off button and that deep voice was silenced.

"Is that what he sounded like?" Kelsey asked.

Mariah nodded and loosened her grip on the steering wheel. "There was nothing my father loved more than preaching about damnation, unless it was hitting me with that willow switch."

"I'm glad he's dead," Kelsey exclaimed.

Jed Sayers's death had brought them here. He'd passed two weeks before and to Mariah's stunned surprise had left her the house and everything in it.

Her father's lawyer had contacted her three days ago to let her know that her father was dead and buried and she needed to let him know what she intended to do about the estate.

During that phone call she'd learned her mother had died a year before. The bastard who had been her father hadn't even let her know that her mother was ill.

"Everything is so green," Kelsey observed as she stared out the passenger window at the plush pasture.

Mariah smiled. "It's spring." The only real sign of spring Kelsey saw at their high-rise apartment in Chicago was the flowers that Mariah bought to fill pots that decorated their balcony.

Kelsey was an urban teenager, accustomed to taking the train or grabbing a taxi to get wherever she needed to go. In Chicago she and her friends had shops, restaurants, theaters and museums at their fingertips.

Plains Point, Missouri, was definitely going to be a culture shock. When Mariah had left town, there hadn't even been a McDonald's anywhere in the vicinity.

"How long are we gonna be here?" Kelsey now asked. She twisted a strand of her long dark hair around one of her fingers in a nervous gesture from childhood.

"I can't answer that," Mariah replied. She tightened her hands on the steering wheel as she saw the exit ramp for the small town. "It depends on what we find when we get there. I have to figure out what to do with all the contents of the house, then see what needs to be done to get it on the market. The only thing I can promise is that we'll be back in Chicago when school starts in September."

"This summer is gonna suck," Kelsey announced with all the authority a teenager could muster.

Mariah didn't reply as she slowed and turned on Main Street. She had expected Plains Point to have gone the way of so many little towns in the Midwest. She'd expected to see boarded-up storefronts and a small town gasping its final breath.

She was surprised to see that Main Street seemed to be thriving with new businesses that hadn't been there when she'd left town years ago.

"At least they have Chinese," Kelsey said as she pointed out a maroon awning announcing the establishment as the Red Dragon.

An office-supply store, a dress boutique and a veterinarian's office were just a few of the new businesses. Mariah supposed the small town had thrived because of its close proximity to Kansas City. It was only an hour's drive from Plains Point to the bigger city.

Mariah had read an article recently that indicated that people were choosing to drive long distances to work in exchange for small-town living.

The tension built inside Mariah's chest as they passed the town square. In the center of the square was not only City Hall, surrounded by a grassy park, but also a public swimming pool and the gazebo where a teenage boy had once proclaimed his undying love for her.

She wondered what had happened to Clay Matheson. In the back of her mind she would always wonder if he had been the one who had followed her home that night and taken what she hadn't been willing to give him.

"At least there's a pool," Kelsey said, breaking into her mother's thoughts.

"During the summers all the kids used to hang out there," Mariah replied.

"I've never seen you swim," Kelsey exclaimed.

"That's true. My parents never let me go to the pool, so I never learned how."

"Maybe I can teach you while we're here. There probably won't be much else to do." The last sentence was muttered beneath Kelsey's breath.

Mariah sighed. "Honey, I know this isn't how you wanted to spend your summer. It wasn't what I had in mind either, but we both just have to make the best of things."

As she turned off onto a small lane, the tension in her stomach knotted like a fist when she saw the two-story house nestled amid a grove of thick, mature trees.

The house itself held enough bad memories to make an oversized scrapbook, but it was the wooded area that surrounded the house that screamed of a horror she'd never quite gotten past.

She tried to keep her gaze off the spot where she'd stood and waited for her father to go to bed, the place where she'd been brutally attacked.

"Ugh, it looks like a dump," Kelsey said as Mariah pulled up in front of the house and parked.

"It definitely needs a coat of paint." Mariah shut off the car engine and sat for a moment, staring at the house, with its sweeping front porch and detached garage. It had once been a pristine white with black shutters, but now the paint had weathered to a dull gray and several of the shutters hung askew.

She'd heard from the lawyer that her father had been ill for some time before his death. He'd apparently been too ill to take care of things and too proud to ask for help.

The yard was in even worse shape than the house, with knee-high weeds that choked off any promise of spring flowers that might attempt to grow.

The ghosts she'd feared would grip her upon reaching the town now slithered fingers up her spine as her gaze drifted from the house to the grove of trees alongside it.

Who? That single question had whispered in the back of her mind for the past sixteen years. Who had attacked her that night?

She heard the rumble of thunder and smelled the scent of the forthcoming storm, and the back of her throat closed up as she imagined the slick plastic over her face, the press of somebody hard and heavy against her.

"Mom!"

Mariah stifled a scream as Kelsey's voice brought her back to the present.

"Are we going to go inside or are we going to sit in the car for the rest of the night?" Kelsey asked, a touch of exasperation in her voice.

"We're going inside," Mariah replied. She knew Kelsey was tired from the long car ride, hungry for something other than junk food and not looking forward to a summer without her friends back in Chicago.

"Let's get settled in and then we'll try out that Chinese restaurant we saw as we drove through town," she said.

"Now you're talking," Kelsey replied as she got out of the car.

It took three trips from the car to the porch to get everything that they'd brought with them. Mariah used the key her father's lawyer had sent to her to open the door.

A musty, closed-up scent greeted them as they stepped into the foyer. Mariah's gaze shot to the corner where the familiar umbrella holder stood, and nestled next to the old black umbrella were two long switches, the wood now pale and brittle.

A touch of bitterness welled up inside her. He'd kept them there all these years as if in anticipation of one last opportunity to punish his errant daughter.

"Phew, we need to open up some windows," Kelsey said as she dropped the suitcase she'd carried in.

As she went around opening windows, Mariah stood in the hallway and tried to think of one moment of joy that she'd experienced within these walls.

Her father had presented himself to the world as a pious, godly man, but in truth he'd been domineering and abusive. Her mother had been a cold woman who never should have had the privilege of bearing a child. Mariah wasn't sure which of her parents she blamed more for her unhappy childhood— the father who beat her or the mother who silently condoned it.

"Mom?" Kelsey walked back to the foyer. "You're going to freak when you see the kitchen. It doesn't look like it's been cleaned for about ten years."

"I don't think I'm ready to face that just yet. Why don't we go upstairs and see where we're going to sleep while we're here."

Kelsey bounded up the stairs with more enthusiasm for exploring than Mariah felt. She followed her daughter more slowly, trying to shake off the faint edge of depression that had fallen over her the moment she'd opened the front door.

The carpeting going up the stairs was threadbare and the wooden spindles were dusty. A little lemon oil would take care of the dust and she suspected beneath the carpeting was oak flooring that would be beautiful when sanded and varnished.

The house was free and clear of debt and Mariah figured she could afford to put a little money into it in order to get top dollar when it resold. That would put a tidy sum of money into Kelsey's college fund.

Kelsey had disappeared and Mariah hurried up the rest of the stairs to find her. The first bedroom was a small guest room that held only a bare double bed and a dresser. The second bedroom had been Mariah's and it was there she found Kelsey.

The girl stood at the window and when Mariah entered the room, she turned to face her mother. "This was your room, wasn't it?" She pointed to the window. "That was the tree you used to climb down to sneak out."

Mariah moved to stand next to her at the window. The big, leafy oak tree had been her vehicle of escape. "That's it." She placed an arm around Kelsey's shoulder. "Now that I look at the tree, I'm surprised I didn't break a leg or an arm on one of my rare escapes."

Kelsey leaned her head against Mariah. "You know what I think?"

"What's that?"

"I think we should have a switch-burning party tonight. Maybe we could pick up some marshmallows and roast them in the fireplace as we watch those stupid sticks burn."

Mariah tightened her arm around her daughter,

love welling up inside her. She'd told Kelsey a lot about her childhood, but there were many secrets she hadn't told her and some lies that had been told as truths.

"Just think of it this way. If things hadn't been so terrible here, I never would have run away. And if I hadn't run away, I wouldn't have met your father and had you. And having you was the very best thing that I've ever done in my whole life."

Kelsey laughed and moved out of her mother's embrace. "You're just trying to butter me up so I won't be a pain in your ass while we're here."

"There is that," Mariah agreed with a laugh.

"Can I have the guest room across the hall?" Kelsey asked.

"Sure. Let's see if we can find some clean linens in the hall closet."

The closet yielded the required linens and as Kelsey got busy making up the bed where she'd sleep, Mariah wandered down the hallway. The bathroom was in relatively good shape, although she was surprised to see the same blue flowered guest towels hanging on the rack as when she was still living at home. When Mariah had lived here, there had never been a guest in the house; it was no wonder they still looked new.

Her parents' room was at the end of the hallway and she stepped inside and gazed around, unsurprised that the room was smaller than she remembered. The double bed had been stripped to the mattress and the only thing on the wall was a large silver cross that hung just above the bed.

Why had her father left her everything? Had it been a desperate act of contrition from a dying man?

Or had he simply wanted to pull her back here one more time, back to the place of her misery? If she was to guess, it was the latter. Jed would have considered it one last act of domination to know that even in death he'd had the power to bring her back here.

It took them a little over an hour to get the bedrooms ready for occupancy and carry up their things. While Kelsey was setting up her computer, Mariah wandered back downstairs.

She peeked into the kitchen and stifled a groan. The old linoleum on the floor was stained and curling up at the edges. The countertops looked as if they hadn't seen a soapy sponge in decades. She refused to look in the refrigerator, afraid of what horrors might await her there.

Tomorrow, she told herself. She'd face this mess tomorrow. From the kitchen she went into what had once been a dining room but for as long as she remembered had been her father's study.

This had been her father's kingdom, the big black leather chair behind the old wooden desk his throne. And it had been in this room where he'd mete out his punishments.

She moved around the desk and took a seat in the large overstuffed chair where her father had so often sat. She ran her hands across the top of the desk, her mind flitting back in time, seeking one single moment when she'd felt loved, felt wanted, by her parents.

Her mind remained blank. Sighing, she pulled open the first desk drawer and stared at the bundle of letters that lay inside. She picked up the bundle and stared at the return address written in her own hand.

Over the years she'd written to her mother to let her know what was going on in her life. She'd written about Kelsey's birth and about getting her teaching degree. She'd chronicled each of Kelsey's special moments of childhood, thinking her mother would want to know about the grandchild she'd never met.

The letters had been her attempt to maintain contact with the only two people in the world who *should* have loved her. And the letters had never been opened.

A small bitter laugh escaped her lips as she shoved them back into the drawer. This would be the first place where she'd start the changes to the house. She'd have the furniture hauled away, repaint the walls, then buy a dining room set so the house would show nicely when it was placed on the market.

She'd give herself a month to take care of things. Then she and Kelsey would get the hell out of here and go back to the life they'd built in Chicago.

Chapter 2

"Mom, are you going to feed me or what?" Kelsey called from the living room.

Mariah stirred from her dark thoughts and glanced at her watch. It was after five and lunch had been a hamburger on the road a long time ago. "I'm going to feed you," she said as she left the dining room. "We'll see what the Red Dragon has to offer a couple of weary, travel-worn women."

Exhaustion weighed heavily on Mariah as they got back into the car to head to the restaurant on Main Street. The long drive that day, coupled with the emotional baggage of coming home, had taken its toll.

She just wanted to eat a meal, then tumble into bed for a long night's sleep. Anything else could wait until the morning.

The tension that had tightened her shoulders slowly dissipated as they drove into town. At least here lay some of Mariah's best memories. School had been nirvana, a break from the house and her parents. And on the rare times she'd been allowed to come into town after school or on the weekends, she'd reveled in the sense of freedom and the joy of meeting up with friends.

Kelsey sat up straighter in her seat as they passed a coffee shop where half a dozen young people were standing out front. "Maybe it won't be such an awful summer," she said.

"You won't have any problem making friends. You never do," Mariah replied. "And I'll contact the phone company and get some Internet juice in the house so you can keep up with your e-mail to your friends back home."

"Cool," Kelsey replied.

Mariah found a parking space in the same block as the restaurant and together she and Kelsey got out of the car. Clouds had begun to form in the southern sky and the air-conditioning in the restaurant was a welcome relief from the thick humid outside air.

An attractive Asian woman led them to a booth in the back and then left them alone with oversized menus. There were several other diners and Mariah eyed them curiously, wondering if she knew them, but none of them looked familiar.

She turned her attention to her daughter, who studied the menu with single-minded focus. For years Mariah had studied her daughter's face, seeking a physical clue to the identity of the man who had raped Mariah that night so long ago. But Kelsey was the spitting image of her mother with her heart-shaped face, dark hair and blue eyes.

"I know what I want," Mariah said, and set her menu aside.

"Let me guess, sweet-and-sour chicken and some crab rangoons," Kelsey replied. Mariah nodded. "You never want to try anything new."

Mariah shrugged. "I know what I like. You're the adventurous one when it comes to food."

At that moment the waitress arrived and took their orders, and Mariah sat back against the bench seat and drew a weary sigh.

"Does it feel weird to be back here?" Kelsey asked.

"I think I'm too tired to process everything at the moment." Mariah picked up her water glass and took a sip. She set the glass back down and frowned. "There's so much more to do than I thought there would be. I don't even want to talk to a Realtor until some of the basics in the house are taken care of."

Kelsey gave her mother a sly grin. "Don't you have any old boyfriends that could give us a hand?"

Mariah laughed. "I imagine all my old boyfriends are married and have families of their own."

"Then maybe you could hire some single hot dude to help with the work," Kelsey said.

Kelsey, at the age where she was discovering the attraction of the opposite sex, had decided her mission in life was finding her mother a boyfriend, or preferably a husband.

Mariah had had one fairly serious relationship when Kelsey had been seven years old. Tom Lantry had been a fellow teacher at the school where Mariah worked. It didn't take long for Kelsey to bond with Tom.

Mariah thought Tom was great. Kelsey thought Tom was great, and unfortunately Tom thought he was great, far too good to limit himself to one woman and a kid that wasn't his.

Kelsey had been far more upset than Mariah when Tom had walked away, and it was at that time that

Mariah decided no more dating until Kelsey was grown.

The one thing the relationship with Tom had done was prove to Mariah that she could enjoy a healthy sexual relationship with a man as long as the man let her set the rules.

As they ate, Kelsey kept up a steady stream of conversation that would be of most interest to any person her own age. She talked about the latest CD release from her favorite singer and gossiped about her friends back in Chicago and as usual worked in the fact that she was probably the only teenager left in the world who didn't have a cell phone.

Mariah pretended to give her daughter her full attention while her mind whirled with all the work that lay ahead of her. Maybe she would take Kelsey's advice and hire a handyman to help out, although she wasn't looking for a hot dude, just a man who knew how to paint and use a hammer.

They were just finishing up their meal when the door opened and a tall, portly man walked in. He wore the khaki uniform of law enforcement and swaggered like a man who enjoyed his position.

His gaze met hers and he stopped, a look of surprise on his face, and in that moment she recognized him. Clay Matheson.

A vivid flash of memory filled her mind, a memory of youthful love and promises never fulfilled. He approached the table, a wide smile curving his mouth. "I'll be damned," he said. "If it isn't Mariah Sayers."

"Hello, Clay," she said. There was little left of the young man she remembered. His handsome features had coarsened over the years and he had the telltale broken vessels in his nose that said he was probably a man who liked his booze.

"I wondered if you'd show up here. Sorry about your dad, may he rest in peace." He grinned at Kelsey. "It's easy to see where you came from. You look just like your mama did when I knew her." He looked back at Mariah. "We need to get together and talk about old times. I'll let Sherri know you're back in town, and maybe you could come over for dinner one night."

"Sherri? Sherri Weaver?" Mariah asked.

"Yeah. She chased me until she caught me ten years ago. We've got four boys who keep her on her toes." He gazed at her for a long moment. "I always wondered what happened to you. You just disappeared one day."

"Long story for another time," she replied.

"How long you planning on staying in town?"

"Just until I can get the house in order and on the market," she replied.

He drew his shoulders back, the gesture doing little to lessen the thick paunch around his middle. "You need anything or have any problems, you let me know. As the sheriff and as an old friend, I'll do whatever I can to help you."

"Thank you, Clay. It was nice seeing you again."

He nodded, gave Kelsey another smile, then left their table. "Wow, it's nice to know my mom knows all the important people in town," Kelsey exclaimed.

Mariah laughed. "The last time I saw Clay, his biggest claim to fame was that he could catch any football that any quarterback could throw to him."

"He looks like he's been catching more pizzas than footballs lately," Kelsey said.

Mariah tried to give her daughter a stern look, but it was impossible to do with Kelsey's eyes dancing with humor. "I'm sure he's a great sheriff," she finally managed to say. "And now let's get out of here and head back to the house. I'm so exhausted I feel like I could sleep for a hundred years."

"What are we going to do for groceries? There's nothing in that kitchen that I'm going to eat tomorrow," Kelsey said as they got out of the booth.

"When we get up in the morning, we'll head to the grocery store and get some supplies in. I just don't feel like doing it tonight."

When they left the restaurant, dark clouds hung heavy overhead and a distant rumble of thunder accompanied a brisk wind.

"Looks like a storm is coming," Kelsey said as they got into the car. "Hmm, I'll sleep good tonight."

Thankfully Mariah hadn't transferred her own dislike of storms to her daughter. Kelsey had always slept like a baby when it rained.

The rain held off as they drove to the house. When they arrived, Kelsey went directly to her room and Mariah followed after her. She sat on the edge of the bed while Kelsey went into the bathroom and changed into her pajamas; then she tucked her daughter in with a good-night kiss.

"I'm sorry this screwed up all your summer plans back home," she said as she stroked a strand of Kelsey's dark hair away from her face.

"It's okay." Kelsey grinned. "You'll pay for it later. When I want you to buy me a car, I'll remind you of the sacrifice I made this summer."

Mariah leaned forward and gave Kelsey another kiss, then rose from the bed. "You have a long time before you need to think about what kind of car you want to drive."

"In two months I'll be fifteen and can get my learner's permit," Kelsey yelled after her mom.

"Talk to me in two months," Mariah said with a laugh as she left the bedroom.

The laughter faded as she went into the small room she'd called home for all the years she'd lived in this house. Kelsey believed her birthday was in two months' time, but the truth was she'd turned fifteen three months ago. Only one other person knew the true date of Kelsey's birth . . . exactly nine months to the day following Mariah's rape.

Mariah had always feared that one day she'd have to come back here and she'd never wanted anyone to know that Kelsey had been conceived by someone in this town.

Mariah's best friend in the whole world, the nurse who had taken her in when she'd been eight months pregnant and living at a shelter, had not only helped Mariah in a home birth but had also fudged the dates of the blessed event. Fifteen years ago it had been easier to pull off such a feat than it would be today. Mariah had obtained a birth certificate and Social Security number based on the falsified record of Kelsey's birth date.

It had been important to Mariah, a way to distance the daughter she loved from the act that had resulted in her birth.

She quickly changed from her slacks and blouse into her pale blue silky nightgown and then went into the bathroom to brush her teeth and wash her face.

When she returned to the bedroom, she turned off

the light and went over to the window. The storm was upon them, lightning streaking across the sky as the wind shrieked around the eaves of the house.

It had been easy to focus on her dysfunctional relationship with her parents, so much easier than dealing with what had happened the night beneath the trees while a storm raged overhead.

There were moments of that night that were burned into her memory, forever a part of her nightmares. The weight of the man on top of her, the slickness of the bag against her face as she tried to scream, still lived in her as if the rape had happened mere hours before instead of years ago.

But there were also moments of that horrendous event that were vague, moments that she felt if she could just focus in on, then she would know who had attacked her. And even after all these years she wanted to know.

She leaned her head against the window and listened to the wind. It sounded like the screams that had been trapped inside her on that night so long ago.

She was back.

He'd watched her get out of her car and go into the Chinese place on Main, a quivering fear coupled with an edge of excitement racing through him.

He'd thought of her so many times over the years. She'd been his first, but certainly not his last.

That first time had been magical to him, an epiphany of sorts that had forever changed his life.

Now standing in the grove of trees on her property, he stared up at the darkened window on the second floor. He'd thought about her often, wondered if she'd ever return to Plains Point and what he would do if she did return. She was a joker in his house of cards.

Over the years he'd grown smarter, been more careful to make sure that nobody would ever be able to identify him and connect him with his crimes.

But with her he'd been less careful, made mistakes that had haunted him over the years. She'd never reported the crime . . . not that night and not in the weeks following. Then she'd simply vanished.

And now she was back and he wasn't sure what that meant for him. For the moment he'd watch and listen and if he felt that she was a threat, he would deal with her.

He'd learned a valuable lesson since that first night with her. He'd learned that dead girls couldn't tell; especially dead girls whose bodies were never found.

Chapter 3

Mariah was up before dawn and in the kitchen to tackle the mess. Sleep had been a long time coming the night before. Along with the storm came the haunting of ghosts to keep her awake.

Many nights she'd fallen asleep listening to her father practicing his Sunday sermon, his deep voice booming from the basement of the house to the rafters overhead.

Even though she knew that he was dead and in his grave, his voice had filled her head until finally she'd slipped from her bed and gone downstairs to the foyer.

She'd grabbed the willow sticks from the umbrella stand and snapped them into pieces, then thrown the pieces out the front door and into the storm. She'd gone back to bed then and slept the rest of the night through.

It had been strange this morning to awaken to the silence of the house in the bed she'd slept in for the first seventeen years of her life. Despite her lack of sleep, a warm shower had invigorated her. She was ready to kick this old house into shape and get it on the market.

She pulled on an old pair of denim shorts and a navy blue tank top, yanked her long hair into an untidy ponytail, then found cleaning supplies beneath the kitchen sink.

She'd always found cleaning cathartic. She'd done a lot of cleaning of this house when she'd been young. Cleanliness was next to godliness, as her father had reminded her a million times. But she'd never minded her chores, found the act of taking something dirty and making it clean strangely fulfilling.

Her best friend, Janice, thought that her enjoyment of cleaning was nothing short of psychotic. "If you ever decide to jump back into the relationship game, you'll make some man a great wife," Janice often said, then laughed. "Hell, I'd marry you if you could cook as well as you clean."

Mariah smiled as she began to scrub down the countertops, her thoughts filled with the woman who had, in all probability, saved her life.

Janice Solomon had been a twenty-nine-year-old nurse and trained midwife when she'd come to the shelter to talk to a very pregnant Mariah. That day Janice had taken a chance. She'd taken Mariah into her apartment. It had been Janice who had risked her career to fudge the dates of Kelsey's birth. She was the only person on the face of the earth who knew the truth about the rape.

Over the years she'd become like an older sister to Mariah and a favorite aunt to Kelsey. She'd encouraged Mariah to go back to school to get her teaching degree at the same time Janice had returned to school to get a degree in psychology.

Janice now had a private practice and worked as a life coach and counselor for troubled teens. She'd never married, although over the years she had often dated. Now at forty-five years old she believed she was far too set in her ways to ever entertain the idea of marital bliss.

Mariah lost herself in the cleaning, occasionally stopping only long enough to write down something on a list she'd begun to keep of what needed to be done.

The kitchen floor was hopeless. The old tiles not only dated the house horribly but also looked just as bad after she cleaned them as they did when they were dirty. She definitely needed to find a handyman who could do the work she couldn't.

"Wow."

Mariah jumped at her daughter's voice and whirled around to see her standing in the doorway. She threw the rag she'd been using to scrub the floor in the sink, then smiled at her daughter. "Better, yes?"

"At least now I won't be afraid to touch the countertops." Kelsey scratched her stomach, then hitched up the pajama bottoms that hung precariously low on her slender hips. "The floor still looks gross."

"Yeah, I'm going to have to find somebody to replace it. Now that I have everything clean, I think it's time we make a trip to the store to stock the fridge and pantry."

"Cool, I'll go get dressed." Kelsey disappeared from the doorway and a moment later Mariah heard her climbing the stairs. The fourth and fifth stairs still creaked just like they had when Mariah had lived here.

God, how she'd hated the creak of those stairs when she knew her father was coming up to confront her about some sin or another. She'd hear that first creak and her stomach would tie into a million knots.

Mariah washed her hands, hoping all thoughts of her father would go down the drain with the dirt. Then she headed up the stairs to get herself ready for a trip into town. She cleaned up, considered putting on makeup, then decided it was too hot. Besides, she'd be coming right back here to get some more work done.

She refastened her hair into a neater ponytail and then grabbed her purse and car keys from the bedroom. Kelsey waited for her at the front door.

"We're not just buying frozen junk, Mom," Kelsey said as they got into the car. "We need to buy stuff that I can cook with, too."

Mariah smiled. Kelsey was her budding chef. After watching several reality shows focusing on cooking competitions, Kelsey had decided she wanted to become a chef and eventually run her own restaurant.

"Whatever you think we need, we'll buy," Mariah replied.

It was almost ten when they pulled up in front of the Bag and Save, the only grocery store in town. The parking lot was half-full and Mariah regretted not putting on at least a dab of lipstick in case she ran into somebody she knew.

Too late now, she thought as she got out of the car. She spent the next thirty minutes chasing after her daughter, who drove the shopping cart like it was a sports car.

With her ATM card singing the blues, they were back in the car. Mariah pulled out of the grocery-store parking area and back onto Main Street, her thoughts once again on all the work that remained ahead of her.

"Mom, look out!" Kelsey screamed just as Mariah caught the flash of something dark running in front of her car. She slammed on the brakes, but not before she heard a sickening thump and a high-pitched yelp.

Kelsey jumped out of the car before Mariah could peel her shaking hands off the steering wheel. A horrible feeling filled her as she got out of the car and walked to the front, where Kelsey was crouched down by a scruffy little dog who lay just to the right of Mariah's tire. The dog whimpered and didn't even try to get up. One of his legs twisted unnaturally.

"Mom, we've got to do something," Kelsey said, tears streaming down her face.

Mariah looked around wildly, wondering where the dog belonged. Seeing nobody in the immediate area, she got back into the car, grabbed an old sweater from the backseat and returned to Kelsey. "Let's see if we can get him into the car. I remember seeing a veterinary clinic as we drove into town."

Kelsey took the sweater from her mother, then gently wrapped it around the hurt animal. Mariah worried about the dog biting, but he allowed Kelsey to pick him up into her arms.

They jumped back in the car and Mariah headed toward the clinic. She still felt shaky, sickened by the fact that she'd hurt the poor dog. "I didn't see him. He darted out of nowhere," she said as much to herself as to her daughter. "I couldn't stop in time."

Tears coursed down Kelsey's cheeks as she murmured soft words of comfort to the whimpering dog. He licked her hand and that only made her cry harder.

"He'll be okay," Mariah said. "It looks like it's just his leg." She hoped that's all it was. A broken leg could be fixed. She prayed there weren't any internal injuries. She'd hate to be the reason that somebody lost a beloved pet.

The veterinary clinic looked like a new building and a small sign out front indicated that Dr. Jack Taylor was the practicing vet.

Jack Taylor. The name was vaguely familiar, but Mariah didn't have time to place it as they scrambled from the car and into the cool interior of the clinic.

There was no receptionist behind the desk and only a low deep bark from someplace in the back heralded their arrival. "Hello?" Mariah called out.

A dark-haired man in a white lab coat came out of a back room. Despite the situation that had brought them in, Mariah felt an immediate jolt at his attractiveness. His green eyes widened slightly as if in recognition as his gaze landed on Mariah. But when he looked at Kelsey and the dog in her arms, he quickly waved them into an examining room.

"I didn't see him," Mariah said. "He darted right out in front of me and I couldn't stop the car fast enough. I didn't mean to hit him."

Kelsey laid the dog on the steel table, then backed away as the doctor took over. "He's been running the streets for weeks." His voice was deep and pleasant. "I've tried to pick him up a couple of times, but he wouldn't let me get near him."

As he spoke, his fingers roamed over the dog's

body. The dog quivered beneath his touch, but didn't protest. "It's okay, little guy," he said as he came to the twisted front leg. "Nobody knows where he came from. I have a feeling somebody passing through town might have dumped him. I'm going to have to get an X-ray on this leg and see what I can do." He scooped up the dog in his arms and flashed them a reassuring smile. "This will take a few minutes."

As he left the room, Mariah sank into a chair and Kelsey paced back and forth on the tiled floor in front of the examining room steel table.

"He's going to need some tender loving care," Kelsey said, and moved closer to her mother. "Poor little thing was dumped and probably hasn't slept in a bed or had anything good to eat for who knows how long. And now he's hurt and it's our fault." She looked at Mariah expectantly. "You know I've always wanted a dog."

"Kelsey, we don't know anything about him. We don't know if he's sick or mean. Besides, what would we do when we go back home?"

"Mrs. Ellis on the third floor has a dog. You'd probably just need to make a pet deposit or something. You know I'm responsible and he's not sick or mean. He just needs me, Mom. I could tell. It was in those big brown eyes of his."

Mariah sighed, unsurprised by her daughter's plea. Kelsey had always loved animals and over the past year had been asking if they could get a dog or a cat. It seemed the Fates were conspiring to attempt to grant her wish.

"Let's wait and see what Dr. Taylor has to tell us when he's finished," Mariah hedged.

It took thirty minutes before Dr. Taylor returned

to the examining room with the dog sporting a plaster cast on his front leg. "Almost as good as new," he said as he handed the docile dog to Kelsey. "I've got him sedated. The break was clean, so I don't anticipate any problems with the healing process."

There was no denying it—the man was a hunk, Mariah thought, and there was something about his voice, something familiar, that niggled in the back of her mind. "I'm sorry, do I know you?" she asked.

He flashed a smile that warmed her to her toes. "Junior year, second-period English. I sat behind you, but there's no reason why you would have remembered me. I was one of the nerds, barely seen and rarely heard."

For a moment Mariah didn't know what to say. It was difficult to reconcile the confident and very hot man in front of her with the vague mental picture she got of the shy, skinny boy who used to sit behind her in English class.

"Don't worry. It's okay if you don't remember me. But I do remember you, Mariah. Are you back in town to stay?"

"No, just for as long as it takes to settle my parents' estate."

"Yeah, I heard your father passed away. It's always hard to lose a parent."

She nodded and opened her purse to withdraw her checkbook. "How much do I owe you?"

He leaned back against the table and cocked his head to one side, a lock of his dark hair falling across his forehead in charming fashion. "Here's the deal. My receptionist took the day off today and she's the one who takes care of all that."

He reached out and gave the dog a scratch beneath

his chin. "I've been worried about this little guy and it looks like maybe he's going to get a home?" He exchanged a conspiratorial glance with Kelsey and then both of them looked at Mariah.

"Yes, I guess he's going to get a home," she replied reluctantly. What else could she do? Besides, maybe the little dog would make the summer away from home and her daughter's friends more palatable for Kelsey.

Kelsey grinned and held the dog close to her chest. "Did you hear that? You're coming home with us."

"Don't worry about any bill," Jack said. "Use the money you would have paid me for all the things you'll need to buy for your new pet." They walked out of the examining room and into the lobby. "Call tomorrow and make an appointment with my receptionist to bring him back in for a checkup in a couple of weeks. I'll give him a round of shots at that time."

"Thank you," Mariah said. "And it was nice seeing you again."

He smiled at her and a faint flutter stirred in her stomach. "Oh, we'll see each other again."

As she and her daughter walked out of the clinic, Jack went to the front window and watched them. Mariah Sayers. He'd been stunned by the old feelings that had rushed back to claim him at the sight of her.

She'd been his high school obsession, the girl who had stirred every teenage hormone he'd possessed. Day after day he'd sat behind her in class, smelling the clean scent of her long dark hair, wishing he had the nerve to reach out and touch the shiny strands, wanting to summon the courage to talk to her.

It hadn't been just pure lust that unraveled him at the very sight of her. There had been something in her eyes, a hint of darkness, of pain, that had both intrigued him and called up a protectiveness that made him want to fix whatever needed fixing in her life.

On the day he'd finally worked up the nerve to speak to her, she'd vanished.

And now she was back and he was surprised that she still stirred a touch of that old youthful lust. She'd looked amazing.

Maybe it was just his imagination. But he thought there was still a shadow of sadness that clung to her. He turned away from the window and shook his head ruefully.

The young girl had obviously been her daughter. Most likely Mariah was happily married and couldn't wait to get back to whatever life she'd built for herself elsewhere.

Rescue complex, that's what his best friend, Josh, told him he suffered, and that desire to play the role of hero protector was what had gotten him into a heartbreaking mess with his ex-wife.

He wondered where Rebecca was now. It had been almost four months since she'd called him wanting money. That was the longest she'd gone without having contact with him since their divorce four years ago.

He'd learned his lesson with Rebecca. Working with animals was far less complicated than dealing with human beings. And Jack had come to enjoy uncomplicated.

Chapter 4

"I can't believe you went to school with him and you didn't remember him," Kelsey said a moment later as they got into the car. "He's so hot."

"Yeah, I noticed that," Mariah replied. There had been little hint in the boy of the man he would become, she thought. She dismissed Jack Taylor from her mind as she pulled into the parking lot of a discount store. "You can wait here with the dog and I'll run in and get what we need to welcome him into the house," she said.

As Mariah raced through the pet-care aisle of the store, she wondered whatever had possessed her to agree to take the dog. Maybe it had something to do with Jack Taylor's gorgeous green eyes looking at her so expectantly.

She still found it hard to believe that the skinny young man who had sat behind her in English class had matured into a hottie like Dr. Jack Taylor. She didn't remember any of the girls in school paying attention to Jack. She'd bet there were plenty of women paying attention to him now.

Dismissing thoughts of the handsome vet, she got

busy and filled her basket with necessities. Dog food went into the basket along with a bed, a leash and collar, food and water bowls and a cute little kerchief that read TOP DOG.

By the time she got back into the car, she was more than eager to get home and hoped half the groceries they'd bought hadn't been ruined by the unexpected delays.

Kelsey greeted her with a beatific smile. "He's so sweet, Mom. He's just been lying here licking my hand. I think he knows that I'm going to take care of him."

"If we're going to keep him, then you need to come up with a name for him," Mariah said.

Kelsey frowned. "I'll have to think about it. I need to pick the perfect name for him."

As they drove home, Kelsey chattered about the kinds of meals she intended to cook for them. "Since I don't have any friends here, I'll have plenty of time to try out new recipes. I was thinking maybe tonight we'd have steak smothered in a sauce of portabella mushrooms and scallions," Kelsey said.

"Sounds good to me. I have a feeling I'd better enjoy whatever you're cooking before you meet some of the local kids. Once you find a band of friends, I'll be back to eating frozen Salisbury steak dinners."

Kelsey frowned, the gesture doing nothing to take away from her prettiness. "I can't imagine what I'd have in common with anyone here."

"You're probably right. I'm sure none of the other almost fifteen-year-old girls in town are interested in boys, fashion or music. They're probably all into milking cows and making their own candles and sewing clothing for the poor."

Kelsey giggled. "Okay, I get your point." She sat

up straighter in her seat as the house came into view. A red pickup was in the driveway. "Who is that?" she asked.

"Beats me," Mariah replied. She pulled up next to the pickup, then spied the man sitting on the front porch. Although she didn't initially recognize him, there was something familiar in the way he sat, with long legs sprawled carelessly in front of him.

As she opened her car door, he stood and stepped out of the shadows of the porch. She certainly didn't recognize the bald head that gleamed in the sunshine, but the blue eyes that twinkled and the open smile that curved his lips to expose a chipped front tooth were achingly familiar and she raced for the arms that he opened wide.

He laughed as he pulled her into a bear hug that almost stole her breath away. When she stepped back from him, she gazed into the eyes of the man who had been her best friend, confidant and neighbor throughout her childhood.

"Finn," she said, then stood on her tiptoes and reached up to rub his bald head. "What happened to all that glorious red hair?"

"Male-pattern baldness. When I realized I was having to comb the hair on my shoulders up around my head, I decided it was time to go cue ball." He stepped back and grabbed her by the shoulders. "But look at you. If I didn't know better, I'd swear I just stepped into a time machine. You look exactly like I remember."

Mariah laughed in delight. Of all the people she'd thought about over the years, Mitchell Tanner Finnigan—Finn to his friends—had come to mind most often.

"And it's an easy guess who this is," Finn said as Kelsey approached where they stood, her new pooch held tight in her arms. "My God, Mariah, is she your daughter or is she your clone?" He offered Kelsey one of those smiles that Mariah remembered, a smile filled with the warmth of the sun. "Hi, I'm Finn. Your mother and I used to be very best friends."

"I'm Kelsey, and sometimes she's my friend and sometimes she isn't," Kelsey replied, making both Finn and Mariah laugh. "Mom, can I take him up to my room?" Kelsey asked, and gestured to the half-snoozing pooch.

Mariah smiled at Finn. "New dog, long story. Let me just get the door unlocked for her. Then I need to get these groceries inside."

"I'll help with the groceries," Finn offered, and began to grab bags as Mariah hurried to the porch to unlock the door for her daughter.

It took only minutes to get the groceries from the car to the kitchen counter; then Mariah put on a pot of coffee, eager to play catch-up with her old friend.

Finn sprawled in one of the kitchen chairs as Mariah set to work putting away the perishable groceries in the fridge and waiting for the coffee to brew.

"I can't tell you how many times I thought about you over the years," he said. "You didn't even tell me good-bye." There was a hint of an old wound in his voice.

"Finn, I didn't even know I was leaving the night that I did." She put the last of the frozen food into the freezer, then sat in the chair opposite him. "You know how awful things were here. The night before I left, my father went ballistic because I hadn't folded some clothes to his measure of perfection. He got the switch and while he whipped me, I decided that was it. That was the last time he was going to lay a finger on me. I either had to leave or I was going to go to prison for murdering him."

Of course that wasn't the complete truth. She'd left when she'd missed her period and realized she was pregnant. She'd run away rather than tell her father that she was going to have a baby.

Finn leaned forward, bringing with him the scent of hay and sunshine. "So, what did you do? Where have you been for all these years? What have you been doing?"

She got up to pour them each a cup of coffee, then sat down once again at the table and gazed at Finn. Finn and Mariah had bonded early in their childhood. It had been a bond of the abused and powerless.

She wrapped her fingers around her cup of coffee. "That night I waited until my mother and father were in bed. Then I packed whatever clothes I could get into a tote bag, stole the money that my mother kept in the freezer for household expenses, and I caught a bus to Chicago."

"Jesus, weren't you terrified?" he asked.

"I was scared spitless," she admitted. "But on the bus ride out I met a guy. He was in the army, on an eight-week furlough, and it was magic." After years of practice the lie fell effortlessly from her lips. "A month later we got married and five months after that, I realized I was pregnant. Unfortunately when I was six months pregnant, my husband, Brian, was killed in a car accident."

His eyes darkened. "That was a tough break. And so you've been living in Chicago all this time, being a single parent?"

"And a teacher. You know that's what I said I always wanted to do."

He reached across the table and grabbed her hand in his big one. "And you've been happy?"

She cast him a rueful smile. "Yes, for the most part I've been happy, although I know I don't have to tell you about the inner demons that occasionally raise their heads." He squeezed her hand, then released it and grabbed his coffee cup. "But enough about me. Tell me about you. How are Susan and Kim?"

"Great." His face flushed with pleasure. "Susan is married and she and her husband live in Virginia. Kim lives here in town and works at the bank." His pride in his two younger sisters was evident in his voice.

He should be proud. Finn had raised them both from the time they were little. "And what about you? Married? Single?"

He grinned. "You remember Hannah Richards?"

"Hot Pants Hannah? You married Hot Pants Hannah?" She looked at him incredulously. Hannah had been the fantasy of most of the guys in high school with her long shapely legs and penchant for short skirts and tiny shorts.

He nodded, his eyes twinkling. "We're celebrating our eighth anniversary next month and she's still got the best-looking legs in town."

"Oh, Finn, I'm so happy for you. Kids?"

"Two. Jeffrey is six and Gracie Ann is four. We need to have a party, get some of the old gang together while you're here."

"We saw Clay last night while we were having dinner. He said the same thing."

"Ah, now, there's a bitter man." Finn took a sip

of his coffee. "He had big dreams of playing professional football and that didn't pan out. His wife was a bitch in high school and hasn't changed much over the years."

"I was surprised when I heard he was married to Sherri," she replied. "I figured she would have left Plains Point years ago. She was always talking about a career as a model."

"The only thing she could model now is maternity clothes. About every other year she pops out another baby and acts like she's the grande dame of the city." He eyed her with a touch of amusement. "I imagine she won't be too happy to hear you're back in town. Way I remember it, you and Clay were pretty thick before you left."

Mariah laughed. "Ancient history. A high school romance that probably wouldn't have lasted until graduation." She smiled as her daughter came into the kitchen. "Did you get the pooch all settled in?"

She nodded. "He's sleeping in his new bed." She looked at Finn. "Mom ran over him with the car. The vet fixed him up and now he's going to be our dog."

"Then you've seen Jack Taylor." Finn laughed and shook his head. "Every single woman in Plains Point has decided to get a dog or a cat since he moved back to town," Finn said drily. He smiled at Kelsey. "What are you? About sixteen?"

Kelsey preened at what she considered a compliment. "Actually, I'm almost fifteen."

"I've got a friend who has a couple of girls about your age. I'll be sure and let them know you're in town." Finn stood. "As much as I'd like to sit here all day and visit, I've got to get back to the farm. I've got chores to do."

"One more thing before you go," Mariah said. "Do you know anyone who does odd jobs?"

"You remember Joel Clarkson? He was a couple of years older than us."

"No, I don't remember him," Mariah replied.

"He's always looking for work. He drinks a bit, is sometimes unreliable, but he's a pretty decent carpenter and will do almost anything for a fair wage. I'll call you later with his number."

"Thanks, Finn." Mariah walked with him to the front door, where he gave her another hug.

"I'm so glad you came back." He released her and smiled. "I always wondered what you were like all grown up."

She reached up and placed a hand on his lean cheek. "I missed you, too." She dropped her hand and stepped back.

"I'll call you with that number," he promised as he went out the door.

"He seems nice," Kelsey said when Mariah returned to the kitchen.

"He's a great guy who had a terrible childhood." Mariah sat at the table and her daughter joined her.

"Terrible how?"

"Finn's mother died when he was thirteen and his little sisters were three and four. His father was a raging alcoholic and most weekends he'd just disappear, leaving Finn to take care of the little girls. Then one weekend when Finn was sixteen, his father never returned home. Finn didn't get to be a normal teenager. He was too busy being a father."

"What happened to his thumb?"

Mariah knew instantly what Kelsey was talking about. Finn had no left thumb. "Right after his mother's death he and his father were out chopping wood. His father was drunk, missed the wood and took off Finn's thumb."

"Oh my gosh," Kelsey exclaimed, obviously horrified.

"It was pretty awful at the time, but Finn found a way to make the best of it. Over the next couple of years I heard him tell a dozen stories as to how he lost his thumb. He made up a story about catching a catfish so big it bit off his thumb. Then there was the story about him wrestling with a bear."

Kelsey laughed. "He sounds like fun. You guys were close?"

Mariah picked up her cup and took a sip of the now lukewarm coffee. "He lives in the house next door. We walked to and from the bus stop together each day and tried to meet in the field between our houses at least once a day. We talked about how much we hated our home life and, as silly as it sounds, drew strength from each other."

"That doesn't sound silly," Kelsey replied. "You never dated him or anything like that?"

Mariah smiled and shook her head. "It wasn't like that between us. Finn and I were very best friends. He was like the brother I never had."

"Speaking of brothers, it's not too late for you to give me a little brother or sister," Kelsey said with a sly grin.

"I'm not sure I could handle a teenager and a toddler at the same time," Mariah said with a laugh.

Kelsey tilted her head slightly and smiled. "I think you could handle almost anything, Mom."

Mariah's heart expanded. She wasn't sure how she'd managed to do something so right, but she'd raised a loving, intelligent daughter who made her proud every day.

"And I still think you should get me a cell phone," Kelsey added.

"Get out of here. A new dog is enough for one day."

Kelsey got up from the table. "Okay, but you haven't heard the last of the cell phone problem."

"Thanks for the warning," Mariah replied.

Kelsey left the kitchen and Mariah got up to pour herself a fresh cup of coffee. She returned to the table and stared out the open window, where the faint scent of rain-washed grass still lingered from the storm the night before. The sky was a blue she rarely saw in Chicago.

She should be working. She should be pushing herself to get everything done and get back to their high-rise apartment. But she remained sitting, enjoying the warmth of seeing Finn again, surprised to discover the pleasant memories his visit had evoked.

Somehow in the years she'd been away from Plains Point, she'd remembered only bad things. But now happy memories bloomed in her mind, memories of her and Finn lying in sweet-smelling grass and looking up at the clouds overhead, of making clover chains to wear around their necks and sipping from a bottle of Scotch to try to figure out why Finn's father loved it so much.

Although Jed had kept a hard thumb on her, there had been moments of freedom made all the more sweet because they came so rarely. There had been the occasional birthday parties and school functions that she'd been allowed to attend. When she was

fifteen, she'd been allowed to go to a carnival in town
with a bunch of kids and their parents.

It had been one of the best nights of her life. The
thrill of the rides couldn't compete with the thrill of
her temporary independence from her parents and
her home.

And when she'd gotten home that night, she'd
paid for her good time. Her father had beaten her
black-and-blue for not dusting the living room to his
satisfaction. But it had been worth every lick of the
switch. As he'd whipped her, in her mind she'd gone
back on the Ferris wheel with the wind in her face
and Finn's laughter ringing in her ears.

She startled as she realized her purse was ringing.
She dug in it and retrieved her cell phone, the caller
ID letting her know who was calling.

"Hey, girlfriend," she answered.

"Ah, you survived your first night in hell," Janice said.

"I not only survived, but I've cleaned a kitchen,
bought groceries, seen my old boyfriend and ac-
quired a dog."

"Wow, you have been busy. How's the boyfriend?"

"Older, paunchy and a drinker," Mariah said.

"And the dog?"

"Little, dark gray and with a broken leg." Mariah
explained to Janice about hitting the dog and the
rush to get him to the vet. As she talked, a vision of
Jack Taylor filled her mind. It had been a long time
since a man had crossed her mind more than once.

"How's everything else? You doing okay? Did you
have nightmares last night?" Janice, ever the counselor, asked.

"No, no nightmares and I'm doing fine." Mariah leaned back in the chair and cast her gaze out the window once again. "There's a ton of work to get done before I can get this place on the market. I haven't told Kelsey yet, but I can't imagine us getting back home for at least a month or so."

Janice was silent for a long moment. "You going to be okay there for that long? I mean, it's one thing to have to spend a week or two in a place where bad things happened, but to stay indefinitely is quite another."

"Actually, right before you called, I was sitting at the kitchen table and remembering some of the good times. You remember me telling you about Finn? He stopped by and we caught up a little bit. It was fun."

"You sound good," Janice replied, relief in her voice. "You'll call me if things get rough."

Mariah smiled, thanking her lucky stars for such a friend. "You're on my speed dial."

"You know, I've been meaning to take a vacation. I could come out there and help you with the house."

"Janice, if you're going to take a vacation, go to Mexico or to Hawaii. Don't waste it coming here to work," Mariah replied.

The two spoke for just a few more minutes, then hung up. The rest of the day passed quickly. Mariah moved from the kitchen to the living room, where she took down draperies, swiped at cobwebs and scrubbed woodwork.

Kelsey and her new pooch, officially named Tiny, moved from her room to the kitchen so Kelsey could work on dinner. Kelsey kept up a running monologue directed at the dog, whose cast clunked on the floor each time he took a step.

Mariah had agreed that the dog could sleep in Kelsey's room at night, but during the day he would be relegated to the kitchen. An old screen propped across the kitchen doorway provided a workable barrier to keep the dog in the room.

It was after six when they sat down to eat the steak that Kelsey had prepared. Tiny sat next to Kelsey's chair, looking up to her with big brown begging eyes.

"Don't you dare give him anything from the table," Mariah said. "You don't want to start a bad habit. He has his own food in his bowl."

Kelsey cast a sympathetic look at Tiny. "Sorry, baby, you have to eat your own food." Tiny cocked his head to one side, then clumped over to his own food bowl and began to eat.

It didn't take long to realize that although, according to Jack Taylor, Tiny had been running the streets for several weeks, he was surprisingly domesticated. He responded to simple commands and after he was finished eating went to the back door.

"I think we need to put up some flyers around town about Tiny," Mariah said when Kelsey came back from taking the dog outside. "It's obvious he's been trained and somebody might be missing him."

Kelsey held the dog in her arms and sighed. "I guess you're right. But if nobody claims him, then I get to keep him, right?"

Tiny barked, as if to add his two cents to the conversation. Mariah laughed and scratched the dog behind one ear. "That's right. You can print the flyers on your computer and tomorrow we'll put them around."

Kelsey nodded and placed the dog on the floor and then together she and Mariah cleared the table.

There was no dishwasher in the old kitchen and as they washed dishes, they talked about what they'd do when they got back to Chicago.

After dinner Kelsey went up to her room and Mariah moved into her father's study and sat at his desk. She'd picked up several empty boxes while they'd been at the grocery store and she began to empty the contents of the desk into one of them.

She'd worked about an hour when Kelsey found her and gave her the flyers she'd made. "I think I'm going to go to bed," Kelsey said. "I don't know why, but I'm pooped."

"It's all this fresh country air." Mariah got up from the desk and wrapped her arms around her daughter. "I'm going to work a while longer, so I'll just tell you good night now." She kissed Kelsey's forehead. "I'll see you in the morning."

As Kelsey headed back upstairs, Mariah returned to the desk. She turned on the desk lamp against the encroaching darkness of nightfall. The sound of crickets drifted in through the open window, a familiar sound from her childhood.

Most of the contents of the desk were trash. Old bills already paid and sermons previously delivered filled the drawers. She threw most of it into a plastic bag, but kept the records of the most recent utility bills that had been paid.

It was after nine when she decided to call it a night. It had been a long day and she was exhausted. She rose from the desk and stretched with her arms overhead, trying to work out the kinks that had tightened her muscles. She wasn't used to the kind of physical work she'd done that day.

As a third-grade teacher, the most physical thing

she did was occasionally run a footrace with a stu-
dent on the playground during recess.

She turned off the desk lamp, then glanced toward
the window into the face of a man standing outside
in the darkness staring back at her.

Chapter 5

She kept her scream trapped inside, not wanting to frighten Kelsey. The man was there only a moment, then gone. Mariah remained in the darkness of the office, frozen in place.

Move, a voice screamed inside her head. There was no phone in the office and her cell phone was in her purse in the kitchen. Call somebody. Get help!

She hadn't recognized the man. What had he been doing peeking in her window? Who was he? Questions crashed inside her head as she backed out of the office.

Had she locked the front and back doors? She couldn't remember. She ran into the kitchen and checked the door. Locked. She grabbed her cell phone and was about to dial for help when a knock sounded on the front door.

Once again she froze, fingers poised to dial. Would somebody who wanted to harm them knock on the front door? There were a dozen windows open in the house. If he wanted to hurt them, he could have just waited until the middle of the night, slit a screen and crept inside.

She moved to the front door, turned on the porch light and then shouted through the locked door. "What do you want?"

"Finn sent me. Said you had some work. Name's Joel Clarkson."

Relief flooded through her. Her fingers relaxed around her phone and she cracked open the door a couple of inches.

"Didn't mean to scare you none," he said. "I knocked and nobody answered. I saw the light on and figured I'd look in to see if anyone was around." Dark hair hung lank around his face, emphasizing hollow, acne-scarred cheeks. He looked thin, but with wiry strength.

"Mr. Clarkson, it's a little late to discuss anything tonight. If you want to come back in the morning, we can talk then."

He backed away from the door with an apologetic shake of his head. "Sorry, I should have realized it was too late. I'll be back in the morning." He didn't wait for her reply, but headed for a rusty black pickup truck parked in front of the house.

She watched until his headlights disappeared down the long, dark driveway; then she closed the door and locked it once again.

Until this moment she hadn't realized how vulnerable she and Kelsey were in this house. Without air-conditioning she'd gone to bed the night before with windows open wide, providing a perfect entrance to anyone who might want to get inside.

She now went around the lower level, closing and locking the windows tight. They could sleep with the upstairs windows open and if necessary she would invest in a couple of fans. Installing central air was an expense she didn't even want to consider for a house she wasn't going to live in.

With everything secure downstairs, she climbed to the second floor, her heart still racing faster than normal. For a moment as she'd stared at that face at the window, she'd thought *he'd* come back for her.

As she stood beneath a hot shower, her thoughts once again raced back in time, back to the night of her rape. She'd always wondered if she'd been raped by a transient passing through town or if it had been somebody she knew, somebody who lived in Plains Point.

There was some comfort in clinging to the belief that it had been a stranger, that it couldn't have been any of the locals who knew her, somebody who still lived in town, shopped where she shopped and ate where she ate.

There would always be a part of her that wondered why he'd picked her. Had it simply been a horrifying chance encounter or had she specifically been targeted for the brutal attack?

As she got into her nightgown, she dismissed these thoughts from her mind. When she'd left Plains Point as a scared, pregnant seventeen-year-old, there had been little time to think of that night. The mere act of surviving had taken all her energy, leaving none left to obsess about the who and why of her attack.

It was only in her sleep that she went back to that place beneath the trees with the scent of the storm in the air, and the memories seeped into her brain like toxic fumes, creating nightmares that pulled her screaming from her sleep. Many times the horror of the attack had gotten all mixed up with the agony of her mother's betrayal that night.

But time was a healer, as Mariah had discovered.

The memories, although never forgotten, became less intrusive as the years had gone by and the nightmares became less frequent.

Kelsey had learned at a young age that sometimes Mommy woke up screaming, and when she got older, she solved the issue of waking up to screams by wearing an iPod with earphones or earplugs to bed.

Mariah slept later than usual the next morning and woke up to the scent of coffee and frying bacon drifting up the stairs.

There were times she couldn't believe how lucky she was to have Kelsey. Although she'd love to take the credit for her daughter's maturity and caring nature, the truth was Kelsey had been born an old soul with a peaceful nature that had rarely given her mother a moment of worry.

She got out of bed and pulled her comfortable but ratty old robe around her, then went down the stairs to see Tiny staring up at Kelsey adoringly as she flipped strips of bacon in the skillet.

"I'm not sure if that dog has that heavenly grin on his face because he loves you or because he loves bacon," Mariah said as she shuffled over to the coffeemaker on the cabinet. "But if you see me looking at you lovingly, it's definitely because you have the coffee waiting for me."

Kelsey grinned. "I woke up early and figured I might as well get breakfast going." She raised an eyebrow. "You were a lazy slug this morning."

Mariah raised her hands over her head and bent her body first to one side, then to the other. "I think maybe I overdid it yesterday. I have aches where I didn't even realize I had muscles."

"Maybe you should just take it easy today," Kelsey said as she removed the skillet from the burner.

"I don't have time to take it easy," Mariah replied, and carried her coffee to the table, where she sat and watched as Kelsey broke eggs into a bowl. "I want to finish packing up the things in the office and then start on the master bedroom. The handyman Finn told me about yesterday stopped by last night and is supposed to be back sometime this morning."

Kelsey began to cut up mushrooms and green peppers. "What's he like? Could he maybe be the man of your dreams?"

Mariah laughed. "I don't think so, not unless I like long-haired Peeping Toms." She explained to her daughter about Joel peeking in the window and scaring her the night before.

Kelsey frowned. "He sounds kind of creepy."

"I can deal with a little creepy as long as he can do what needs to be done around here." Mariah took a sip of her coffee, making a list in her mind of all the work she hoped Joel Clarkson could accomplish. "Finn wouldn't have recommended him to me if he weren't safe," she added.

They had just finished eating when the sound of a vehicle's tires crunching on the gravel drive drifted in through the open window.

"That's probably Joel," Mariah said.

Kelsey looked out the window, then looked back at Mariah, her eyes wide. "You'd better go pull on some clothes and do something with your hair. It's not your handyman. It's the vet, Dr. Hot."

Mariah sprang to her feet as she remembered the electric spark she'd felt when she'd looked at Jack Taylor the day before. She had no idea what he was doing here, but she sure didn't want to greet him in the robe that was almost as old as her daughter and with her hair, not sleep-tousled, which sounded charming, but rather sleep-tangled, which was definitely not charming.

"Go," Kelsey said urgently. "I'll keep him occupied until you're dressed. And put on some lipstick," her daughter demanded as Mariah raced for the stairs.

Upstairs in her room Mariah hurriedly changed from her nightgown and robe into a pair of shorts and a T-shirt. As she brushed the tangles from her hair, she heard Jack's pleasant deep voice talking to Kelsey.

She had the tube of lipstick halfway to her mouth when she stared at her reflection in the mirror and wondered what in the hell she was doing.

The last thing she was looking for was a man. She was here to take care of family business; then she'd go back to her life. Okay, Jack was easy on the eyes, but he was most certainly not here to see her—he'd probably come to check up on their furry little friend.

She threw the lipstick to the side of the bathroom counter and headed downstairs where Jack's and Kelsey's voices came from the kitchen.

He'd been hot in his white lab coat the day before, but this morning, wearing a pair of jeans that molded to his long legs and with a white T-shirt stretching taut across his broad shoulders, he positively sizzled.

He smiled as she entered the kitchen and she felt a kick of attraction punching her midsection. "Good morning." His deep voice felt like a physical caress.

"Dr. Taylor stopped by to check on Tiny," Kelsey said.

"I didn't realize doctors in this day and age made house calls," Mariah replied. She tried not to stare at him, but she was still trying to find some semblance of the skinny young man she had barely known in high school in the handsome, buff man in front of her.

"Only in special circumstances." He crouched down and Tiny sniffed his hand suspiciously. "He looks like he's in good hands," he said as he rose to his feet. "How's his appetite?"

"Good, and he slept through the night," Kelsey said. "Would you like a cup of coffee, Dr. Taylor?"

Mariah flushed as she realized her hostess skills had momentarily fled her. "Yes, would you like a cup of coffee?" she repeated.

"No thanks, I've got to get to the office, and please, call me Jack," he said to Kelsey. He redirected his gaze to Mariah. "Kelsey mentioned that there wasn't a man around the house. I was wondering if maybe she and you would be interested in grabbing some pizza tonight with me. There's an all-you-can-eat pizza buffet in town."

"Oh, I don't think—"

"I love pizza," Kelsey exclaimed, interrupting whatever Mariah had been about to say. "Can we go, Mom?"

Mariah knew that pizza wasn't one of Kelsey's favorite meals, that this was obviously some sort of matchmaking ploy. "Okay," she agreed. "We'd love to go out for pizza with you."

"Great. Why don't I pick you up around six?" He started out of the kitchen.

"That sounds fine and I'm sure you'll be surprised

by how many pieces of pizza my daughter can eat," Mariah said with a pointed glance at Kelsey.

"Then I'll see you at six," Jack said. His eyes gleamed with a light that once again danced an electric flicker through Mariah. "I'm looking forward to it," he said, then walked out the front door.

Mariah stood at the door and watched him get into his car, unable to help but notice how fine his butt looked in the tight jeans. As he pulled away from the house, she went back into the kitchen, where her daughter was loading the sink full with their breakfast dishes.

"Since when do you love pizza?" she asked.

Kelsey shot her a wicked grin. "I just all of a sudden got a craving for it." She turned away from the sink to face her mother. "You were going to tell him no. Anytime anybody asks you out, you say no. You never have any fun. It's just pizza, Mom. You don't have to sleep with him. Just go out and have a good time."

Mariah stared at Kelsey, surprised by the uncharacteristic outburst. "Well, I'm glad you made that clear to me. I was afraid I'd have to strip naked and have sex in the middle of the buffet table."

Kelsey giggled and bent down to scoop up Tiny in her arms. "I just want you to have some fun, Mom."

"I do have fun," Mariah protested. "I have fun spending time with you."

Kelsey looked at her soberly. "But I'm not always going to be around. Eventually I'll go off to culinary school and get married and I don't want you to spend your whole life all alone."

Mariah leaned forward and kissed her daughter on

the cheek. "You aren't doing any of those things for several years and you shouldn't be worrying about me." Mariah laughed as Tiny licked the underside of her chin. "Now, why don't you go do something typically teenagerish like make a mess in your room or call one of your friends long-distance and talk too long?"

Kelsey grinned. "Actually, I was kind of wondering if maybe this afternoon I could go to the pool for a couple of hours."

"I think that's a great idea. How about I take you and drop you off at the pool right after lunch? You can hang out until about four. Then I'll pick you up."

"Cool, and in the meantime I'm going upstairs to mess up my room and make a long-distance phone call." Kelsey carried her dog out of the kitchen and up the stairs.

At that moment another knock sounded on the door. It was Joel to discuss what work she might have for him to do. He had a faint reek of alcohol but appeared clear-eyed and freshly showered.

They sat at the kitchen table and discussed the various jobs she needed done, agreed on a fair price and decided that the first task for him to tackle was the overgrown yard.

It was twelve thirty when she left to take Kelsey to the pool. Joel was on a lawn tractor, making headway on the front yard, and he waved as they pulled out of the driveway.

"Call me if you want me to come and get you before four," Mariah said as she pulled up in the parking lot in front of the pool. She handed her daughter her cell phone. "Don't get it wet and don't lose it."

Kelsey rolled her eyes. "I'll guard it with my life and I'll see you at four."

Mariah watched her walk toward the pool entrance, her slender hips swaying beneath the bright pink cover-up she wore. Matching sparkly flip-flops adorned her feet, and Mariah knew beneath the cover-up was a pink and white polka-dot bikini that Mariah thought was half-obscene and her daughter thought was too conservative.

She was growing up so fast and her boyishly slim body now sported a hint of the curves to come. Mariah watched her until she disappeared behind the large fence that surrounded the pool.

What she wanted to do was run after her, wrap her up in a dozen beach towels and tell her to get back in the car. She wanted to lock her in a closet where nobody could ever hurt her, where nobody could ever throw her down in the grass and brutalize her.

Mariah had spent most of Kelsey's life fighting these impulses, knowing that her own fear could emotionally cripple her daughter if she allowed it to.

As she drove home, she wasn't alone in the car; the ghosts of the past sat in her backseat, whispering of all the bad things that could happen to young girls.

Chapter 6

It was ridiculous to feel so damned nervous about a simple pizza date, Mariah thought as she grabbed first one blouse, then another from her closet. She'd already decided on jeans, but couldn't make up her mind what to wear on top.

Whenever she was under stress, even the simplest decisions became difficult. And she was definitely stressed right now as she thought about seeing Jack Taylor again.

She closed her eyes and grabbed the first hanger her hand landed on. It was a purple T-shirt decorated with the logo of the school where she worked. It wasn't her favorite, but without giving herself the opportunity to second- or third-guess herself, she yanked it on over her head.

"Kelsey, he'll be here in fifteen minutes. Are you about ready?" she called down the hallway.

Kelsey had come home from the pool chatting about a handful of kids her age that she'd met. Suddenly the summer in Plains Point didn't look so bleak after all.

She now came out of her bedroom wearing a pair

of navy capris and a matching tank top. She frowned as she saw Mariah. "Gosh, Mom, could you pick an uglier T-shirt?"

"We're just going out for pizza. I didn't know I needed to adhere to a dress code."

Kelsey gave her the pained-teenager look. "Still, it wouldn't have hurt for you to put on something a little prettier."

Mariah gazed at her daughter patiently. "Kelsey, honey, let's get something straight. I'm here in Plains Point to get this house ready for sale and nothing more. Tonight is a one-shot deal, an evening out with you and Jack for pizza. Don't try to turn it into something bigger than it is."

"Okay," Kelsey said, obviously disappointed. "But could you at least put a little lipstick on so he won't notice how ugly that shirt is?"

"All right," Mariah relented, and went back into her bedroom. She held no expectations for the evening. She simply thought it might be fun to chat with him and catch up on everyone they had gone to school with.

The butterflies in her stomach were hunger, nothing more, she told herself firmly as she walked down the stairs. Tiny was in the kitchen and barked at the sound of her footsteps. She moved to the gate that kept the little pooch on the tiled floor, and leaned over to give him a pat on the head.

"We won't be long," she said, and laughed as he cocked his furry head to one side, as if listening intently to what she had to say. "A couple of slices of pizza, then home."

The phone rang and she hurried back into the living room and lifted the receiver. "It's on for tomorrow night," Finn said. "Barbecue and beer and half the people we went to school with, and you'd better not tell me you and your daughter can't come, because you two are the official guests of honor."

Mariah laughed. "What time and what can I bring?"

"Six o'clock and nothing but your gorgeous self and your charming daughter," he replied.

"We'll be there. Thanks, Finn." She hung up the receiver as Kelsey came down the stairs. "That was Finn. We're invited to a barbecue at his house tomorrow night at six."

"Sounds like it might be fun," Kelsey said.

At that moment the doorbell rang. Dr. Hot had arrived.

Kelsey answered the door and he walked in, imbuing the entryway with palpable energy. A pair of jeans hugged his legs and a short-sleeved polo shirt perfectly matched his green eyes.

"Hi," he greeted Kelsey, then turned his gaze on Mariah, and she suddenly wished she'd put on something pretty and feminine. "Are we ready to go?"

"Just let me grab my purse," Mariah said, and hurried into the kitchen. Jesus, what was wrong with her? One look at him and her stomach began to break-dance and heat fired through her.

She grabbed her purse from the table, made sure the back door was locked, then rejoined Jack and Kelsey in the living room. "Ready," she exclaimed.

Instead of the pickup truck he'd arrived in that morning, a sleek sports car awaited them. "Wow, nice ride," Kelsey said as she slid into the backseat.

"My truck is pretty much a work vehicle. Charlie Barclay got this in on his car lot and I couldn't resist it." He opened the passenger door for Mariah.

"Boys and their toys," she said lightly as she slid onto the beige leather seat.

He laughed, shut her door, then walked around the front of the car to the driver door. There was a quiet confidence in the way he held himself, as if he was a man who knew and liked his place in life.

As he slid behind the steering wheel, the car filled with his scent, a minty soap coupled with a spicy cologne. "Looks like somebody has been making headway on your yard," he said as they pulled away from the house.

"Joel Clarkson. I've hired him to do some work around the house," she said.

"He likes to drink, but I've heard he's pretty handy when he's sober. I just wouldn't expect much from him on the weekends."

"That's what Finn told me when he recommended Joel," she replied.

"Speaking of Finn, I've been invited to a barbecue tomorrow evening in your honor." Jack turned left on Main.

"Yes, he called right before you came to pick us up, and told me he'd invited a bunch of the gang we went to school with. It sounds like it should be fun."

Jack laughed, the sound deep and so pleasant it wove a wave of heat through her. "Finn's barbecues are legendary here in town. Everyone eats too much, drinks too much and talks about old times."

"I'd like to hear some of the gossip from when my mom was in high school," Kelsey said from the backseat. "You know, maybe gather some blackmail information for the future."

Jack laughed once again along with Mariah. "I'm afraid you're going to be out of luck. As I remember, your mother wasn't one of the wild ones at school. You'll be hard-pressed to find blackmail material in her background."

"That's what I keep telling her," Mariah said.

At that moment they pulled up in front of Ken's Pizza Buffet and Arcade. "Hey, this looks pretty cool." Kelsey was the first one out of the car.

Jack turned and looked at Mariah with a hint of apology. "This isn't the usual place I take somebody, but I thought your daughter might enjoy it."

"It's fine," she assured him. "It looks like fun." And that's what she wanted. Not candlelit dinner and romantic music, not soft glances and the promise of something deep and lasting. She just wanted an evening of fun.

Together they got out of the car and joined Kelsey on the sidewalk just outside the restaurant. As he opened the door, the robust aroma of tomato sauce and garlic spilled out, making Mariah realize she was starving.

Jack paid and they all went down the buffet line, filling their plates with pizza and salad. Then they found a booth not far from the entrance to the arcade room.

"Now, I want to know where you've been and what you've done since you just disappeared from school," Jack said.

"Left town, got married, had Kelsey, lost my husband and became a teacher." Mariah smiled. "That's the short version."

He raised a dark eyebrow. "There's a lot of living in that short version."

She shrugged, picked a piece of pepperoni off one

of the slices and popped it into her mouth. "What about you? What's your short version?"

"Went to college, became a vet, got married and got divorced."

"Did you marry somebody from here in town?"

"No, I met Rebecca in college. She was from Kansas City. After our marriage I started a clinic there, but when we divorced four years ago, I decided to move back here. I like the small-town living."

"I'm still trying to adjust to it," Kelsey said as she dug her fork into the salad on her plate.

"I'm sure after spending your whole life in Chicago, Plains Point probably seems like a pioneer town," Jack replied.

"It's not that bad," Kelsey conceded. "At least I met some kids at the pool today and they all seemed pretty cool."

"How long do you think you'll be here in town?" he asked Mariah.

"I'd thought just for a week or two, but that was before I saw the condition of the house. I'm thinking now it will take at least a month, maybe two, to get everything done." She looked down at her plate, finding it easier to look at her pizza than into the evocative warmth of his green eyes.

For the next few minutes Jack and Kelsey chatted about movies and video games and music. He was good with Kelsey, not talking down to her in a way some adults did with teenagers. He seemed genuinely interested in her opinions and Kelsey responded easily.

Mariah found herself staring at him. His facial features radiated strength. A lean face with a well-defined jawline, a straight nose, dark brows that slashed straight and even over each eye. The only thing that softened him was the slight curl of his dark hair and the warmth that radiated from his gorgeous eyes.

"Mom?" There was just enough exasperation in Kelsey's tone to let Mariah know it wasn't the first time she'd tried to get her attention. With a flush of heat in her cheeks she pulled her gaze away from the man across the table and to the teenager seated next to her.

"A couple of girls I met at the pool today just went into the arcade room. Can I go, too?"

Mariah wanted to tell her absolutely not, that she needed to sit in the booth and not leave Mariah alone with Jack for one minute. But even as she thought this, she knew it was crazy. "Okay." She opened her purse and pulled out a ten-dollar bill. "Here. I imagine none of the games in there are free."

"Thanks." Kelsey grabbed the ten and shot out of the booth.

Jack smiled at Mariah. "She seems like a good kid."

"She's so good it's sometimes scary," Mariah admitted.

"It must have been tough, being a single parent."

"She's made it pretty easy by being such a great kid. Of course the worst years are just ahead." She smiled ruefully.

Jack leaned back in the booth. "I imagine you've laid the foundation right so that the teen years will be a snap."

"From your lips to God's ears," she replied. She'd hoped that some of the simmering tension inside her would dissipate as they chatted, but it hadn't. She couldn't remember the last time she'd felt so nervous around a man.

"I always wondered what had happened to you," he said. "One day you were sitting at your desk in front of me and the next day you were gone and never came back. The gossip was that you'd run away, but nobody knew why."

"My father used to beat me." The words fell from her mouth before she realized she was going to speak them.

His eyes widened, then narrowed. "The good Reverend Sayers was a child abuser?"

She reached for her water glass, needing to moisten her dry mouth as she thought of her father. "He'd preach charity and love on Sunday, then beat the hell out of me the rest of the week."

"What about your mother?" he asked.

Mariah shrugged. "She bought into the 'Spare the rod, spoil the child' theory."

Jack's features tightened at once. "Nobody knew? Nobody could help?"

"Finn was the only person who knew and he had enough problems of his own." A new flush filled her cheeks. "I didn't mean to get into all this. I left the last time my father took a switch to me. I decided that night that he would never hurt me again. I took a little money, a few clothes, and caught a bus to Chicago."

He leaned forward, the warmth of his gaze washing over her. "You are an amazingly strong woman."

She released an embarrassed laugh. "Not really. I just did what I thought I needed to do to survive."

He shook his head. "I always knew there was

something sad about you. Even though you smiled and laughed and on the surface seemed like a normal teenager, there was something in your eyes that made me sad for you."

She looked at him in surprise. He certainly had paid more attention to her in school than she had to him. She didn't know whether to feel flattered or uncomfortable.

He seemed to sense her discomfort. "I was an observer in high school. Nobody paid much attention to me, so that made it easy for me to see things that others didn't."

"You've definitely changed since high school," she replied. Talk about stating the obvious—could she say anything more stupid?

He smiled. "My mother tells everyone I was a late bloomer. My first year in college I shot up four inches and gained some weight."

"Finn told me that half the women in town went out and bought dogs or cats when you started your clinic here."

He laughed. "It's amazing what a difference a few years can make in the way people see you. Girls who never looked my way in school are suddenly bringing me casseroles and dropping off perfectly healthy animals who they think need my attention."

"Hmm, I guess I should feel privileged that you asked me out for pizza," she said lightly.

"I guess you should," he agreed teasingly, but with a bold hot light shining from his eyes.

A crazy breathlessness swept over her. She'd have to take care. She had a feeling Jack Taylor had the potential to rock her world and that's the last thing she wanted or needed in her life.

*   *   *

It was back.

The hunger.

The rage.

The ravenous need to feel the potent power of ultimate control. He'd managed to keep it at bay for almost six months, but now it was back, burning in his gut, tearing apart his brain.

He knew how to sate it. It had all begun so long ago with her. With Mariah. That was the first time the rage had become so great he'd felt he'd die from it. That night he hadn't known where to find relief, what would stop the maddening demons from screaming in his head.

He'd scarcely remembered leaving his house with a garbage bag wadded up in his pocket. He'd run like a wild animal being chased by a predator, only for him the predator was an unrelenting growl inside his head.

Then he'd seen her. Standing in the grove of trees by her house. She was all that was good, all that was kind, and he wanted to smash that goodness and destroy as he'd been destroyed.

And he had. He'd taken her with a brutality that later would make him puke. But in her terror, in the very act of dominance, he'd reached a place he'd never been before, a place of utter and complete nirvana.

After he'd left her lying broken on the ground, after he'd puked up his guts, he realized the rage that had tormented him was gone and he was at peace like he'd never been before.

That had been the beginning. And for a year it had been enough. When the rage began to build again, filling him up to the point that he thought his skin would crawl right off him, he'd known exactly what to do.

Her name had been Gina and she'd been sitting in the town square. He'd come up behind her, thrown the bag over her head and raped her. This time he'd been smart—he'd worn a condom. He'd left her scared and broken and run like the wind when he was finished.

It had been good, but it hadn't been as good as with Mariah. In all the times after, it had never been as good as it had been that first time.

Even when he'd escalated it by not covering their faces, by staring into their eyes as he raped them, it hadn't been the same. Even when he'd choked the life out of them, then carried them to his secret place and buried them, it hadn't been as good.

And now the hunger was back.

The hunger and the rage.

Tonight somebody would pay. Tonight some woman would die and as he raped her, as he choked her until the life flicker in her eyes vanished, he'd think of that first time.

And Mariah.

Chapter 7

Mariah stood on the back porch and surveyed the work Joel had done. The yard finally looked like a real lawn instead of an abandoned lot, and in the flower beds, now without the cover of the weeds, a few petunias and impatiens she'd bought and planted that morning bloomed in reds and purples.

Wafting on the summer breeze was not only the scent of freshly mowed grass but also the faint whiff of hickory smoke coming from the direction of Finn's place. Kelsey was in the yard with Tiny, the little dog chasing her as if the cast on his leg were a tiny booster rocket.

Kelsey's laughter rose in the air as she played with her companion and for a moment Mariah was filled with a contentment she hadn't known in a very long time.

This house and this land weren't bad. She'd once believed they were, but in fact they had the potential to bring somebody years of happiness.

Kelsey's laughter helped change her perspective, but she knew that part of her good feeling this morning came from the residual glow of the night before.

There was no denying that she'd enjoyed the dinner with Jack.

They'd chatted until Kelsey had returned to the table, talking about the town, bits and pieces from high school days and their present lives. It had been superficial chat that seemed appropriate for a casual date. As the evening went on, she found herself relaxing, but the electricity she felt between them never completely went away.

It had been close to nine when he'd brought them home and left them with the promise of seeing them at Finn's barbecue. She didn't like the fact that she wanted to see him again. She knew it would only complicate things for her to get close to anyone here in town.

She'd said good-bye to Plains Point years ago and within a month, two at the longest, she would say good-bye again. There was no room in her life for a relationship with a hot vet from a small town she wished to escape.

With a sigh she went back into the kitchen and into the utility room, where a load of curtains was waiting to be moved from the washing machine to the dryer.

The odor of bleach greeted her as she opened the washing machine door. She loved the scent of bleach, so clean and fresh. It would be nice if a jug of bleach could be poured over the first seventeen years of her life, leaving behind a whitewash of her memories rather than the harsh stains of reality.

For eight months after she'd run away, she'd drifted from homeless shelter to homeless shelter in Chicago, afraid for herself and the life she carried inside her. But even though those days and nights had been frightening, she'd been filled with a wondrous love for the baby growing inside her.

She remembered lying on a cot and rubbing her growing tummy, thinking this was finally somebody who would love her. This child would love her as her parents hadn't, and she'd vowed to be the best mother she could be.

And so far she had been. She'd been the mother she'd never had, loving and available. She'd been a room mother and a Brownie leader. She'd gone on the school field trips and encouraged Kelsey to have her friends over whenever she wanted.

The ringing phone pulled her from the past and out of the utility room. It wasn't the house phone but rather her cell on the kitchen counter.

"Tell me you still can't cook," Janice said.

"I still can't cook."

"Good."

Mariah laughed and sat at the table. "What's this all about?"

"I was thinking about all the movies I've seen about small towns and I started worrying that you might be turned into a Stepford Wife."

"That might be difficult, considering there's no evil husband around. Besides, it would take more than a miracle and modern science to make me a cook."

"How's it going otherwise? Is Kelsey screaming to come home yet?"

Mariah gazed out the window where Kelsey was still being chased by Tiny. "She spent a couple of hours at the public pool yesterday and met some kids. Then last night we went out to dinner with the veterinarian who fixed the new dog and she hung out with some of the kids at the arcade. She seems fairly satisfied here for now."

"Whoa, back up. What's this about dinner with a vet? Who is he and what does he look like?"

"His name is Jack Taylor and I went to high school with him. As far as what he looks like, suffice to say that Kelsey calls him Dr. Hot."

"Hmm, if he passes the Kelsey test, he must be hot. Are you seeing him again?"

"I'm sure I'll be seeing him again. It's a small town," Mariah replied.

"You know that's not what I mean," Janice replied impatiently.

"Honestly, Janice, it would be pretty stupid for me to look for a relationship in a town I'll soon be leaving," Mariah exclaimed.

"And it's about time you did something completely stupid in your life," Janice countered. "A brief affair with a man nicknamed Dr. Hot would probably be good for you."

"Have you been talking to my daughter?"

"No, I just don't want you to wind up like me, alone and so set in my ways I scare off most men. You're young and gorgeous and you deserve to have a healthy, loving relationship with a special man."

Mariah laughed once again. "How did we get from brief hot affair to happily ever after?"

Janice's familiar low chuckle filled the line. "I'm being a pain, aren't I?"

A deep affection for her friend rose up inside Mariah. "I know you only want what's best for me."

"We've talked about this before. If you allow that

night to keep you from falling in love, then you remain a victim for the rest of your life."

"Are you through?" Mariah asked. This time it was her turn to feel slightly impatient. They'd been over this a million times before.

"I'm through," Janice agreed.

For the next few minutes the two caught up on news from Chicago and by the time they hung up, it was time to start getting ready for the barbecue at Finn's.

What Janice had never understood about Mariah was that she'd found her happiness without a man in her life. She was fulfilled by her work as a teacher, warmed by her love for her daughter. She'd never needed a man to fill empty spaces or make her complete. She was complete on her own.

Sure, it might have been nice to find some man to share her life with, one who admired and respected the choices she had made, one who shared the same likes and dislikes.

There were times she admitted that it would be nice to have somebody to whisper to in the quiet, somebody to share a pot of coffee with in the mornings, somebody to make love with late at night. But she didn't need that in her life.

At a quarter to six Mariah checked her reflection in her dresser mirror. She'd pulled her long hair back and fastened it at the nape of her neck with a mother-of-pearl clasp. She wore one of her favorite outfits, a turquoise sundress that would be cool and airy for a night spent in the late-spring heat and fun turquoise flip-flops. She'd even taken time to paint her nails a pearly pink.

She felt nervous as she turned away from the mirror. Tonight she would be seeing people she hadn't seen in years. Classmates she'd laughed with, fellow students she'd seen on a daily basis.

But in the back of her mind as she thought of the young men she'd known in high school, she'd always wondered if one of them had been waiting for her that night, hiding beneath the cover of the woods and the storm.

Was she going to eat barbecue tonight, drink a beer and exchange old memories with the man who had raped her?

She shoved these thoughts away, refusing to allow her evening to be tainted by something that happened so long ago. "Wow, you look nice," Kelsey said as Mariah met her in the hallway and they went downstairs.

"Back at you." Mariah smiled at her daughter, who looked achingly fresh and pretty in a pair of pale pink shorts and a pink and white tank top.

"We can't leave yet," Kelsey said. "You're the guest of honor and so we can't be one of the first to get there. It's so uncool."

Mariah sat on the edge of the sofa. "Well, we certainly don't want to be uncool." Kelsey perched on the sofa's arm, the clean scent of her shampoo battling with the latest had-to-have perfume.

Tiny yipped from his confines in the kitchen and Kelsey popped up to run to the gate and sweet-talk him. "We'll be back before you know it," she said. "I'll bring you home a nice barbecued hot dog."

"You're spoiling that dog," Mariah exclaimed.

"I know, but he deserves to be spoiled. He's just so cute." Kelsey reached over the gate and patted Tiny on his head. "I really don't think we need to keep him gated like this. He lets us know when he needs to go out. Maybe tomorrow we can just forget about the gate?"

"Maybe," Mariah agreed, and stood. "Come on, squirt, let's get over to Finn's. I'm sure nobody will say anything if the guest of honor is right on time."

Mariah tamped down a touch of nervous tension as they got into the car. She didn't know if her nerves came from the prospect of seeing old friends or the anticipation of seeing Jack again.

It was the crazy male-female thing that she'd briefly felt for Tom Lantry, a kick that in his case had lasted only until she realized he got that same kick looking at his own reflection in a mirror.

When they pulled down the long dirt drive that led to Finn's place, Mariah noticed the changes that had occurred. The old farmhouse sported fresh white paint and a new large porch. A pristine white barn had replaced the old one that had listed precariously to one side.

The place looked prosperous, although there were some things that had remained the same. The old smokehouse stood in the distant pasture along with an old feed shed that had been mangled by a rampaging bull when Finn and Mariah had been twelve.

The driveway was already full of vehicles as Mariah nudged her car between an SUV and a pickup. As she and Kelsey got out of the car, the sounds of merriment coming from the back of the house drifted in the still evening air.

"Looks like there's a big crowd," Kelsey said.

"Sounds like it, too," Mariah replied.

Finn greeted them at the front door. He grabbed Mariah in one of his signature bear hugs, then released her. "You look gorgeous as always. Come on in, most of the gang is already here."

He led them through a pleasant living room decorated in earth tones with framed pictures of two red-haired little kids on nearly every surface.

"Hey, Mariah." The woman Mariah had known as Hot Pants Hannah smiled from the kitchen doorway. She wore a pair of Daisy Duke shorts that exposed the long, shapely legs that had given many a teenage boy a moment of breathless fantasy. Her brown hair, once almost boyishly short, now touched her shoulders, enhancing her prettiness.

"Hannah, it's nice to see you again. This is my daughter, Kelsey."

"It's nice to meet you," Kelsey said.

Hannah smiled. "Not only gorgeous, but she has good manners, too."

Mariah smiled. "Thanks for doing this."

She smiled and nodded toward Finn. "It's no big deal—he looks for opportunities to throw these shindigs. Last summer we threw together a barbecue because he had a cold sore on his lip and thought it would cheer him up."

"She's making that up," Finn exclaimed, the look he gave his wife one of obvious adoration.

Hannah winked at Mariah and Kelsey. "Okay, maybe it was a stubbed toe."

They all laughed; then Finn herded Mariah and Kelsey toward the sliding glass doors that led to an immense patio complete with a barbecue pit as big as Mariah's master bath in Chicago. Half a dozen picnic benches filled the area along with folding lawn chairs.

People were everywhere, standing in groups, sitting on the benches and hovering around the two beer kegs surrounded by ice and chilling in oversized plastic garbage cans.

Kids played in the yard, both on a swing set and with dozens of lawn toys. Some chased one another in a game of tag. A handful of kids around Kelsey's age sat at one of the picnic tables slightly away from the adults.

One of the girls, a cute little blonde, waved to Kelsey as they stepped outside. "Go on," Mariah said, and smiled at her daughter.

Finn grabbed Mariah by the arm and led her to a group of people. Within minutes her head was spinning as she tried to put faces with names from her past.

Although she didn't see Clay Matheson in the group, his wife, Sherri, greeted Mariah coolly. "Nice to see you again," she said, although the brittle hardness in her brown eyes said otherwise.

Sherri had been the mayor's daughter in high school. A pretty blonde who many of the girls had thought was stuck-up, she appeared to have put on about forty pounds since the old days.

"Nice to see you again, too," Mariah replied.

"I heard you've been living in Chicago." Her gaze swept down the length of Mariah. "I just assumed they'd have great clothing there, but maybe not."

Bitch, Mariah thought even as she smiled, but before she could reply, an arm fell on her shoulder and she looked up into Jack's knowing eyes.

"Hey, you," he said. "I've been waiting for you to arrive. Sherri, you don't mind if I steal her away, do you?" He didn't give her a chance to answer, but steered Mariah away.

"You scare the hell out of her," he said into Mariah's ear, the warmth of his breath shooting that crazy electricity through her.

"Why should I scare her?" Mariah asked, half-glad and half-sorry when he dropped his arm from her shoulder. Wearing a pair of dark brown cargo shorts and a beige polo shirt, he looked cool and handsome.

His gaze swept over her in the same way Sherri's had moments before, only in his case she felt his gaze like a physical caress. "Why should you scare her? Because you've come back here all sexy, sassy and single and everyone knows that years ago you and Clay had a thing for each other."

"High school stuff, not real-life stuff," she replied. She glanced over to where Kelsey sat with the other teens, her head thrown back in laughter.

Mariah looked back at Jack. "Speaking of Clay, I notice our good sheriff is absent."

"Somebody said that something came up and he'll be here later. How about I bring you a beer?" He gestured toward a nearby empty picnic table.

"Okay," she agreed.

By the time Jack returned to the table with their beer, several others had joined them and for the next hour they chatted about old times.

The kids and teens ate first; then the adults fixed their plates and returned to the tables to feast on barbecued brisket and fresh ears of corn and a dozen other side dishes that had been brought in to add to the spread.

No matter whom Mariah visited with, she remained acutely aware of Jack. He mingled with the others and each time she heard his deep laugh, a tiny rivulet of heat flooded through her. It was obvious he was well liked and admired by everyone.

As night fell, Finn and Hannah lit tiki torches. Most of the young kids fell asleep and the group thinned to eight couples.

Kelsey and the cute blond girl named Katie, who Mariah now knew belonged to Joe and Gretchen Arrowood, had their heads together whispering and giggling like long-lost best friends.

"There he is, finally," Finn said as Clay joined the party. He went directly to his wife, kissed her on the cheek and then flopped into a lawn chair.

"Missing kid," he said.

"Oh no, who?" Linda Graham asked. Linda had been a cheerleader in high school and she'd married one of Clay's best friends, Charlie. She still had her pretty smile and the sweet personality that had made her liked by both the girls and the guys in school.

"Missy Temple. Her mother went in to wake her up this morning around ten and she wasn't there. The bed hadn't been slept in and Mrs. Temple didn't know where she might have gone." Clay took the beer Sherri offered him with a grateful smile.

"She has a reputation for being wild," Roger Francis said. "Maybe she's just holed up with one of her friends."

Clay raised an eyebrow. "You into teenage girls, Roger?"

Roger grinned easily. "Nah, I'm just into gossip. As coach of the football team I hear plenty. Nathan Wilkens, my star quarterback next year, mentioned one day that Missy liked to smoke more than her share of weed and she talked about dating college boys."

"Maybe one of those college boys ran off with her," Sherri said.

"Maybe," Clay replied, and took a drink of his beer. "I'm hoping she'll show up in the next couple of days, sorry for worrying her mama." He smiled at Mariah. "What's it like to see all these ugly mugs again after all this time?"

"It's been wonderful," Mariah replied. "We've been talking over old times the whole night."

"We've all changed, that's for sure," he said. "Take Jack there." He pointed a finger toward Jack, who stood nearby. "I remember a time when I could bench-press his squirrelly ass with one arm. Then he went off to college and had a makeover or something."

Jack smiled. "It was self-defense. I figured if I was eventually going to come back here to live, then I'd better bulk up so you wouldn't pick on me anymore."

Clay snorted. "Everyone knows if any man would hurt a hair on your head, half the single women in town would lynch the perpetrator. That's the problem with being so damned good-looking. Everyone wants you. Believe me, I understand the problem." He preened and ran a hand through his thinning hair as everyone else jeered him.

"I don't get it, Jack. You can have most any woman, but you care more about the dogs and cats in town than the women who own them," Roger exclaimed.

Jack's gaze flickered to Mariah. His eyes glowed in the illumination from the torches. "Maybe I'm just waiting for some special woman to come along and change my ways." Heat flamed in Mariah's cheeks and she breathed easier as Jack broke the eye contact.

"How long you going to be in town, Mariah?" Linda asked.

"Initially I figured on being here just a week or two, long enough to get the house set up with a local Realtor. But I hadn't anticipated all the work that needed to be done on the place. It's probably going to be a month or two before we head back home."

"I heard you have Joel Clarkson helping you out." Roger's wife, Marianne, wrapped her arms around her shoulders as if staving off a shiver. "That man gives me the creeps."

"Ah, he's all right," Finn replied. "Joel's a loner and kind of weird, but you can't argue that he does good work when he's sober."

"He always seems to be lurking around in the shadows like somebody who has something to hide," Marianne exclaimed.

Roger laughed and leaned over and patted her leg. "Marianne sees boogeymen in all the shadows."

"And I think on that note, it's time for me and Kelsey to head home," Mariah said as she stood.

"So soon? Hell, I just got here," Clay exclaimed.

"Your loss," Roger said, also getting up from his chair. "We've got to head out, too."

"I'll walk you to your car," Jack said to Mariah, who motioned to her daughter that they were leaving.

"That's not necessary." It was a weak protest. It was dark and in truth she would welcome his presence next to her.

"I know, but it's what I want to do," he replied. He took her by the elbow, his touch warm and with a hint of possession.

If any other man had touched her like that, she would have pulled away, but she didn't from Jack. "It was fun, wasn't it?" he asked as they walked around the side of the house toward the front where all the vehicles were parked.

"Other than the fact that Sherri's gazes were sharp enough to cut skin, it was very nice."

"She'll be fine once she realizes you haven't come back to steal her husband."

Mariah laughed. "A husband is the very last thing I'm looking for," she replied.

"And why is that?"

"My life is pretty full as it is."

"It's been four years since I've been in any kind of a relationship. I don't need a woman to cook or clean for me. I don't *need* anyone for much of anything. But there are times I think it would be nice to have somebody to share the good times and the bad with me."

"I feel the same way, but most of the time I'm okay alone." She pulled her keys from her purse and looked for her daughter, who had yet to round the back of the house.

"There's that strong woman talking," he said teasingly.

She shrugged and smiled. "I guess that's just who I am."

"I'd like to kiss you," he said. His voice was low and intimate in the darkness that surrounded them. "That's just who I am."

"That's crazy," she said with a half-breathless laugh. Her heart beat so fast in her chest she felt as if she couldn't draw a full breath.

"You used to drive me crazy years ago," he replied. He ran his index finger down the side of her face. "I've never admitted this aloud before, but I had a terrible crush on you years ago."

"Oh, I never knew."

"I would have been horrified if you'd known." He dropped his hand from her face as Kelsey appeared at the corner of the house. "I just want to let you know, I've waited all this time to get a kiss from you and I intend to get one before you leave town."

He stepped back from her. "Good night, Mariah." He turned on his heels and headed toward his car.

It was later that night as Mariah lay in her bed that she wondered if a high school crush could have led to rape. And she hated the fact that whoever had raped her had stolen the pleasure of a man wanting to kiss her.

"You certainly were friendly to her," Sherri Matheson said the minute she and Clay were in the car and on the way home from Finn's.

Clay shot his wife a quick glance. "No more friendly than I would be to anyone," he replied.

Sherri made that *hrump*ing sound deep in her throat that tightened all of Clay's stomach muscles. Jesus, he'd rather face a hopped-up meth head than Sherri when she made that familiar little noise.

"Sherri, honey, I don't know what you're talking about," he exclaimed. "I sure as hell wasn't overly friendly to Mariah. Do we need to swing by and pick up the kids?"

"No, Mom is keeping them overnight." Sherri slapped the air-conditioning vent to blow more fully on her face. "She certainly seemed plenty friendly with you. I saw her looking at you when she thought nobody else was watching her."

There was no point in arguing with her. Clay knew after ten years of marriage that when Sherri got something in her mind, nothing could persuade her otherwise.

With four kids, aged eight, six, four and two, the nights that he and his wife got alone were rare. And a quick glance at his wife's stony expression let him know he'd better do something or this childless night would go to waste.

"Sherri, honey. Mariah Sayers doesn't mean anything to me. There's only one woman I'm crazy about and that's you." He pulled into the driveway of their neat little ranch house and parked the car, then turned to further reassure his wife.

But she was out of the car with a slam of her door. "Ah jeez," Clay muttered as he got out of the car and followed after her.

"I'll bet her house doesn't smell like dirty diapers and old sneakers," she snapped as she waited for him to unlock the front door. "I'm sure it would be much nicer for you to go home with her than come here with all the chaos of the boys and me as fat as a cow."

"Sherri, baby, you're overreacting here." He opened the door and she flew in ahead of him, her footsteps thundering as she flipped on lights and headed toward the master bedroom.

He got there just in time to see her ripping the blanket from the bed and grabbing her pillow. "Sherri, what the hell are you doing?" he asked.

"I could tell by the way you looked at her that you'd love to have Mariah Sayers in your bed. After all, she was the one you really loved. I just got you by default." She pushed past him.

"She was just somebody I dated. We were kids. Sherri, what are you doing?"

She whirled around to face him, her pretty brown eyes awash with tears. "I'm sleeping in Benny's room. I refuse to lie in bed with a man who's probably going to dream about another woman."

He watched her stomp off toward their eldest son's bedroom, her bottom jiggling with each step as if to torment him with a visual reminder of what he wouldn't be getting that night.

He thought about going after her, trying to talk some sense in her, but truth was he was just too damned tired. Sherri was high maintenance on most days, but when she got like this, no matter what he did to try to appease her, it was wrong.

She'd probably cool off by morning and maybe sneak into bed with him for a little slap and tickle before he left for work.

Work. The knot in his stomach suddenly twisted into a burning coil of fire. He left the bedroom and headed for the kitchen. He was too wound up to go to sleep and there was a cold brew in the refrigerator calling his name.

He grabbed a beer and popped the top as he sank into one of the chairs at the table. He tipped the bottle to his lips and took a deep swallow. He was drinking too much, had been for the last six months.

The booze was the only thing that took the edge off the fear that had been a constant companion for the last few months. If he was drunk, he wouldn't think about the secret he had, a secret that could destroy him.

Chapter 8

A warm lick on the bottom of one foot awoke Jack the next morning.

"I know you're not up on the bed," he said without opening his eyes.

A low whine was his answer, followed by another lick. "It's my day off, Rover. I don't need to get up before the crack of dawn."

Rover, a black schnauzer, understood many things, but he didn't understand sleeping in. He jumped up with his front paws on the bed and barked, two short yips. *Get Up.*

"All right, all right." Jack sat up and swung his legs over the side of the bed. Rover watched him with intelligent brown eyes as Jack got to his feet and stretched with arms overhead.

Rover danced with excitement around his feet. After three years the dog knew Jack's habits better than Jack's ex-wife had known them. He went to the bathroom, pulled on a pair of running shorts, grabbed the leash and fastened it on Rover's collar and then headed for the front door.

Jack had discovered the joy of running when he'd

been in college. He stepped out of the door into the predawn air and headed at a moderate pace up Main Street. He loved this time of the morning, long before the stores opened and when the streets belonged to him alone.

The slap of his feet echoed on the sidewalk and Rover easily kept up at his side. Every important decision Jack had made in his adult life had been made while he'd been slapping pavement.

He'd been jogging when he'd decided to ask Rebecca to marry him and he'd been jogging when he realized he had to divorce her.

They'd met their junior year in college. Rebecca had been a smart vivacious blonde who wanted to be a nurse. They'd married after graduation and for the first year of their marriage things had looked bright.

Jack was establishing his own animal clinic and she was finishing up nursing school. He thought they were working together, supporting each other both in their career choices and in their life in general.

Rebecca was an overachiever and had the energy of three people. She kept the house in perfect order and prepared elaborate meals while juggling her school load and working part-time as Jack's receptionist. Jack had tried to get her to slow down, but she'd insisted she was fine.

Then one night at three in the morning he woke up to find himself alone in the bed. He found Rebecca in the kitchen scrubbing one area of the tiled floor and from her jerky gestures, from her fierce concentration on that single spot of tile, he realized she was high.

That night had been the beginning of broken dreams and financial ruin. It had taken him two years after that night before he finally recognized he couldn't fight her meth addiction, that he couldn't heal whatever wounds lay deep inside her that made her need to self-medicate. He spent an exhaustive amount of money sending her to rehab twice and after the last failure he'd given up on their marriage.

Rover's bark pulled him from the past and he realized he'd been running too fast. "Hey, sorry, buddy," he said as he stopped, his breaths coming in deep pants. He picked up the dog and bent over partway in an effort to catch his breath, unsure if the physical activity or thinking about Rebecca had exhausted him.

He didn't want to think of her anymore. Thinking about her brought a bitterness to his soul, a hardness to his heart that was at odds with the man he believed himself to be.

He'd rather think about Mariah and the way she'd looked last night at the barbecue. Hot and sexy. The minute she'd arrived in that blue sundress, he'd felt like a horny teenager again.

When he'd seen her for the first time after she'd arrived back in town, he'd thought he'd seen shadows in her eyes that whispered of old wounds. But last night she'd looked strong and independent, and after the years of his trying to heal a woman who didn't want to be healed, Mariah's assertion that she didn't particularly *need* a man in her life had merely intensified his desire to make her want him.

He'd spent his high school years watching everyone else get the girl. He'd suffered a crippling shyness that had kept him from talking to the girl he wanted more than anything else on earth, a girl who had grown into a strong, vibrant woman he still wanted.

She wasn't immune to him. He'd seen the flutter of her pulse at the base of her throat when he'd told her he wanted to kiss her. If Kelsey hadn't appeared when she had, Jack would have had Mariah in his arms.

He set Rover back on the ground and turned around to head home. Mariah Sayers was back in town. As his feet began to slap the pavement again, Jack smiled. Things were definitely looking up.

"You were right—it's hardwood underneath." Joel dropped the piece of living room carpeting he'd ripped up, and straightened to look at Mariah.

"I knew it. How long would it take to rip out all the carpet and sand and varnish the floors beneath?"

Joel shrugged. "About a week."

"Then let's do it," she replied.

He raised an eyebrow and hitched up his pants with a thumb. "You sure you want to go to all that trouble and expense for a place you're just going to sell?"

It was foolish, she told herself. She should just put the place on the market now, warts and all, and take whatever anyone offered for it. She should escape before things got sticky between herself and Jack. She should run before the memories of her attack grabbed hold of her and refused to let go.

Last night she'd had a particularly vivid dream about the attack. She'd awakened herself with a scream, the details of the dream already faded by the time she opened her eyes. Yes, she'd be smart to cut her losses and run.

But she had a crazy need to transform this house, to take something that had been ugly and hated and transform it into something beautiful. It was as though she believed that if she fixed the house, she could somehow fix her past. Wouldn't Janice have a field day with that little bit of delusion?

"Ms. Sayers?" Joel stared at her, obviously awaiting an answer to a question she no longer remembered.

"Rip it up," she said, decision made. Foolish or not, perhaps a bit delusional, she didn't care. When she left here, this house would no longer be one of nightmares, but a showcase for a new family to love and a place to build good memories.

For the next hour she and Joel moved all the furniture to one side of the room so he could work on the other, ripping up the ancient carpet and pad.

"I'm donating this furniture to charity. I'll call somebody and see if we can get it out of here by tomorrow or the next day."

"I'll take it," Joel said. "We could do a little bartering. I get any furniture you want to get rid of and I'll knock some money off my bill."

"Sounds good to me, although Finn is taking the desk in the office." She glanced at her wristwatch. "He should be coming to get it anytime now." She'd mentioned last night at the barbecue that she wanted it out of her house and Finn had told her he would buy it from her. She'd insisted that if he hauled it away, that was all she wanted.

As Joel got to work ripping up the rug, Mariah went into the kitchen, where Tiny was curled up on a rug. As she sat at the table, the pooch limped over to her and gave a small whine.

Mariah reached out and scratched him behind the

ears. "I knew it was going to be like this, buddy," she said. "You know how teenagers are. They want to spend time with you unless a better offer comes along."

In this case the better offer had been the pool with Kelsey's new best friend, Katie. "She'll be home later this afternoon," Mariah told Tiny, who sat for another minute of scratching, then went back over to his little rug and curled up.

I'd like to kiss you.

Jack's words exploded unbidden in her mind. What shocked her was for just a minute as she'd stood in front of him, she'd wanted him to kiss her. Maybe it was the result of the two beers she'd drunk, she told herself even though she knew better.

It hadn't been the alcohol; it had been the man. The glint in his eyes had warmed her and the scent of him had stirred her on a lustful level she couldn't remember feeling before. Oh yes, she'd wanted him to kiss her . . . badly.

A rap at the back door pulled her from her crazy thoughts and she smiled as she saw Finn. "How's my girl?" he asked, and leaned over to kiss her cheek. He thrust two Tupperware containers into her arms. "Leftovers from last night. Hannah thought you might like them. Potato salad and that green bean salad that Kelsey liked."

"That was so thoughtful," she replied, and gestured him inside. She put the containers in the refrigerator, then turned back to face him. "I want to thank you again for last night. It was fun seeing everyone again."

"It was fun, wasn't it?"

"Hannah is great and your kids are darling."

He grinned, that wide, open smile that had always managed to make her feel better no matter what the circumstances. "You know what I think? I think we've both overcome the crap of our youth very well."

She nodded. Finn had no idea about what had really driven her from here. He didn't know about her rape and the resulting pregnancy and even though he'd been her best friend in the whole world, she didn't want him to know. She didn't want anyone to know.

There was one reason she would forever keep the secret. Kelsey. She never wanted her daughter to know that she'd been the product of rape.

"I saw Joel's truck parked out front. Maybe he'll help me load up the desk," Finn said.

"I'm sure he wouldn't mind, but you might want to take a look at the old thing and see if you really want it," she suggested.

He followed her into the office, where Mariah had packed up most of the things and all that was left was empty shelves and the desk and chair.

"Are you sure you want to get rid of it?" he asked as he ran a hand over the polished mahogany top.

"Positive. What am I going to do with it? Everything in the house is going." She walked to the desk and found the tiny grooves that had been worn there over the years, grooves her fingernails had left when she'd been commanded to bend over and take her punishment.

"Then in that case I'd be glad to take this off your hands. Hannah has been wanting a nice desk for a corner of the living room and this will just fit the bill."

"Then it's all yours." She dropped her hand from the tiny grooves that radiated with her youthful pain.

With Joel's help they got the desk out of the house and into the back of Finn's pickup. The minute the hated piece of furniture was driven away, Mariah felt a new lightness in her heart. The desk, more than anything else in the house, had represented all the power that her father had yielded and the powerlessness that she had felt growing up.

Joel had knocked off for the day and it was just about time for Kelsey to come home when Jack called. "Have you recovered from last night?" His deep voice washed over her in a pleasant wave.

"Thankfully I didn't have enough beer that I had to recover," she replied, wishing he didn't affect her on some primal level that was both exhilarating and a little bit frightening.

"I was wondering if you and Kelsey would like to have dinner with me tomorrow night here at my place. I'm not a bad cook and you can meet my significant other."

"Your significant other?" Had she missed something? Read his signals wrong? How could she possibly read "I'd like to kiss you" wrong?

"A miniature schnauzer named Rover," he replied.

She smiled in relief. "I'm surprised you don't own a dozen cats and dogs. You know, a hazard of your profession."

"I love animals, but I have tremendous self-control." There was something intimate in the words and again a flash of heat swept through her. "So, how about it? Dinner tomorrow night?"

"Why don't you come here? There's nothing my daughter would love more than to cook a meal for a visitor." And she'd feel better on her home turf, at least until she sorted out the crazy feelings Jack Taylor stirred in her.

"Now I feel like I'm imposing," he said.

"Not at all, I wouldn't have offered if that was the case."

"Okay," he agreed. "We'll do it your way for now. What time would be good for you and what can I bring?"

"Around six and absolutely nothing," she replied.

"Then I'll see you tomorrow evening. Oh, and Mariah, I still want to kiss you." He clicked off, leaving her hanging on to the receiver as a wave of warmth swept over her.

It was crazy that a skinny, nerdy kid from high school could heat up her insides sixteen years later. But there was nothing skinny or nerdy about Jack now.

She was seated at the table making a list of things she wanted to take care of the next day when Kelsey came in. Her long hair was still damp and she was wrapped in a beach towel.

"Did you tell Katie's mom thanks for bringing you home?" she asked.

"No, I didn't. You know, because you didn't raise me right and teach me manners. Duh, Mom."

"A simple yes would have sufficed," Mariah said drily. "And you're not going to believe what I did."

"What?" Kelsey grabbed a cold can of Coke from the refrigerator, then joined her mom at the table.

"I invited Jack over for dinner tomorrow night and told him you'd love to cook him a great meal."

Kelsey rolled her eyes. "Mom, you seriously need Dating 101 classes. You shouldn't have told him that

I was going to do the cooking. You should have let him think you did the cooking."

"I couldn't do that," Mariah said. "That would be dishonest. If a man's going to like me, he's got to know the real me and the real me doesn't do much cooking."

"Yeah, I guess you're right. It's like the girls in my class who wear totally huge padded bras. It's so fake, but I'm not sure the boys my age are smart enough to know fakes from the real thing."

Mariah laughed. "So, what's on the menu for tomorrow night?"

Kelsey frowned. "I'll have to give it some thought. I'll let you know after I take a shower and get the chlorine out of my hair."

"Did you have a good time?"

"Yeah, Katie has some cool friends and they were all nice to me. There was only one guy that was kind of a creep. He told me his dad hated Grandpa."

"What's his name? Maybe I know his dad."

"Ryan Kent."

Mariah frowned. "I remember a Doug Kent who was two years older than me." What Mariah remembered about Doug was that he had been mean to her in high school, always glaring at her or bumping into her accidentally on purpose. "I wonder if Ryan is his son." Kelsey shrugged. "So, what did you say to him?"

"That I didn't even know my grandpa, but what I knew of him I didn't like too much either." She shrugged. "It wasn't a big deal." She raised the soda can to her lips and took a long drink, then scooted back and got up from the table. "I'm gonna take a shower. I'll be down in a few minutes."

"I'll make us some sandwiches for supper," Mariah said. "And we have some leftover potato and green bean salads that Finn brought over earlier."

"Sounds good," Kelsey said as she left the kitchen.

When she was gone, Mariah leaned back in her chair and wondered why she had a feeling that having Jack over to dinner wasn't a great idea. What point was there in getting close to anyone here?

Oh, and Mariah, I still want to kiss you. His words echoed inside her head.

She jumped up from the table and got to work setting the table for dinner, refusing to spend another minute thinking about kisses and Jack.

As she and Kelsey ate, Kelsey talked about the kids she'd met and how she and Katie almost seemed like sisters. They liked the same music and television shows; they were both good in science and hated math. Katie even liked to cook, although not on the same scale as Kelsey.

Kelsey started talking about a couple of the boys she'd met and Mariah saw a spark in her daughter's eyes as she talked about a particular young man named Justin. Thankfully they had already had their talk about dating and had agreed that when Kelsey was sixteen, she could date. Until that time she could go out in a group, but not with a boy alone.

After dinner Kelsey went up to her bedroom to listen to music and talk on the phone to Katie, and Mariah cleared off the table.

She'd just finished in the kitchen when a knock fell on the front door. She peeked out the side window and saw that it was Marianne Francis.

"Marianne," she said as she opened the door.

The pretty woman smiled with a touch of apology.

"I'm sorry to drop in without calling, but I was driving home from the store and passing right by and just decided to stop on impulse."

"Please, come in." She opened the door to allow the petite brown-haired woman inside. "Come on into the kitchen. Would you like a glass of iced tea or a soda?"

"No, no thanks. I'm fine." She sat at a chair at the table and smiled. "I just wanted to stop in and tell you how much I enjoyed seeing you again last night. It made me remember school lunches with you and Clay and Roger and me."

Mariah remembered and returned Marianne's smile. Clay and Charles and Roger had all been best friends in high school, so it was only natural that when Mariah started seeing Clay, she starting hanging out with Marianne. The two might have become best friends if fate hadn't intervened.

"I know Sherri was kind of tough on you last night," Marianne continued.

Mariah smiled wryly. "If she thinks I've come back here to claim my long-lost high school sweetheart, she's definitely mistaken."

"I know, but Sherri has been feeling bad about herself since her last baby. She gained more weight than usual and hasn't been able to take it off. She's prickly as a pear these days and you were just an easy target for her unhappiness."

"You and Sherri are friends?"

Marianne nodded. "Sherri and I have been friends since seventh grade, when my family moved here. Even then she was crazy about Clay. It nearly broke her heart when he got so serious with you. Anyway, that's not why I'm here. I wanted to tell you that anytime you feel like having lunch out and want company, just give me a call." Her gaze went to the nearby window and she stood. "I've got to get home."

"You don't have to rush off," Mariah exclaimed, jumping to her feet as Marianne headed for the front door.

"But I do," she replied. "Roger wasn't kidding last night when he said I see boogeymen in all the shadows." A tiny frown danced across her forehead as she looked to the west where the sun was quickly sinking into the horizon. "I don't like to be out after dark. I try never to be out after dark. Call me," she said as she went out the door.

"I will," Mariah promised. She watched as Marianne hurried toward her car. She half ran with her keys at the ready, as if frantic to beat the sun to bed.

When Marianne's car had disappeared down the driveway, Mariah locked the door, turned off all the lights downstairs, then went up to check on her daughter.

Kelsey was on the phone and when Mariah came into the room, she cupped her hand over the receiver and looked at her mother with a hint of impatience. "Do you want something?"

"No, I was just going to sit and talk to you for a little while before heading to bed."

"I'm talking to Katie right now."

"Okay, then I'll just see you in the morning," Mariah said, an unexpected pang resounding in her heart. As she turned away from the doorway, she heard Kelsey whisper, then giggle.

She was growing up, Mariah thought. She didn't need her mother to tuck her in anymore. She would rather talk to her friends. And that was the way it was supposed to be, but that didn't make it any easier.

Mariah went into her bedroom, changed into her nightclothes, then sat on the edge of the bed and used her cell phone to call Janice.

"What are you doing?" she asked when her friend answered the phone.

"Eating a bowl of ice cream and watching some dumb reality show on the tube," Janice replied. "What about you?"

"Sitting on the side of the bed feeling sorry for myself because my daughter would rather talk to her new friends instead of me," Mariah said honestly.

Janice chuckled. "Ah, the pains of motherhood. You realize that's going to happen more and more often. You've been a great mother, Mariah, but you've pretty much built your life around your daughter."

"That's not true." Mariah stretched out on the bed. "I have my work."

"True, but most of your time and attention has been focused on Kelsey. You need to get a hobby. You need to get a man."

"I don't need a man," she retorted. "I've done very well with my life by myself. I don't need anyone."

"Okay, you're right," Janice replied. "But as Kelsey gets more involved with her friends and spends more time away from home, wouldn't it be nice to have a companion? We human beings, we're social animals. We enjoy the company of others."

"This conversation was supposed to be about Kelsey, not about me," Mariah finally said with a touch of aggravation.

"I just want to tell you that I admire you tremendously," Janice said. "Not many women would be able to do what you did, to have a baby under the circumstances you had and love that baby wholeheartedly."

"I couldn't have done it without you," Mariah replied softly. "If you hadn't rescued me from that shelter, I don't know what would have happened to me."

"You would have been fine. You're a survivor, Mariah. You're so strong. And you'll survive Kelsey's teenage years just fine," she finished with a laugh.

They talked a few more minutes, then hung up. Night had fallen outside and Mariah got up and went to Kelsey's room. She was off the phone and her room was dark except for the small night-light she'd slept with since she was a child.

She was already asleep, her iPod next to her on the pillow and the earphones firmly planted in her ears. Nothing short of a bomb blast beneath her bed would wake her now. She'd always been a hard sleeper and that combined with the music that would play all night in her ear made it next to impossible to wake her up until she was ready.

Mariah stood in the doorway for several long minutes, simply watching the rise and fall of her daughter's chest, loving the sight of her face in slumber.

Mariah had never regretted her decision to make up a husband, to give Kelsey the comfort of believing that she'd been conceived in love. It was certainly easier to be the child of a man who had been killed in a car accident than of one who had raped and brutalized.

She fought the impulse to walk over and kiss

Kelsey on her cheek and instead returned to her bedroom and turned off the light.

Rather than get right into bed, she walked to the window and stared outside into the darkness. A full moon overhead illuminated the tops of the trees and spilled shimmery silver light to the ground.

Her window was open and the sound of crickets and insects created a rhythmic hum that was almost soothing. Her gaze automatically went to the grove of trees in the distance, the place where she'd been attacked.

In the moonlight the area looked tranquil, almost beautiful, but it was a place where evil had visited. The trees should be misshapen and ugly to reflect the evil that had been in their midst. But instead they were magnificent, beautiful oaks with leafy canopies.

She drew a weary breath and started to turn away from the window, but something gave her pause. She froze, a faint alarm ringing softly in the back of her head.

The night breeze fluttered in the window, bringing with it complete silence. Something had disturbed the insects. Everything that had been singing and creaking moments before had stilled.

As she stared at the stand of trees, a shadow detached itself from one tree and ran to disappear into the darkness surrounding another.

The alarm screamed inside her. Her heartbeat crashed in double time.

Somebody was outside.

Was it him?

Oh, God, had he come back for her again?

Chapter 9

"If somebody was there, they aren't there now," Clay said as he stood in Mariah's kitchen. "Are you sure it wasn't some animal? We've got good-sized raccoons around here."

Mariah shook her head and belted her robe more tightly around her. She felt foolish, but she was certain of what she'd seen. "It was a person."

"Could you tell if it was a man or a woman?" he asked.

"No, it was just a shadow, but definitely a person running from tree to tree."

Clay frowned. "Did you see where they went?"

She shook her head. "I backed away from the window and called you," she replied. Her heart still pounded too fast, although she was grateful that Clay had responded to her call as quickly as he had. "I just can't imagine what anyone was doing out there in the dark."

Clay leaned against the counter and smiled. "You've got a pretty teenage daughter, a new girl in town, who I imagine has all the boys stirred up. It's possible one of them decided to come out here and try to get a peek at her through a window, or was lurking out there trying to get up his nerve to knock on the door and talk to her."

"At this time of night?" Mariah glanced at the kitchen clock. Almost eleven.

"It's late, but it's summertime and besides, nobody ever said teenage boys had a lick of sense."

Mariah felt herself begin to relax at his words. Maybe he was right. It certainly made more sense that a teenage boy was sneaking around to get a peek at Kelsey than a rapist was coming back for Mariah sixteen years later.

"Maybe you're right," she agreed. "I'm sorry I called you out here for this. I guess I overreacted."

"Nonsense, that's my job." He pushed off the counter and straightened. "I can understand you being a little nervous out here with it just being you and your daughter. I don't want you to hesitate calling me if you feel unsafe about something." He headed toward the back door. "I'll do one more sweep around the house and the yard before I go."

"Thanks, Clay," Mariah said. "I really appreciate it." She locked the door after him, then leaned heavily against it. Those moments between the time she'd seen the shadowy figure and Clay's arrival had seemed an eternity.

There was no question that Clay's scenario of a love-struck teenage boy made more sense than her own fear that her attacker had returned for her.

She shoved off the door and after double-checking that all windows and doors were locked up tight, she climbed the stairs once again to her bedroom.

A view from the window showed Clay with his flashlight searching the general area where she'd told

him she'd seen somebody. She watched until he finished up his final search, then got into his patrol car
and drove off.

Thankfully Kelsey had slept through the whole
thing. Mariah didn't want Kelsey to know what a
fraidy-cat she was, so she was grateful that her
daughter usually slept like the dead.

Getting beneath the clean-smelling sheets of her
bed, she tried to calm herself, tried to will her heartbeat to slow. When she'd recognized she would have
to return to Plains Point to deal with the estate, she
hadn't really realized how much it would bring back
the fear, a fear that she had put behind her over
the years.

She swallowed against that fear now and hugged
one of her pillows against her chest. She had to fight
against it, refused to allow it to rule her during her
time here. If she gave in to it, then she wasn't a
survivor—she was a victim once again. If she gave
in to the fear, then he won—his words to her were
true, that he'd broken a piece of her and she belonged to him forever.

Chapter 10

"Beef Wellington," Kelsey said the next morning as they were eating breakfast. "I think that would be good for dinner tonight."

"Isn't that kind of difficult?" Mariah asked. She figured anything that had a duke's name in it had to be hard to make.

"On a scale from one to ten, with ten being the most difficult, it's about a six. But I'm a seven on the cooking scale, so I should be able to pull it off." Kelsey flashed her a confident smile. "With it I'll serve steamed broccoli spears, a corn medley and dinner rolls. For dessert we'll have to check what fresh fruit they have in the store."

"Sounds great, my little Emeril."

"You know what this means?" Kelsey paused to take a sip of her orange juice. "This means a major grocery shopping trip this morning."

"We'll have to wait until Joel gets here before we can leave. He's going to work some more today on ripping up the carpeting."

"How are you going to entertain a gentleman caller with the living room all torn up?" Kelsey asked.

"He's just coming over to eat. Any entertaining I do can be done right here in the kitchen," Mariah said. "At least Joel hasn't started on this floor yet." She looked at the ugly tile beneath her feet.

At that moment a knock on the back door indicated Joel had arrived to begin his work for the day. By ten thirty Mariah and Kelsey were in the grocery store, Kelsey armed with a list the length of her hair.

As Mariah followed behind her daughter, she tried to tamp down the impulse to call Jack and cancel the whole night. What had she been thinking when she'd agreed to dinner? She'd obviously had a momentary lapse of sanity.

What was it about the handsome veterinarian that made her forget that she wanted no ties here in Plains Point? What was it about him that sent her pulse racing in a wild, exciting way? Why did the thought of him kissing her weaken her knees and form a ball of fire inside her stomach?

"I think that's it," Kelsey said forty-five minutes and a full cart later.

"If you keep this up, I'm going to have to take a second job to keep you in the gourmet food you like to cook," Mariah said as they headed to the cashier.

"It will all pay off when I'm writing best-selling cookbooks and have my own show on the Food Network," Kelsey replied.

They rounded the corner and nearly collided with another cart pushed by Sherri Matheson. "Sorry," Kelsey exclaimed.

"Hi, Sherri," Mariah said.

The plump blonde curled up her lip in obvious disdain. "Mariah," she said with a curt nod of her head, then pushed ahead of them to a cashier on the opposite side of the store.

"What's her problem?" Kelsey muttered as they got in the nearest line.

"Ancient history," Mariah replied. "I think she's pegged me as a big-city, man-hungry woman who's after her husband."

Kelsey giggled. "It would be closer to the truth if she thought you were an undercover nun."

Mariah slapped her daughter's arm playfully.

By the time they returned to the house, Mariah's nerves about the evening to come were in full scream. As Kelsey began the food preparations, Mariah went upstairs and indulged in a long, hot bubble bath.

As she lazed in the water, the scent of jasmine filled the air and she leaned her head back against the cool porcelain and tried to calm herself.

The meal meant nothing. Jack Taylor meant nothing. They'd share some pleasant conversation, a good meal; then it would be over and Jack would go back to his life and she'd eventually get back to hers.

It was silly to stress about a simple meal. By the time she got out of the bathtub, wonderful scents drifted up the stairs from the kitchen. She grabbed a long cotton skirt and a matching T-shirt from the closet and dressed.

At least if the conversation was stilted and awkward, the food would be good, she thought as she put on her makeup. An hour and a half, two at the most, how long could a meal take to eat?

She pulled her hair into a ponytail at the nape of her neck, then checked her reflection in the mirror.

She looked cool and casual, perfect for a simple dinner. But her eyes shone with an anticipation that she tried hard not to acknowledge.

"Something smells good," she said as she entered the kitchen.

Kelsey closed the oven door and turned around. "You look pretty, Mom."

"Thanks. How's it going?"

"All that's left is last-minute stuff, so I'm going to go upstairs and clean up. Then I'll finish everything once he's here." She scooped up Tiny in her arms. "And since this one doesn't have very good table manners, I'll make sure he stays in my room until after dinner."

As Kelsey disappeared from the kitchen, Mariah glanced at the clock. Quarter till six. Fifteen minutes and he'd be here. She knew instinctively that Jack Taylor was a man who was rarely late.

The table was already set, so she made a pot of coffee and by the time it had brewed, Kelsey returned to the kitchen clad in a clean pair of shorts and a T-shirt.

"Are you nervous?" she asked Mariah.

"Why would I be nervous? It's just dinner with an old friend," Mariah countered, although she thought the tone of her voice sounded higher than usual.

Kelsey grinned. "Yeah, an old friend who looks like a movie star."

"But he's not a movie star. He's a small-town veterinarian and there's nothing for me to be nervous about."

Kelsey checked the temperature on the oven, then turned back to look at Mariah, her brow wrinkled in thought. "When you met Daddy, did you know right away that he was the one?"

"Not right away, but fairly quickly," Mariah replied, surprised by the question. It had been a long time since Kelsey had asked any questions about her father. "Why?"

"I don't know. I was just wondering. When you first saw him, did you feel butterflies in your stomach?"

Had Kelsey met somebody who gave her butterflies? Had she already met a boy here who attracted her? Before Mariah had a chance to find out where the conversation was leading, the doorbell rang and it was Mariah who had ridiculous butterflies in her stomach.

"We'll talk about this later," Mariah said as she left the kitchen to answer the door. The butterflies intensified as she pulled open the door to greet Jack.

Wearing a pair of jeans and a short-sleeved blue polo shirt, he looked amazing. He grinned at her and raised his hands, a bottle of wine in each. "I come bearing gifts," he said as she opened the door to let him inside. "I didn't know what was being served, so I picked up a bottle of white and a bottle of red."

"Red would be the wine of the night," she replied. "And please excuse the mess. As you can see, I'm having the carpeting pulled up in here."

"Looks like the floors are nice beneath."

"A little sand and varnish and I think they'll be beautiful," she replied.

"Speaking of beautiful, you look great." His gaze went from the top of her head to the tips of her toes, evoking a heat wave inside her.

"Thanks. Come on into the kitchen. Kelsey has

been slaving over a hot stove all afternoon." She'd feel more comfortable with Kelsey chaperoning. Then maybe he wouldn't look at her like he wanted to eat her up.

"Something smells terrific," he said as they entered the kitchen.

Kelsey grinned at him. "I hope it tastes as good as it smells."

"Kelsey is my budding chef." Mariah took the two bottles of wine from him and gestured him into a chair at the table. "Would you like a glass now?"

"Only if you're joining me."

Those green eyes of his should be outlawed as too sexy, she thought as she found wineglasses and poured them each a glass. "Thanks," he said as he took his from her, his fingers lingering on hers a fraction too long.

As Mariah sat in her chair at the table, Jack directed his attention to Kelsey, who was arranging dinner rolls on a baking sheet. "So, you like to cook."

"I love it," she exclaimed.

"Janice, my best friend back in Chicago, says that Kelsey learning to cook was a matter of her own survival," Mariah explained. "She was raised on frozen dinners and fast food."

"You don't cook," Jack said.

"Mom thinks she's cooking when she makes a box of macaroni and cheese," Kelsey quipped.

Jack laughed. "I have to confess, I'm not much of a cook either. I eat a lot of meals at the café."

"What made you decide to be a veterinarian?" Kelsey asked as she popped the dinner rolls into the oven.

"I always liked animals. From the time I was a

little boy. My mother used to complain because I was always dragging home dogs and cats, frogs and whatever else I thought might need some help. Being a vet just seemed natural. And speaking of animals, how's Tiny doing?"

"Great," Kelsey said. "I've got him locked up in my room right now because he likes to beg at the table, but I love him. He's smart and sweet."

"And seems totally devoted to Kelsey," Mariah added. She was beginning to relax as the conversation flowed easily.

"That's one of the best things about dogs. They are loyal to a fault," Jack replied. "What about you? Did you always want to be a teacher?"

"Not really. It wasn't until Kelsey was a baby that I really started thinking about where I wanted to go with my life. I liked kids, so teaching seemed the way to go. I also knew the hours would be the most accommodating for a single parent. I'd be off work on the same days that Kelsey was out of school and have all summer at home with her."

"You like Chicago?"

Why was it that when he looked at her, she felt like she was being caressed? She took a sip of her wine before replying, hoping the drink would lower the spike of her internal temperature.

"Chicago is okay," she answered. "There are a lot of things about city living that don't thrill me. But my work is there and it's been home for a long time now."

Within minutes the food was ready and they began to eat. The conversation continued to flow comfortably as they talked about movies they'd seen and shared memories of high school.

Kelsey joined in, asking questions about those distant school days and giggling as Jack teased her about being the new hot chick in town.

The food was delicious and Kelsey beamed beneath Jack's effusive praise. When they were finished eating, despite Mariah's protests to the contrary, Jack insisted he help with the cleanup.

Mariah washed, Jack dried and Kelsey put away the dishes. It was during this process that the butterflies began to soar once again in Mariah's stomach. Jack stood close enough to her that she could smell his scent, a crisp, clean smell that was intensely attractive.

The large, airy kitchen shrank as he filled the space right next to her with his presence. Each time he took a dish from her, their fingers touched and a spark shot off inside her.

Maybe it's the wine, she told herself. She'd had three glasses, more than she usually drank. But she knew it wasn't the alcohol. It was Jack.

The minute the dishes were done, Kelsey made a quick exit. "I've got e-mail to do," she said as she headed out of the kitchen.

Mariah wanted to stop her, to insist that she stay in the kitchen, but she knew she was being foolish. She didn't need her daughter to chaperone her. She was a grown woman, for crying out loud.

"Would you like to take our coffee and sit outside on the porch?" she asked. Surely in the great outdoors she wouldn't be so aware of him. The night air would diffuse the dizzying scent of him, and the old wicker chairs on the porch were far enough away from each other that he wouldn't be able to inadvertently brush her thigh or touch her hand.

"Sure, that sounds nice," he agreed.

They carried their coffee cups to the front porch, where the evening breeze was pleasant and dusk was just beginning to fall.

"These chairs have been on this porch for as long as I can remember, but I don't think my parents ever enjoyed them," she said as she sat.

"Too bad, they didn't know what they were missing." He held his coffee with one hand and used the other to move his chair closer to hers. He sat and grinned at her, the sexy cast of the smile once again torching her internal temperature to combustible levels. "There's almost nothing better than sitting on a porch with a beautiful woman and watching the sun set."

"You've certainly overcome the shyness you suffered in high school," Mariah said drily.

He flashed her a grin. "It was my sophomore year in college when I realized the meek might inherit the earth, but shy people rarely get anything they want. I spent a lot of time watching other guys get the girls and decided it was time for me to get more assertive. I don't have a problem anymore saying that I want something." There was a heat in his eyes that made warmth flush her cheeks. "What about you, Mariah? Do you go after what you want?"

"Sure, but before I do, I make sure it's something I really want and not just a whim," she replied. She was aware that the conversation had an underlying sexual connotation. How could she not be aware of it with his eyes gazing at her so boldly and that damnable sexy smile curving the corner of his lips.

It was the most intimate conversation she'd ever shared with a man and the fact that she was having it made her wonder if perhaps she had reached a place in her life where she was open to the possibility of a relationship.

"You have children, Jack?" she asked, wondering if there were little dark-haired tots living with his ex-wife.

"No, no kids. Rebecca and I were busy with our careers for the first couple of years of marriage and at the time we might have started talking about kids, we were talking about divorce instead."

"I'm sorry," she said.

He smiled. "Don't be. We needed to divorce."

"Is she here in town?"

"No. To be honest, I'm not sure where she is." A muscle in his chiseled jaw became visible. "I hear from her occasionally, but it's been a while since last time I heard from her." He sat back in the chair. "What about you? Any stalker boyfriends I should know about? Ex-husbands?"

She laughed. "I haven't had time to have either. My priority has always been getting Kelsey raised. I figured there would be time enough for a relationship when she got grown."

He lifted his coffee cup to his mouth and eyed her over the rim. "She looks pretty raised to me," he said just before he sipped his coffee.

It had been years since a man had flirted with her and even longer since she'd enjoyed it. But she was enjoying it now. As night fell, they continued to talk, sharing little pieces of information about themselves interspersed with flirtatious banter.

It was close to ten when he stood to leave. "As much as I hate to say good night, I've got to get back to the office and check on a couple of sick animals."

"It's been nice." Mariah got up from her chair, surprised at just how much she'd enjoyed the evening.

"Enough to do it again?" he asked. He stepped close to her, so close she could once again smell him, could feel the heat that radiated from his body.

Her heart hitched in her chest, the beat accelerating to a near fever pitch. He didn't touch her in any way, but she felt touched by the gleam of his eyes as they gazed at her, by the faint stir of his breath against her face.

"You know this is foolish," she said a bit unsteadily. "As soon as this house is ready to be put on the market, I'm heading back to Chicago."

"From what I could see, it looks like it's going to be a while before that happens," he replied. "There's nothing that says you can't be a little foolish in the meantime." He smiled wickedly. "And I'm just the man to be foolish with."

"Call me," she replied.

"I will. I'd also like to kiss you."

"Okay." The single word was a nervous breath.

He leaned forward and pressed his lips against her forehead. She closed her eyes, pleasure sweeping her from the point of contact to her very toes.

She tilted her face upward, fully expecting him to claim her lips. Instead he stepped back from her and she opened her eyes to see his smile. "Good night, Mariah."

"Good night, Jack."

She watched as he walked down the stairs and toward his car. A whispered sigh escaped her. The man was something else. He'd told her he wanted to kiss her, and what he'd managed to do was make her want him to kiss her.

As he got into his car, she raised her hand to touch her forehead where the imprint of his lips lingered. Maybe it was time for her to be a little foolish, to indulge a side of herself that she'd been out of touch with for a very long time.

He gave a short honk as he pulled out of the driveway and she waved even though she knew he probably couldn't see her in the dark.

As his headlights disappeared from view, she became aware of a prickling at the nape of her neck, the odd feeling that she was being watched.

It exploded inside her, a miasma of gray, a sense of impending doom. Her gaze went to the grove of trees where she'd seen somebody the night before.

Was he there now?

Watching her?

Waiting?

She took a step backward, crashed into one of the wicker chairs and nearly fell. Her lungs tried to draw breath, but it was as if a bag were over her head, a plastic garbage bag.

Stumbling to the door, she managed to get inside. She locked it, then leaned forward in an attempt to catch her breath. She closed her eyes and willed herself to calm down.

When she was once again breathing normally, she straightened. The brief panic attack only served to remind her that even though she was a great mother and a woman thinking about indulging in a relationship with a handsome man, there was still a piece inside her that was broken, a piece of her soul that her attacker had taken with him. And in its place he'd left fear and a sense of painful vulnerability.

As she climbed the stairs to her room, she mentally grabbed on to the memories of the time spent with Jack, knowing they would warm the icy center that had formed inside her.

Chapter 11

Clay hated working the night shift, although he supposed he was better off at his office than at home. Sherri was still pissed off at him and had him sleeping on the sofa, and was talking to him only when it was absolutely necessary.

He got up from his desk and walked over to the coffeemaker, where the thick liquid inside the carafe smelled like it had been warming for months.

Most nights in Plains Point were quiet ones. Occasionally on a Friday or Saturday night somebody would get too liquored up and start a fight in one of the bars and Clay or one of his men would have to go out and take care of it.

The call from Mariah the night before had been the first time in a long time he'd left the office at night on any kind of an issue.

He poured himself a cup of coffee, then carried it back to his desk. He'd just sat when Roger Francis came in. It was obvious Roger had spent part of the evening with his nose in the sauce. He swaggered in and plopped himself in the chair opposite Clay's desk.

"What are you doing out this late on a week-night?" Clay asked his friend.

"Had a few beers at Larry's and thought I'd stop in here before heading home to the little woman." Roger rubbed the end of his nose. Beer always made his nose itch. "Any news on Missy Temple?"

Clay shook his head. "Nothing. I talked to her friends and most of them think that she ran off, said she'd been talking about getting out of here for months."

"Marianne told me that Sherri told her you had to run out to Mariah's place last night."

"She thought she saw somebody lurking around in the trees near the house. It freaked her out, but when I got there I didn't find anything." Clay took a sip of the coffee and winced at the bitterness.

Roger leaned forward, a sly grin on his face. "Tell me the truth, she still rev your engine?"

"Jeez, Roger." Clay shot a glance at his doorway, hoping nobody was on the other side listening in. "Of course not. You know I'm a one-woman man. Sherri's the only one who revs my engine."

"Still, you've got to admit, Mariah is as hot now as she was in high school." He itched his nose again and leaned back in the chair. "You know if you wouldn't have gone after her back then, I would have. She was one of the best-looking girls in school. I'll bet she was hot under the sheets."

Clay thought about lying, about telling Roger that he'd knocked off a piece of Mariah every night that they'd been seeing each other. "I wouldn't know," he said truthfully. "Mariah and I didn't do anything but kiss. Back then she wasn't ready to do anything else and I respected that."

Roger sat back in his chair and rubbed the end of

his nose. "Too bad for you. I'll bet Jack won't have that problem with her."

Clay shrugged. "That's between him and her. They're both consenting adults. Besides, I got more important things on my mind than Mariah Sayers and her love life."

"Like what?"

"Like how to get back into Sherri's good graces."

"Has she been on one of her tears?"

"Ever since the night of the barbecue at Finn's. She thought I was too nice to Mariah."

"God save us all from jealous wives," Roger exclaimed. "Speaking of which, I'd better get my butt home. Marianne has been complaining that I've been spending too many nights out lately."

"Have you?"

Roger nodded. "Yeah, guess I have. I've been having trouble sleeping, feel restless and don't quite know what to do with myself."

"You feel this way every summer," Clay reminded him. "As soon as the school year starts and you begin to train your football team, you'll be fine."

"You're right." Roger stood. "Guess I'll head home. See you tomorrow."

As Roger left, Clay took another drink of his coffee and fought an edge of bitterness that rose up inside him. As the high school coach, Roger was doing the job Clay would have loved to have.

When he'd been younger, his life plan had always included football. As the star quarterback of his high school team, he'd been awarded a full scholarship to Missouri University. There he'd played good football for three years and had been scouted by two AFC teams.

Then in his senior year tragedy had struck. A bad fall, a blown knee, and he'd become a cliché of what can go wrong when you bank on a professional-sport career.

After graduating, he'd come home with no idea what he was going to do with the rest of his life. By that time he'd married Sherri and she was pregnant with their first child. Roger was already the high school coach, all his other buddies had settled into jobs and he was drifting.

It had been Sherri who had encouraged him to run for sheriff. She loved the idea of being the sheriff's wife. Nobody had been more surprised than Clay when he'd been elected.

For the last ten years being sheriff had involved little more than directing his men where to set up traffic stops, breaking up fights and dealing with the occasional robbery.

He knew what people said about him. Clay Matheson was a good man, a fair man, adored by his wife and children. He kept the streets of Plains Point safe and shared the same moral compass as most of the fine people in town.

If they only knew the truth.

As he stared out the window into the darkness of the night beyond, he had the impulse to get out of his chair, walk to his car and drive as far away from here as he could get.

He wanted to escape before the people of Plains Point found out the truth, before his image as a good sheriff, a good man, was shattered beyond repair.

Chapter 12

Thunder rumbled in the distance and the air smelled of the approaching storm. Mariah stood beneath the cover of the trees and stared at her father's study window. If he found out she'd sneaked out, he'd take the skin off her legs and butt with that willow switch.

As she thought of what her punishment would be, the old scars on the backs of her legs burned hot. She breathed a sigh of relief when his study light went out. Good, now she could get back into her bedroom and nobody would be the wiser.

The wind had picked up and lightning rent the sky in the southwest. She'd have to hurry to climb the tree that would lead her to the safety of her room.

A rustle behind her froze her in her tracks. Before she could process what the noise might be, a slick plastic bag was yanked over her head.

Someplace in the darkest recesses of her mind, Mariah knew she was dreaming and she tried to wake herself up before the real horror began, but the nightmare continued to play out.

She was on the ground. He was on top of her,

whispering to her. Then his hands splayed and pressed hard on her upper arms, holding her down as he raped her.

Help me. Somebody help me. Her brain screamed the words that she couldn't audibly speak.

She sat straight up in bed, tasting the horror in her mouth, the smell of the storm lingering in her nose. The light of dawn creeping in the window brought her completely out of the dream and she shuddered and gasped in relief.

Usually when she awakened from the nightmare memory, her impulse was to shove it out of her mind, forget about it as quickly as possible.

This time she lay back on the pillow, stared at the faint morning light and tried to remember every detail of that night.

She'd forgotten about his hands pressing so hard against her upper arms, hard enough that for a week afterward she'd had bruises there. She'd been bruised other places as well. By the next morning dark bruises had appeared on her inner thighs, making even the simple task of walking difficult.

He'd been so big, so heavy. At this thought she realized it couldn't have been Jack Taylor who had attacked her that night. Jack had been a scrawny, skinny boy and the person who had grabbed her that night had been big and husky.

She hadn't realized until this moment, with relief flooding through her, that she'd been just a little bit afraid that it might have been Jack, who had confessed that he'd had a crush on her in high school, the man who made her feel special now with just a glance of his green eyes.

With the knowledge of his innocence shining bright inside her, she felt a weight off her shoulders and a new desire to allow whatever might happen between them to continue.

She stared up at the ceiling and tried to remember those last moments with Clay in the gazebo. Had somebody been watching them as they'd kissed and declared their youthful love for each other?

Had somebody been in the shadows of the gazebo watching and waiting? Had she been followed as she hurried home, running through the town park and down Main Street with the euphoria of Clay's declaration of love ringing in her heart?

Knowing that she wouldn't sleep any more, she got out of bed, pulled on her robe and crept out of her room. As she went down the stairs, even the familiar creak of the fourth and fifth stairs didn't ease the residual horror her nightmare had left behind.

"Coffee," she muttered aloud. That's what she needed, a big hot cup of fresh-brewed coffee.

As she waited for the coffee to brew, she stood at the window and watched the sun crest the horizon, shooting pinks and oranges to lighten the night skies.

Had he followed her home from town? Had the attack been a matter of the wrong place at the wrong time or had he been waiting for her in the shadows of the trees, wanting her specifically?

She'd thought it was all behind her. For most of her time in Chicago she hadn't dwelled on that night. She'd lived her life, happy, and it had been only odd moments when the memories had disturbed her.

But now she realized despite the fact that sixteen years had passed, she still hadn't resolved it or been able to put it completely behind her. She wished now she had reported it, but at that time she'd been more afraid of her father than anything else in the world.

That's what bad girls get when they sneak out of the house. Her mother's voice filled her head. *It's your fault this happened, nobody else's.*

"Thanks, Mom," she whispered softly as she poured herself a cup of coffee.

There should be a test that everyone had to take before they became parents, she thought. If you failed, then you didn't get the responsibility of having an innocent, vulnerable child in your care. Both her parents would have failed miserably.

They had spoken often about the love of God, but hadn't had any love in their hearts, and she had to wonder what influences had created them. She'd never known her grandparents, didn't know what kind of upbringing her parents had endured.

She carried her coffee to the table and sat, surprised to discover that the rage, the hatred, that she'd always felt for her parents had tempered into something different. A weary acceptance.

Perhaps they had truly believed that they were decent parents, that the punishments they gave were just and right. They hadn't been evil people, just cold and hard and unavailable to any emotional need Mariah might have had.

As the sun rose higher in the sky and she sipped her coffee, she realized they didn't deserve her hatred. They deserved her pity. If she accomplished nothing else returning to Plains Point, this realization was enough.

She was dressed to work by the time Joel was supposed to arrive at eight thirty. She was going to help him move the rest of the living room furniture into the now empty study so he could begin sanding the living room floor.

She'd told him he could have the furniture but not until she and Kelsey were ready to head back to Chicago. She didn't want her daughter and herself to live in a house where there was no furniture. Joel had been agreeable to waiting.

He was not agreeable when he arrived nearly half an hour late. It was obvious he was suffering a hangover and was sullen and slightly ill-tempered. He reeked of alcohol and his eyes were so bloodshot they looked as if they could bleed at any minute.

Together they moved the furniture, with Joel bitching and moaning at every step. Mariah tried desperately to hold on to her patience, but finally she snapped.

"Go home, Joel. Go home and sleep off whatever is wrong with you," she exclaimed. "You're no use to me today. I don't want you here."

"I'll be all right," he said, although the sullenness of his voice said otherwise. "There's no reason for you to get all hoity-toity. I remember you from high school, you walking the halls like you thought your shit didn't stink."

She wasn't sure who was more shocked by his words, her or him. He stared at her in horror. "I'm sorry. I didn't mean that. I don't know what's wrong with me today."

"Why don't we talk about it tomorrow," Mariah said coolly.

"Look, I said I was sorry," he said, and wrung his hands. "Hell, everyone in high school treated me like dirt. Half the people in this town still do."

"Joel, I don't even remember you from high school," she exclaimed. "And if I was mean to you or ignored you or something, then I'm sorry. But that was then and this is now."

"You gonna fire me?"

She sighed. She so didn't need this. "I'll tell you what, how about you show up tomorrow on time and we'll pretend today didn't happen?"

He nodded, his lank hair falling forward. "That's a fine idea." He grabbed his toolbox and slid out the door. A moment later she heard the spit of gravel and the roar of his engine as he fishtailed out of her driveway.

"What was that all about?" Kelsey said as she came down the stairs carrying Tiny in her arms.

"Joel. I sent him home. He was hungover and cranky and I didn't want to deal with it today." At that moment the phone rang.

"Have lunch with me today," Jack said when Mariah answered.

Giddy pleasure swept through her. "You scarcely give a girl a chance to think," she replied.

"That's the idea. Don't think, just do." She hesitated and he continued. "If you're worried about my intentions, don't. I'm working today, so lunch will be an hour at the café."

Why not? She certainly didn't need to be here to supervise Joel. Why not have lunch with a man who both intrigued and excited her? This trip back to Plains Point didn't have to be about the ugly past; it could also be about pleasure. And she deserved it.

"All right," she agreed. "What time are you planning on taking your lunch hour?"

"Unless an emergency comes up, around one. Would that work for you?"

"Shall I meet you at the café or at the clinic?"

"The clinic. That way if I do get held up, you won't be sitting all alone in the café waiting for me."

"Okay, then I'll see you about one." She hung up and turned to see Kelsey beaming at her. "Wipe that look off your face," she exclaimed. "It's just lunch."

"If you say so," Kelsey replied. "If you're going out for lunch, could you drop me off by the pool?"

"I think that could be arranged," Mariah replied, her head filled with sweet anticipation at seeing Jack for lunch.

At twelve forty-five Mariah pulled to the curb near the swimming pool. "You have your sunscreen? Your towel?" she asked her daughter.

Kelsey rolled her eyes. "Mother, I'm almost fifteen, old enough to know what I need when I go to the pool." She opened her car door. "Should we just go ahead and set a time for you to come back and get me?"

"Just tell me when and I'll be here," Mariah replied.

"Why don't we say about five?" Kelsey slid her long tanned legs out the door. "Oh, and have a great lunch with Dr. Hot."

"Stop calling him that," Mariah protested, then laughed as her daughter wiggled her fingers in a good-bye and took off toward the pool.

She'd expected daily hassles with Kelsey while they were here. She'd thought her daughter would pout and whine about missing her friends back home, hating being away for the summer. But Kelsey had adjusted remarkably well.

As she pulled away from the curb, her thoughts went from her daughter to the man she was about to meet for lunch. A kick of adrenaline shot through her.

"Calm down," she said aloud as she headed toward the clinic. She was acting like a hormonally charged teenager. She'd intentionally dressed down for lunch, as if choosing to wear jeans and a summery tank top would make the meal less important.

As she parked the car in a space in front of the clinic, the beat of her heart belied the casual clothes. Although there was no rhyme or reason for it, this *felt* important.

She got out of the car and went into the cool interior of the building. Behind the receptionist's desk a woman with graying hair and a smile greeted her with a friendly hello.

"I'm here to see Jack," Mariah said.

"Oh, you must be Mariah. He told me to expect you. He's with a client right now, but he should be finishing up any minute if you'd like to have a seat."

Mariah nodded and sat in one of the chairs. She could hear the rumble of Jack's deep voice coming from one of the examining rooms. Just the sound of it created the butterflies taking flight in the pit of her stomach.

She'd been sitting only a minute or two when the door to one of the examining rooms opened and Jack ushered out an elderly woman clutching a cat carrier.

If ever there had been a man born to wear a white coat, it was Jack Taylor. It was a perfect foil for his slightly curly dark hair and green eyes.

"You bring Casper in next week at the same time and I'll check her out," he said to the old woman. He smiled at Mariah as he placed a hand on the woman's shoulder and led her to the door. "And don't forget to bring me pictures of that new great-grandbaby next week."

"I won't." Her face wrinkled with her smile as she gazed up at Jack. "And if Casper has any other problems, I can call?"

"Anytime," he said as he patted her arm. "I'll see you next week, Mrs. Waverly."

As the door closed behind the old woman, Jack turned to gaze at Mariah. "I don't know about you, but I'm starving." There was an almost iridescent glow in his green eyes that made her think he might not be talking about food at all.

"I'm beginning to have an appetite," she replied. Her ambiguous words were met with a new flame of heat from his eyes. "Maybe we should get to the café," she added.

He grinned at her as if knowing she didn't quite trust herself alone with him. "Have you met Beverly, my right-hand woman?" He gestured toward the receptionist, who looked at Jack as if he'd hung the moon.

Mariah smiled at Beverly. "It's nice to meet you."

"It's nice to meet you, too. You two go and have a nice lunch. I'll keep things going here." She made a shooing motion with her plump hands.

Jack grasped Mariah by the elbow, his hand warm against her bare skin. "Ready?"

She nodded and together they stepped out into the warm afternoon air. "Is Casper a sick kitty?" she asked.

"No, that's the healthiest cat I've ever seen. But Mrs. Waverly is the loneliest woman I've ever seen. She lost her husband six months ago and soon after his death she started bringing Casper in with imagined illnesses. It didn't take me long before I realized it wasn't about Casper needing care, but rather Mrs. Waverly needing company. So once a week I tell her I'm doing a free cat checkup and she comes in and tells me about her grandkids and what's going on in her life." He shrugged. "It's no big deal and it keeps her happy."

It was a big deal. Jack's hot gazes and sexy demeanor had her in a slow burn, but the fact that he'd take time for a lonely old widow spoke to her heart.

The café was busy, but they found a table near the back and seated themselves. "If you eat here every day, you must know what's good," Mariah said as she studied the menu.

"It's all good. I don't think I've ever had a bad meal here," he replied. "Today is Thursday, so that means the special of the day is chicken à la king and a side salad."

Mariah closed her menu. "That sounds good to me."

As they waited for the waitress to take their orders, Jack told her about some of his patients, both the furry and fluffy ones and their respective owners. By the time the waitress arrived, he had Mariah laughing at his tale of an escaped pet rabbit and Beverly's frantic efforts to catch it.

"God bless that woman, she was down on her hands and knees making what she imagined were rabbit noises," he said.

"You love what you do," she said, stating the obvious as the waitress left with their orders.

"I do," he agreed. "I've always been a healer." A dark frown raced across his features. "Sometimes I'm successful and sometimes I'm not." He picked up his water glass and took a sip and by the time he placed the glass on the table, the frown had disappeared. "I'd much rather talk about you and me than about my work."

"There is no you and me except for this lunch date," she said.

"I'm hoping to change that." The wicked light was back in his eyes.

"Why? You don't know anything about me. You don't even know if I'm a Democrat or a Republican," she said with a laugh.

He grinned. "I don't care about your politics, but I do know everything that I consider to be important about you."

"Like what?" she asked curiously.

"You're a teacher, so I know you have a lot of patience. You've raised your daughter alone and that tells me you're strong and independent. Your daughter is charming and smart and has a good sense of humor and that speaks volumes about the kind of person you are."

He stopped talking as the waitress returned with their orders and it wasn't until she'd left them alone again that he continued. "And then there are the other things."

"Other things?" Her cheeks warmed as his gaze lingered on her face.

"I like the way you smell, like some kind of a mysterious flower. I like the way your eyes light up just before you laugh." He leaned forward slightly, his gaze holding hers intently. "I like the way you tilt your head to one side when you're thinking, the way your hips move when you walk. You're the first woman in a long time who has made me think about making love."

"Oh." Mariah's breath hitched in her chest at his words and a flutter of pure feminine pleasure swept through her.

He leaned back and smiled. "Now, we'd better eat before our food gets cold."

Eat? How could she eat when her head was suddenly filled with visions of Dr. Hot naked and in bed with her? She looked down at her chicken à la king and let the joy of his desire for her sizzle through her. What was even more exciting was her desire for him.

It had been a very long time since her relationship with Tom and there had been no one who had tempted her since. Until now. Jack Taylor definitely tempted her to be foolish.

Thankfully for the rest of the meal the talk focused on things other than sex, although energy simmered between them. The more time she spent with him, the more she liked him.

Sex had been easy with Tom despite the trauma of her rape. She'd always known that the rape had nothing to do with sex and everything to do with rage and domination and control.

After Tom she'd rarely thought about sex. Life had been too busy, and what was the point of thinking about something you had no intention of having?

Now as she ate her chicken and picked at the side salad, all she could think about was sex with Jack. It was as if his flirtation had tapped into some source of primal desire she hadn't known she possessed.

The sun was warm on Jack's shoulders as they stepped out of the café to walk back to his office. He reached for her hand, and when her fingers curled warmly around his, he felt happier than he had in a long time.

When they reached the door to the clinic, she thanked him for the meal, but when she got ready to leave, he grabbed her arm.

"Do you have time for me to show you around the clinic?" Jack asked. "I don't have an appointment for another half hour or so." He wasn't ready to tell her good-bye. Whenever he was with her, he felt as if he were living in his teenage fantasy. Eventually he suspected the fantasy would fade, but at the moment he was enjoying the hell out of it.

"Okay," she agreed, and allowed him to usher her inside.

"All's been quiet," Beverly said as they walked in.

"Good. I'm going to show Mariah around," Jack said to his receptionist. A dozen women had applied for the job and the best decision Jack had ever made was hiring Beverly. She was efficient and loyal and told him he reminded her of her son.

"I've got three examining rooms," he said as he led Mariah into the inner sanctum of the office. "But this is what I'm most proud of." He opened a door that led to the operating room. "All the equipment is state-of-the-art."

She gazed around the room with its steel table and overhead lights. "It looks like a real operating room, I mean one for people."

He smiled. "Most of my clients think their pets are little furry people." He led her through the operating room into his main office.

It was a pleasant room painted in pale yellow with an oak desk, a matching bookshelf and pictures of animals that some of his smallest clients had drawn for him.

"I spend a lot of time in here," he said, watching her as she went from picture to picture, a smile of delight on her features.

"It's a nice room, so cheerful and bright," she replied.

He took her by the arm and led her to the window and pointed at the small ranch house directly behind the clinic. "That's my place. It's small. It was always meant to be a temporary home, but so far I haven't made the move to a bigger place."

The smell of her made him half dizzy, a smell of exotic flowers in bloom, a sweet feminine scent that aroused him. She turned away from the window and into his arms. Her eyes widened in surprise, but she didn't move away.

"I know a great big farmhouse that's going to be on the market soon," she said.

He heard the slight breathlessness in her voice and he wanted her next breath to be with his mouth against hers. He leaned forward and took her lips with his, pleased when she opened her mouth to him.

The ache that rose up inside him nearly took him to his knees as their tongues battled and he wrapped her in his arms. She fit perfectly, her breasts against his chest and her lean hips jutting forward into his groin.

He wanted her here and now. He wanted to take her clothes off, taste her skin and lay her back over the desk and make love to her until nightfall.

It was she who broke the kiss, taking a half step

back from him, her eyes glowing darkly. "I think we'd better stop," she said, her voice shaky and thin. "You have a client who's arriving anytime."

"Ah, I hate it when nasty reality intrudes on my fantasy."

She tilted her head to one side in the fashion he found so charming. "I'm just an ordinary woman trying to deal with real life, not a fantasy."

"Okay, if you say so," he replied, and reluctantly dropped his arms from around her. "But I have to indulge myself just a little before you go."

Once again her eyes widened. "What do you mean?"

"For almost an entire year I sat behind you in English. Every time you'd turn your head, I'd watch the sun play in your hair and my fingers would itch and burn with the need to reach out and touch it. May I?" He pointed to the clasp at the nape of her neck.

The pulse at the base of her throat throbbed and he wanted nothing more than to press his lips there and feel the pounding of her blood.

Instead he reached behind her and removed the clasp from her hair. The dark strands spilled free and into his hands. Just as he'd imagined all those years ago, it was silky to the touch. "I've waited almost sixteen years to do that," he said as he handed her back her clasp.

She took the clasp and quickly refastened it in her hair. "I don't quite know what to say."

He smiled. "You don't have to say anything. I was just a nerdy kid half-crazy for the girl who sat in front of me."

"But you aren't that nerdy kid anymore and I'm not the same girl I was then," she reminded him as she took another step away.

"You're right," he agreed. "But the minute you and Kelsey rushed in here carrying Tiny, I wanted to know you better, to see how life had treated you and if you were happy. I still want to know you better." He grinned. "So, when can we get together again? I still owe Kelsey a home-cooked meal at my place."

"How about Sunday afternoon?" she said.

"Perfect, just name the time."

"Around one? You don't have to walk me out," she said as she headed toward the door.

"I'll call you," he replied, and with a nod she was gone.

Jack moved to his desk and sat, his head filled with her. As he thought of the kiss they'd shared, his blood pounded inside his veins.

There was no question that his initial interest in her had been to assuage an old crush that had roared back to life at the sight of her. But each moment that he spent with her created a new desire for her, a desire that was very much that of a grown man and not a hormonally charged teenager.

His cell phone rang and as he looked at the clock on his desk, a sense of déjà vu swept through him. Exactly two thirty.

"Hello?" he answered.

No reply, although he could tell it wasn't a dead line, could sense somebody's presence on the other end. "Hello?" he repeated.

Still no answer. He pressed the receiver closer to his ear, a sick dread twisting in his stomach. The pregnant silence continued. Finally he spoke again. "Rebecca?" he said softly.

There was an audible click and the caller hung up.

The caller ID read ANONYMOUS and as he closed his phone, a sense of disaster filled him. If it was Rebecca reaching out to him once again, then he could be sure that destruction and chaos would be right behind her.

Maybe it wasn't her, he thought. Maybe it was a wrong number or some strange glitch in the cell phone system. But he knew better.

Two thirty had always been phone time for him and Rebecca. She got out of her nursing classes at two and by two thirty was home and would call him at his office. He'd schedule his clients so that unless an emergency came up, he was free from two thirty to three to talk with his wife.

He leaned back in the chair and rubbed a hand across his eyes as a deep weariness filled him. He should have known better than to believe the madness was finally behind him.

As a buzzer sounded softly from the intercom, he stood up to go to his next appointment, but he couldn't quite shake the feeling of impending doom.

Chapter 13

Mariah was reluctant to drive home after lunch, since she'd just have to turn around and come back to get Kelsey from the pool. She had two hours to kill and decided to check out some of the stores in town.

Maybe she'd buy a new outfit to wear to Jack's on Sunday. A shiver of delight filtered through her as she thought of the kiss they had shared. Hot and hungry, his lips had taken command of hers and her visceral response had been both surprising and immediate.

She pulled into a parking space in front of the store called Chic Boutique and cut the engine. She was going to sleep with Jack. The minute he'd kissed her, she'd known that before she left Plains Point, she was going to be in his bed.

The realization of her own intentions shot an eager anticipation through her, but also a curious sense of rightness.

Oh, she had no illusions about any kind of long-term relationship with him. This trip to Plains Point was temporary and Jack's place in her life could only be the same.

Maybe he was supposed to be a transitional man. Kelsey was old enough now that Mariah felt as if it was time to come into her own. It was time for her to decide what she wanted from life, whether she wanted to spend the rest of her life alone or whether she would like to share it with somebody special.

Recognizing that she was overanalyzing, she got out of the car and headed for the store, looking forward to losing herself in the simple pleasure of shopping.

With a chatty saleslady and racks of cool clothes, it was easy to spend almost two hours. She tried on dozens of things and finally settled on a pretty pastel-colored floral skirt and a blouse in buttercup yellow. It would be perfect for a Sunday dinner.

She paid for her purchase, then headed for the pool to pick up Kelsey. Kelsey wasn't waiting out front as she usually was, but a glance at Mariah's watch let her know she was a little bit early.

Instead of going directly to the pool area, she walked to the gazebo where Clay Matheson had once made her young heart sing. She stood in the center of the structure, the memories from that night so long ago dancing in her head. That night the air had smelled of the roses that were planted around the gazebo.

She and Clay had been so focused on each other. Had they not noticed somebody lurking in the shadows of the night, watching them as they shared a kiss, listening as they spoke their words of love? Had that person then followed her as she left, silently stalking her until she was in those trees alone and vulnerable?

An icy chill walked up her spine and she quickly left the gazebo and hurried toward the pool. The sounds of laughter and splashing water filled the air, along with the scent of chlorine and hot pavement.

A five-foot-high fence surrounded the pool and Mariah peeked over the top to look for her daughter. She spied Kelsey immediately. Seated at an umbrella table surrounded by half a dozen boys and girls, Kelsey had thrown back her head and Mariah could hear the sound of her laughter.

A swell of intense love filled Mariah's heart. Was there anything as wonderful as the sound of your child's laughter? She wished a lifetime of laughter for Kelsey.

As she watched her daughter, a sudden, inexplicable fear gripped her, the fear that somehow Kelsey would discover the truth about her conception, that all the lies Mariah had told to protect her daughter would be turned into a weapon that would destroy their loving relationship.

She thought of the person she'd seen in the shadows of the trees in front of the house and the creepy feeling she'd gotten of being watched and a presentiment of her life exploding apart nearly brought her to her knees.

What she wanted to do more than anything else was pack up their bags and leave Plains Point tonight, right now. The panic seared up the back of her throat and she feared she was going to throw up.

At that moment Kelsey saw her and waved. Her bright smile instantly dispelled the attack that had seized Mariah. As Kelsey gathered up her things to leave, Mariah calmed and by the time Kelsey joined her at the car, she felt almost normal again.

Kelsey kept up a steady stream of chatter as they drove home. "Katie wants me to sleep over tomorrow night at her house. Can I?"

"Only if I talk to Katie's mother. You'd have to come home fairly early on Sunday because we have a lunch date. Jack has invited us to his place around one so he can cook a meal for you."

"That's cool, but didn't he say he wasn't much of a cook?"

Mariah smiled and turned into the long driveway of their house. "My guess is it will either be takeout or something very easy like burgers." Her smile fell as she pulled in front of the house.

"Oh my God," Kelsey exclaimed. "What's that?"

Spray-painted across the front door, bold red letters read *GO HOME*. Mariah stared at the letters. The paint had run and the impression was of dripping blood, making the whole thing that much more horrifying.

Kelsey started to open her car door, but Mariah reached across and grabbed her arm. "Don't get out." She released Kelsey and fumbled in her purse for her cell phone. "I'm calling Clay."

She punched in the number for the sheriff's department and connected to her old friend, who promised to be out in the next fifteen minutes.

Kelsey stared at her with big eyes. "Do you think somebody is inside the house?"

"I don't know, but we're not about to take a chance. We'll just sit tight until Clay gets here to check things out."

Kelsey looked back at the house. "Why would somebody do that to us? That's so creepy."

"I don't know, honey. I can't imagine." Mariah thought of those moments at the pool, when she'd been nearly overwhelmed by a sense of foreboding.
GO HOME.

Who would want her to leave? Who had wanted to deliver the message that she wasn't welcome in this town? And why do it this way? It was so ugly.

She was somewhat relieved when Clay showed up. He got out of his car, a deep frown etched across his forehead as he hitched up his pants with his thumbs.

"Looks like somebody isn't happy with you," he said as he gazed at the house. "You been inside to see if there's any other damage?"

Mariah shook her head. "We waited for you."

"Smart thinking. I'll just go in and check things out."

Mariah handed him her house key and watched as he climbed the porch, then pulled his gun with one hand as he unlocked the door with the other.

The gun made it all that much more real. Kelsey moved closer to her side and Mariah put her arm around her daughter's shoulder, wanting to comfort her even though Mariah had little comfort to give. She couldn't offer her daughter warmth, for there was nothing but coldness inside Mariah.

Who? Who would do such a thing? Joel. Had he been more upset than he'd let on when he'd left that morning? Was it possible he decided to give her a little payback for some imagined slight?

Clay appeared in the doorway, his gun once again in his holster. "You can come in. Everything looks fine."

Mariah and Kelsey climbed the porch stairs and once inside, Kelsey ran up the stairs to her bedroom to check on Tiny, while Clay and Mariah went to the kitchen.

"It looks like kids' work," Clay said. "Maybe your daughter has pissed off some girl? Gone after somebody's boyfriend?"

Mariah shook her head. "Kelsey's not like that. She doesn't even date."

"That doesn't mean she hasn't made somebody nervous. She's a gorgeous kid. I'm sure all the girls are feeling the heat of competition." He leaned back in the chair and eyed her curiously. "Unless you've managed to piss somebody off since you've been in town."

"Joel Clarkson and I had a little tiff this morning," she admitted.

Clay straightened. "About what?"

"He showed up to do some work for me with a hangover. He was surly, we had some unpleasant words and so I sent him home. I don't think he was happy about losing a day's pay."

Once again Clay frowned. "This just doesn't feel like something Joel would do. Oh, he's an alcoholic and can't hold a real job, but I've never known him to do something malicious or mean."

"The only other person who might be anxious for me to go back to Chicago is your wife," Mariah said.

Clay's face reddened. "Jeez, Mariah. I gotta tell you, this isn't Sherri's style. Sherri's in-your-face, not something like this. I still think this feels like a kid. I'll check around with some of the teenagers and I'll talk to Joel, but I don't think you need to be worried too much about this. It's a pain in the ass and it's going to take a couple of coats of paint to cover, but I don't want you losing sleep over this."

"Easy for you to say," she said, and offered him a small smile.

He got up from the table. "I'll do my best to find out who's responsible, but to be honest, I doubt I'll have any answers for you."

"I understand. I just appreciate you getting out here so fast for the second time." She walked with him to the front door. "I feel like I'm suddenly a high-maintenance newcomer in town."

"Don't be silly." He offered her a warm smile, one reminiscent of the boy he'd once been. "High maintenance is old Mrs. Silvers on Main Street. She calls every couple of days to make me come out to her house and get the aliens out of her attic."

"I'm relatively certain I don't have aliens in the attic," she said with a small laugh. "You'll call me if you find out anything?"

"Of course."

The minute Clay had left, Mariah went upstairs to Kelsey's room. The girl was on the bed, Tiny lying next to her. "You okay?" Mariah walked over and sat on the edge of the mattress.

"Yeah, just kind of creeped out."

"It's just a little spray paint," Mariah said. "Anybody giving you trouble? Any of the kids you've met?"

Kelsey sat up. "You think one of the kids I've been hanging around with did it?"

"Honey, I'm not sure what to think. Clay seemed to believe it might be the work of a teenager. He thinks maybe one of the girls in town is threatened by you. You know you're far prettier than any of the girls here."

Kelsey grinned. "You wouldn't be the slightest bit prejudiced, would you?"

"Who, me?" Mariah gave her a mock look of innocence. "Look, don't worry about it. It was just a bit of spray paint, nothing to be scared about. All it means is that tomorrow you and I have dates with a couple of paintbrushes."

"I can live with that," Kelsey agreed.

Mariah got up from the bed. "Why don't you come on downstairs and I'll fix us some supper? I've got a frozen pizza that has our name on it. I'll even throw together a salad to go with it."

"Okay." Kelsey picked up Tiny and together mother, daughter and pooch went downstairs. When they reached the kitchen, Kelsey sat at the table while Mariah pulled the pizza from the freezer.

"You know that boy I told you about? Ryan Kent? The one who told me his dad hated Grandpa?" she said.

Mariah set the oven temperature, then turned to look at her. "What about him?"

"He wasn't at the pool today. You don't think he spray-painted the house, do you?"

"I don't know. Has he been mean to you?"

"No, not at all." Kelsey stared down at the table, looking miserable. "I hope he didn't do it," she said, a note of desperation in her voice.

Mariah stared at her daughter. "You like him?"

Kelsey shrugged. "He seemed really nice and he's funny. I thought he kind of liked me and I guess I sort of liked him. But maybe it was just an act. Maybe he and his dad hated Grandpa enough that he was just pretending to like me."

"Let's not jump to conclusions, okay? He may be a very nice boy who had nothing to do with this." Mariah hoped so, for her daughter's sake.

Kelsey looked up at her, hope shining in her eyes. "You think? I mean, he seems really nice."

"Then let's give him the benefit of the doubt for now," Mariah replied, but made a mental note to herself to talk to Clay the next day about the Kent family.

Was it nothing more than a teenage prank? Or was it something more ominous? Those thoughts played in Mariah's head during the meal and afterward.

They were still whirling around in her brain late that night as she stood at her bedroom window and stared outside. Somebody had been lurking in the shadows of the trees. Somebody wanted her to leave town. Were the two things related?

Maybe it was time to step up the renovations, get things done as quickly as possible and do what the spray-painting culprit wanted.

Perhaps it was time to go home.

It was back.

The rage and the hunger.

He stood in the cover of the trees, staring up at the window where Mariah's silhouette was visible. As long as he didn't move from his position, he didn't have to worry about her seeing him. The night was dark, with clouds chasing across the sky and obscuring the moonlight.

It was too soon. It had been only a couple of nights since he'd taken Missy. He'd thought that she would ease the pain and calm the beast inside him, but she hadn't.

He leaned with his back against the tree, the rough

bark biting into his bare skin. The night air did nothing to cool his fevered skin, the burn of unrelenting wrath in his heart, in his soul.

He closed his eyes for a moment, trying to gain control. He wasn't a bad man, although he was a man who did bad things. Sometimes he felt as if there were two people inside his skin, both the good man and the crazed, raging bad man.

Most of the time the good man was in control, going about his business and being an upstanding citizen. But lately, especially since Mariah's return to town, the bad man had been rising to the surface far too often.

He believed that in brutalizing those women he took a piece of them. He thought that if he got enough pieces, he'd become whole and the anger and disappointment would go away. On some level he knew it was irrational, but in a stronger, more visceral place inside him he couldn't help but believe it.

He clenched and unclenched his hands at his sides as he once again looked up at the window where *she* stood. She shouldn't have come back here. She should have stayed away. If he hadn't seen her again, then Missy Temple might still be alive. But Mariah had stirred the beast in him.

He'd tried to warn her away and hopefully she would take the warning and go back to where she'd come from. But if she didn't, then he couldn't be responsible for what might happen.

Mariah.

His first.

His best.

Maybe if he took her again, made her disappear like all the others, she'd be the final piece that would fix him. She'd be the cure for his madness.

Chapter 14

Mariah got up late the next morning after a night of bad dreams. The images that plagued her in her sleep were more vivid than they'd ever been and she felt unsettled and on edge as she dressed for the day.

The first thing on the agenda this morning was coffee, and then she intended to get to the job of painting over the message that some creep had left on the house.

She was seated at the table and on her second cup of coffee when her cell phone rang. It was Janice. Her familiar voice was a balm against the riotous emotions that had warred inside Mariah since the moment she'd opened her eyes.

"How's life in the slow lane?" Janice asked.

"Not so slow. Yesterday a graffiti artist decided to leave a message spray-painted across the front of the house."

"You're kidding. What did it say?" Janice asked, concern in her voice.

"*Go home*, that's what it said."

"Okay, who have you managed to piss off while you've been there?"

Mariah laughed. "That's exactly what Clay asked me when he came to investigate. What makes you think it's about me? Clay mentioned that it's possible it's the work of some jealous teenage girl who finds Kelsey threatening."

"Nothing teenage girls do surprises me," Janice replied drily. "They can be the meanest human beings on the face of the earth. I've always said that what we should be doing is recruiting teenage girls into the army because they really know how to kick ass. So, how are you otherwise?"

"If you'd asked me last night, I was ready to pack my bags and leave. Screw the renovations, screw this town, I was out of here. But this morning I'm feeling differently. I'm not about to let a little dab of spray paint scare me off."

"Good for you. But you sound stressed and tired."

Mariah sighed. "I haven't been sleeping well."

"Nightmares?"

"The worst." She closed her eyes for a moment, thinking of the dreams that had tormented her all night long. "They're much more vivid than they've ever been. It's like I'm trying to remember something important in my sleep, but when I wake up, I don't know what it is."

"Returning to the scene of the crime probably has something to do with the increased frequency and intensity of the dreams," Janice said, sounding more like a psychiatrist than a friend. "You need to talk to somebody about getting a tranquilizer to help you sleep."

"No, thanks. And now, on to more positive things. The overgrown yard now looks like a neat lawn, the carpeting in the living room has been pulled up to reveal gorgeous hardwood floors and I've picked out tile for the kitchen floor."

"Sounds like you're sinking a lot of money into the place to turn around and sell it."

"I'll more than get it all back when it sells," Mariah replied.

The two chatted for a few more minutes; then a knock sounded on the back door. "I've got to go," Mariah said. "Somebody's at the door." She said a quick good-bye to Janice, then hurried to answer the door, assuming it would be Joel.

It was Finn. "Is that fresh coffee I smell?" he asked as he entered the kitchen.

"Fresh an hour ago," Mariah replied as she pointed him toward the table. "What are you up to this morning?"

"The usual. Chores and herding kids." He thanked her as she placed a cup of coffee in front of him. "I saw the paint on the front of the house. You have trouble?"

"You tell me. That was left yesterday afternoon while Kelsey and I were out."

Finn took a sip of his coffee. "You called Clay?"

She nodded. "He came out and saw it. He thinks maybe it was some teenager."

Finn shook his head. "When my kids get older, if they ever do anything like that, they'd better get out of town before I get hold of them."

Mariah grinned at him. "I can't imagine those two darling red-haired kids of yours ever doing anything wrong."

"Ha! I tell Hannah all the time that I think those kids are part demon. They understand almost every word in the English language except *no* and they'd rather break a toy than share it with each other."

Mariah laughed. "It's just a stage. They'll out-grow it."

"You promise?" Finn shot her a comical look of desperation. "Speaking of kids, that's why I stopped by."

"You want me to adopt yours?" Mariah teased.

"Don't tempt me," he replied with a laugh. "Actually Hannah and I were wondering if your daughter did any babysitting. Sunday is our anniversary and I'd like to take Hannah out for dinner and maybe a movie. Our regular babysitter is on vacation with her family."

"Yes, she does some babysitting, but I'll have to check with her and see if she's interested," Mariah replied.

"Interested in what?" Kelsey asked as she appeared in the kitchen. Tiny barked and growled as he saw Finn. "Shh." Kelsey stroked his back to calm him.

"Babysitting for Finn and Hannah Sunday night," Mariah replied.

"We pay good and we're great tippers," Finn exclaimed.

Kelsey grinned. "How can I turn down an offer like that? What time do you need me?"

"Why don't I pick you up around five thirty and I should have you home by ten or so," Finn replied.

"Sounds fine to me." Tiny growled again. "I'll just take him back upstairs," Kelsey said.

"Not on my account," Finn said as he stood. "I'm leaving." He smiled at Kelsey. "I'll see you tomorrow night." He leaned over and kissed Mariah on the cheek. "And I still don't feel like you and I have had a really good chance to talk."

"You know where to find me," she replied. She got up and walked with him to the door. "Hey, before you leave, do you know anyone who does outside house painting? I'm keeping Joel busy inside, but I'd like to get somebody working on the outside as soon as possible."

"Roger Francis does a little painting during the summers when he's off work at the high school. You might give him a call."

"Thanks, I will."

He gave a wave and left, taking a large dose of the room's energy with him.

Kelsey placed Tiny on the floor as she got out a bowl for cereal. "I guess you'll just have to make sure we're home from Dr. Taylor's house in time for Finn to pick me up for the babysitting job."

"That shouldn't be a problem. Jack said one o'clock. A simple meal can't last that long." An edge of excitement fluttered in Mariah's stomach at the thought of seeing Jack the next day.

But all thoughts of Jack fled when half an hour later she and Kelsey grabbed paintbrushes and got to work on the bright red lettering on the house.

Maybe Clay was right. Maybe it was nothing more than a jealous teenager's way of expressing anger. It wouldn't be the first time an adolescent grabbed a can of spray paint to communicate emotions.

Joel showed up at noon and began sanding the living room floor. He was quiet and seemed contrite and got right to work. Spray-painting a house might be something a drunk would do, Mariah thought as she cleaned up the breakfast dishes—especially an angry drunk.

She wondered if Clay had questioned Joel, then commanded herself to stop stressing about it. It wasn't as if somebody had left a dead cat on her doorstep or something else more ominous. It was just a little paint, for crying out loud.

Thinking about paint and the sad condition of the exterior of the house, she found Roger Francis's phone number in the book and called. Roger's wife, Marianne, answered the phone and for a few minutes she and Mariah chatted.

"Finn told me that Roger does some painting during the summers," Mariah finally said.

"Whenever he can get the work," Marianne replied. "He hates the summer when he isn't coaching and so a couple of years ago he started taking on paint jobs during that time."

"Is he home? I'm looking for somebody to paint the exterior of my house."

"He isn't here right now, but I can have him call you as soon as he gets in."

"That would be great," Mariah replied. "I'm anxious to get this old place back in shape."

"You should have a housewarming party when you get it all fixed up," Marianne said.

"I'd rather have a wealthy buyer," Mariah said with a laugh.

By evening Mariah was exhausted. She'd arranged with Roger to give her an estimate for the paint job on Monday morning. Joel had sanded the entire living room floor and intended to varnish it on Monday.

She and Kelsey had spent much of the day packing

things up in Mariah's parents' bedroom. Mariah had been pleasantly surprised by how little emotion she felt as she folded their clothing and emptied dresser drawers.

If she felt anything, it was a kind of peace that never again would her father be able to hurt her, that never again would her mother look at her as if she were the spawn of Satan.

And there was pride, that she'd survived them. She hadn't become a drug addict or an alcoholic. She hadn't become a child beater or a person who self-mutilated with a razor blade. She'd simply survived.

She thought of the letters she'd found in her father's desk drawer, letters she'd written that had never been opened. She'd poured her heart and her soul into those pages, hoping for an answer, some sign that they had loved her.

The day she'd found those letters in the drawer, she'd been freed from any more emotional baggage of her parents. You could pick your friends, but you didn't pick your parents. In the grand parent lottery, she'd lost, but from the misery of her own childhood she'd learned the ways to be a pretty terrific parent all on her own.

Kelsey cooked a chicken dish for dinner and afterward they both cleaned up the kitchen. Then Katie's mom arrived to pick Kelsey up to spend the night.

Mariah refused to get spooked in the house by herself. She wandered from room to room, making notes about what needed to be repaired or replaced.

If Roger could get the outside of the house painted and Joel finished up the living room floor and tiled the kitchen, then she could conceivably put the house on the market in the next couple of weeks.

Maybe she should go ahead and contact a Realtor. She wanted somebody who could handle all the details of showing the house when Mariah and Kelsey returned to Chicago. When the house sold, Mariah would make a short trip back here to sign the closing papers. Then she'd be done with this house, Plains Point and her past.

Funny how the idea didn't fill her with joy. In the short amount of time they'd been here, this place had begun to feel like home.

But it's not home, she reminded herself. Home was her apartment in Chicago with its modern furniture and view of the smog.

At eight she turned on the television that Joel had carried from the living room into her bedroom and she curled up on the bed to watch the latest offerings of reality TV shows.

But the crazy antics of ten people living together in a house couldn't compete with the dark thoughts that edged into her head.

Was the painted message meant for her? Was there somebody in town who saw her as a threat? Maybe the man who had raped her? Had that same man been watching the house, standing in the shadows of the trees and thinking about that night so long ago?

Or was the paint meant for Kelsey, as Clay had suggested? Was it possible that Mariah hadn't seen anything in the grove of trees except drifting shadows from the trees blowing in a light wind?

Maybe the sense of foreboding she felt was nothing more than the internal workings of a neurotic woman. Perhaps in returning to the scene of the crime, she was now sensing imaginary monsters in every corner.

It was entirely possible that her "monster" had drifted out of town the night of the attack, or was now in prison for an unrelated crime. Or he could be dead. There was no reason to believe he was still out there waiting to terrorize her again.

She was being foolish, like Marianne Francis, whose husband, Roger, had teased that she saw a boogeyman in every shadow. Maybe that's what Mariah was doing, seeing boogeymen where none existed.

She was just getting ready for bed when the phone rang. "Just thought I'd check in to make sure we were still on for tomorrow," Jack said.

"Unless you're calling to cancel," she replied.

"Not on your life," he replied. She sat on the edge of the bed, warmed by the mere sound of his deep voice. "I've spent the day racking my brain trying to decide what to cook for an important woman and her chef daughter."

"Don't stress it," Mariah replied lightly. "Hamburgers are always good."

"I'll keep that in mind. So, I'll see you here about one."

"I'm looking forward to it," Mariah said softly.

"Not half as much as I am," he replied, then murmured a good-bye and clicked off.

The warm feeling that Jack's voice had evoked carried her through a night of dreamless sleep and into the next day. It was just after noon when she finished her shower and was dressing for the date with Jack when Kelsey came into the bedroom, her arms wrapped around her stomach.

"Mom, I don't feel very good. I think maybe I should skip lunch at Dr. Taylor's." She sat on the edge of the bed and leaned over, as if her tummy was killing her, but Mariah saw a glint in her daughter's eyes that belied the sick belly.

"Then I'll just call Jack and cancel," Mariah said.

"No!" Kelsey's protest was immediate. "I mean, it would be so rude to cancel so late. He's probably been cooking all morning." She offered her mother a wan smile. "You go ahead. I'll just stay here in bed and I'll probably feel okay by evening when Finn comes to pick me up."

Mariah eyed her daughter suspiciously. "Why do I get the feeling that this is all a ruse on your part to give me time alone with Dr. Hot?"

"Mom, how can you even think that?" Kelsey protested, but the twinkle in her eyes told Mariah that's exactly what she was doing. "I'll be fine here. I know all the rules. I'll keep the doors locked and won't let anyone in. I'll just spend some time on my computer and maybe bake a cake or something." Kelsey stood. "Honestly, Mom. I'd be bored to death if I go with you. You go have a good time and let me just hang out here."

"Are you sure?" Mariah knew she should be disappointed that Kelsey didn't want to go, but it was hard to feel dismayed at the idea of spending time alone with Jack.

"I'm positive, and you'd better finish getting ready or you're going to be late."

Mariah gazed at the clock on the nightstand and realized Kelsey was right. Her pulse raced as she finished her makeup, repeated the rules to Kelsey, then got into her car to drive to Jack's.

She had a feeling Jack wouldn't be disappointed that lunch was going to be for two instead of three. She hoped he hadn't gone to too much trouble in an effort to impress Kelsey, and she wished she could control the adrenaline that pumped inside her as she drew closer to the clinic and Jack's small house behind the business.

The house was a small ranch painted creamy beige and sporting hunter green shutters. It looked neat and homey with spring flowers spilling out of a flower bed that bordered the sidewalk leading to the front door.

She got out of the car with sweaty hands, which she dragged down the front of her skirt. The lyrics from the chorus of Madonna's "Like a Virgin" played in her mind and a nervous burst of laughter bubbled to her lips.

She was pathetic. She was suffering a major regression, falling into the hormonal high of a teenager on her first date.

Standing in front of the door, she drew a deep breath, swiped her hands once again down her skirt, then knocked on the door.

Jack answered and she wasn't sure whether it was the warmth of his smile or the silly barbecue apron he wore that calmed her crazy nerves.

"Come in," he said as he opened the door. He looked just over her shoulder. "Where's Kelsey?"

"She came down with a last-minute stomachache," Mariah said as she stepped into the living room.

"Nothing serious, I hope."

"I have a feeling her stomach felt better the minute I left." Mariah gazed around the living room with interest. She'd always believed you could tell a lot about a person by the space he or she inhabited.

Jack's space held comfortable furniture in warm

earth-toned colors that instantly put Mariah at ease. "Nice," she said.

"It's small, only two bedrooms. But for now it's enough for me. Come on into the kitchen. I've got steaks marinating. I'm going to throw them on the grill in the backyard."

The kitchen was just as comfortable as the living room. A round oak table was set for three with white plates, yellow napkins. The predominant colors were yellow and black—black appliances against pale yellow walls.

"Please, sit," he instructed, and pointed to the table. "Would you like a glass of wine? A beer? Soda?"

"A glass of wine would be wonderful," she replied as she sat at the table. "Can I do anything to help?"

"Yeah, just sit there and look beautiful." He went to the refrigerator for the wine.

His gaze held hers for a long moment and she wondered how many times he'd manage to make her breath catch in that wonderful, delicious way before the day was over.

He pulled out a bottle of wine and poured two glasses. "A toast," he said as he handed her one of the goblets. "To teenage fantasies and second chances." His green eyes gleamed with fiery intent.

It was at that moment she knew that before the afternoon was over, she was going to be in Dr. Hot's bed.

Chapter 15

Clay entered the chaos of his house just after one on Sunday. Sherri and the boys had just arrived home from church and he was coming off an all-night shift.

He'd spent much of the past forty-eight hours trying to find out who had spray-painted the Sayers house. He'd spoken to Joel, who insisted he'd been ticked off at Mariah for her uppity attitude but was innocent of doing anything so stupid.

He'd corralled a dozen kids around Kelsey's age at the pool and questioned them about the vandalism, but none of them professed to know anything about it, let alone who might be responsible.

Mariah had called him to tell him that Kelsey had mentioned Ryan Kent. Everyone in town knew that Ryan's daddy, Doug, had hated old man Jed Sayers. The feud had begun years ago when Doug's mother, Lana, had gone to see the preacher for some marital counseling. After the second session she'd gone home, packed some bags and left her husband and son for parts unknown.

Doug had been a senior in high school when this

had happened and Clay had been a sophomore, but Clay remembered the scandal. Apparently Jed had convinced Lana that her husband, Lenny, and her son were demons and the only way to save her soul was for her to get as far away from them as possible. Fool woman that she'd been, she'd believed him and left behind devastation for the two men who had loved her.

Clay had connected with Doug that morning at Raymond's Auto Works. Over the years Doug had become a quiet loner. He worked as a mechanic and seemed to care only about cars and his son, Ryan.

Doug laughed when Clay told him why he was there. "If I was going to spray-paint the Sayers house, why would I wait until that old man died?" Doug wiped greasy hands on an equally greasy towel. "That's old history, Clay. I got no bone to pick with Mariah."

Even though Doug had said all the right words, Clay couldn't help but notice how his eyes had narrowed when he'd talked of Jed Sayers.

Clay left the garage, unsure whether he believed the man, but unable to do anything else. It had just been a bit of ugly vandalism, not a major crime spree.

As he walked into his living room, where his three oldest boys were wrestling and the two-year-old was squalling from his playpen, he carried with him the memory of what Mariah had said to him when he'd asked her whom she might have upset.

The only other person that might be anxious for me to go back to Chicago is your wife.

GO HOME, the paint had said. Two weeks ago Clay would have scoffed at the idea that his wife might grab a can of spray paint and damage somebody's property, but two weeks ago he hadn't been sleeping on the sofa. There was no question that since Mariah had arrived in town, Sherri hadn't been herself.

"Hey, boys, knock it off," Clay commanded to his little wrestlers as he walked through the living room in search of his wife. The boys ignored him. They'd wrestle until one of them got hurt. Then they'd come crying to him.

He paused at the playpen to give Robbie his pacifier and then went into the kitchen, where Sherri sat at the table and stared out the window.

"Hi, babe." He would have leaned over and kissed her on the cheek, but since the night of the barbecue at Finn's, Sherri had acted like she'd rather slap him than kiss him. "How was church?"

"Same as always."

He sat in the chair next to hers. "I feel like it's been a month since I've had a little time at home."

"You've certainly been putting in the hours the last week or so," she replied, her gaze still directed outside.

"I told you Aaron had the flu and I've been covering his time as well as my own. Hopefully he'll be back to work tomorrow and I can slow down." He wished she'd look at him. He'd like to look into her pretty brown eyes. "So, what have you been doing the last couple of days? What did you do Friday?"

She finally turned to look at him, her eyes giving nothing away of her thoughts or feelings. "Friday? Mom kept the boys, I had lunch with Linda and then I did a little shopping. Why?"

Clay drew a deep breath. "Somebody spray-painted *GO HOME* across Mariah's front door sometime on Friday afternoon."

Her eyes narrowed to dangerous slits and Clay knew in that instant he'd handled it badly. "And you think I'd do something like that?" She shot out of the chair, which sent it careening backward, and it toppled over with a crash. "You checking my alibi, Sheriff Butthead?"

When Sherri called him butthead, it was the same as that *hrump*ing noise she made just before she exploded. "Hell, Sherri, I don't know what to think. You've been acting like a crazy woman since she got into town."

"Crazy enough to paint her house? Have you considered that maybe she spray-painted it herself so she could call you and you'd come running to her rescue?" Sherri exclaimed, her face mottling with her anger.

"That's the dumbest thing I've ever heard," Clay scoffed. "She doesn't want me and I sure as hell don't want her."

"So you say," she replied. "But why have hamburger when you can have filet mignon?"

"I'm telling you that I love you and you're talking about steak," Clay said in frustration.

Sherri stared at him for a long minute, her lush chest heaving as she shook her head. "Sometimes, Clay, you're dumber than a doorbell." With that, she whirled out of the kitchen and seconds later he heard the slam of their bedroom door.

Robbie started crying again and Benny ran into the kitchen to tattle on one of his brothers. Clay drew a weary sigh.

How was it that a woman who'd been absent from this town for the past sixteen years could wreak such havoc in his life?

Chapter 16

The steaks were amazing, the salad was crisp and fresh and the potatoes were baked to perfection. For a man who professed he didn't cook, Jack had put on a terrific meal.

The conversation had been just as good. They'd talked about their lives and what they'd like to see for themselves in the future.

"I liked being married," Jack said as they cleared the table. "I enjoyed sharing my life with somebody. What about you?"

Mariah averted her gaze from him as she put one of the plates in his dishwasher. "I wasn't married long enough to really know what true marriage is all about."

"That's too bad. When a marriage is good, I think it's one of the most valuable things in the world. My parents have been married for forty years and I watch them and I want that closeness, that comfort that they have together."

"Where do they live?" Mariah asked.

"In a retirement village in Kansas City. They travel

a lot, so I don't see them much, but my mother is a great letter writer."

"A lost art," Mariah said. "The young kids today don't know how to write a letter. They either e-mail or text message everything."

He placed the last dish in the washer, then straightened and smiled. "I used to write notes to you when we were in school."

"Really? Why didn't you ever give me one of them?" she asked.

He looked horrified. "I would have died if you'd actually read one. You were dating Clay, the star of the football team. I was a nothing, a nobody. I could only yearn for you from afar."

Mariah smiled at his dramatics. "You appear to have survived that time of unrequited love just fine."

"True, I managed to suck up my heartache and go on." He stepped closer to her. "But you never forget your first crush." He reached out with his index finger and traced it down the side of her face. "Especially when the girl you had a crush on grows up to be an amazing woman."

"I'm not so amazing," she protested. Her mouth suddenly grew dry as he continued to trace her jawline with strong fingers.

"Oh, but you are," he countered. He took one of her hands in his and placed it on his broad chest, where she could feel the strong, rapid beat of his heart. "Only an amazing woman could make my heart do that."

"Then you must be a pretty amazing man." She took his hand and placed it just above her breast where the beat of her heart was so fast, so strong, it felt as if it would burst right out of her chest.

He held his hand there for only a moment, then dropped it to his side. She knew by the look in his eyes that this wasn't going to be a slow seduction. The pulsing energy between them indicated an explosive storm about to come and Mariah wanted it. She wanted wild and frantic, sensation without thought, pleasure without recriminations.

"I've told you before, but I'll tell you again—you drive me crazy," he said as he rubbed her lower lip with his index finger. She drew his finger into her mouth and sucked, tasting the slight saltiness of his skin.

His entire body tensed and he looked at her as if he was dazed. "Jesus," he managed to gasp just before he backed her up against the refrigerator. He crashed his mouth down to hers and the storm was unleashed.

Her hands found his broad shoulders and swept down his muscled arms as their tongues battled and swirled. His fingers fumbled with the tiny buttons down the front of her blouse and her nipples hardened as if in anticipation.

With the cool surface of the refrigerator at her back and Jack's fiery heat in front of her, she felt wild and needy. She thrust her hips against his, reveling in the fact that he was fully aroused.

He pushed back with his groin as he parted her blouse and pulled his mouth from hers. She threw her head back as his mouth trailed down her throat, frantically nipping and licking, as if he wanted to taste every inch of her. And she wanted him to. Oh God, she wanted his mouth all over her.

As his mouth worked down her chest to her belly, his hands cupped her breasts, still covered by her wispy silk bra. She shrugged off her blouse and reached behind her to unfasten her bra.

She plucked at his shirt, wanting to feel his hard, muscled chest against hers. With Tom she'd been a passive lover, but Jack demanded more and she willingly gave it, wanting her own pleasure as well as giving it to him.

As she cast aside her bra, his hands moved up her skirt, caressing her legs with hot hands. He stopped only when he reached the backs of her upper thighs.

He froze.

He looked up into her eyes, his dark gaze holding an unspoken question.

"Don't stop," she hissed, and arched against him. She knew what had stopped him, but she didn't want to talk about it—she didn't want to think about it right now. All she wanted was him, touching her, tasting her.

He fell to his knees and she raised her skirt as he pulled down her panties. Her knees almost buckled as his mouth kissed her upper thighs, her lower abdomen. His warm breath on her fevered skin drove her half-mad.

Everywhere but where she wanted him, he tormented her with teasing nips and his hot mouth. He licked her inner thighs and she wanted to scream for him to take her now before she went insane with need.

She cried out as he cupped her buttocks and pulled her tight against his mouth. Electric sensations sizzled through her. She grabbed his hair, tangled her fingers there and hung on tight as an orgasm ripped through her.

He didn't give her time to recover. He unzipped

his pants and pulled himself out. Hard and eager, he entered her and at the same time his mouth found hers again.

Her gasps mingled with his as he pumped into her. She raised a leg and curled it around his back, allowing him to drive deeper into her. He was so deep inside her she felt as if he were a part of her.

She clung to him, her arms wrapped tight around his neck as the waves of pleasure intensified. She was on fire, mindless with want.

Harder, faster, they moved and her body screamed for a second release. She was almost there and a sob escaped her as it overtook her, shuddering through her with the force of a tornado.

He groaned as he came. With his head thrown back and neck muscles taut he pulsed inside her. When he was finished, almost as if by silent communication, the two of them slid to the kitchen floor and stared at each other.

"Is that what you fantasized?" she finally managed to ask.

A slow, sexy grin curved his lips. "In a million years at seventeen years old I couldn't have fantasized that." He blew a puff of air and warmed her with his gaze. "My fantasy had more to do with the backseat of a car and the possibility of touching your breast."

Mariah laughed, then gazed around the room. "This is definitely a first for me, looking for my panties in a man's kitchen." She had no idea when exactly they had completely left her possession.

He pointed next to the kitchen island where the lacy underwear lay on the floor. He stood and held out his hand to help her up. Grabbing his hand, she went into his embrace.

His lips touched her forehead softly, tenderly. Then he framed her face with his hands. "Next time it will be slow and romantic." He smiled. "And definitely in a bed."

With just those words he made her want him again. Nodding, she moved out of his embrace, grabbed the clothing that had come off during their lovemaking, then hurried toward the bathroom.

As she re-dressed, his words played and replayed in her mind. *Next time. Next time it will be slow and romantic.* How was it possible to be stirred by the idea of making love to him again when her body still tingled with the aftermath of their explosive, intense coupling that had just taken place?

God, Kelsey, your mother has become a slut. She almost laughed out loud at the thought.

Once she was cleaned up and dressed, she lingered for a moment in the bathroom and stared at her reflection in the mirror. Swollen lips. Tousled hair. Cheeks red and eyes too bright. She looked like a woman who had been ridden hard and put away wet, as the old saying went.

She finger-combed her hair and then got a cool damp tissue to run across her face. Nothing she had experienced with Tom had prepared her for what she'd just shared with Jack. Jack had tapped into a primal sexual energy she hadn't known she possessed and she embraced it, loved the fact that she was wonderfully, magically human.

She left the bathroom and found Jack in the living room staring out the window. He turned to face her as she entered the room. He gestured her toward the sofa and together they sat side by side.

"I'm not usually so reckless when it comes to birth control," he said as he reached for her hand. "I was just so crazy. You made me so wild."

"Don't worry. I'm on the pill." She'd started taking birth control pills when she was seeing Tom and had never stopped even when that relationship bit the dust.

He tightened his grip on her hand and gazed at her with steady intent. "The scars on the back of your thighs? Want to talk about it?"

She rarely thought about the remnants of her father's rages, the flayed skin that had healed into raised welts. As far as she was concerned, they were her father's shame, not hers.

"My father's favorite form of discipline was a willow switch," she said.

The green of his eyes darkened to near black and he squeezed her hand painfully tight. "Then it's a good thing he's already dead," he said. "Otherwise I would have been happy to use a switch on him." He eased his grip.

She smiled. "Thanks, but I've pretty much resolved that part of my past. Unfortunately there are far too many kids who are abused by people who profess to love them. You know what they say—what doesn't kill you makes you strong."

Jack reached out and smoothed a strand of her hair away from her face. "I always knew there was something going on with you. I sensed a sadness inside you."

"This time when I leave Plains Point behind, I won't carry any sadness with me," she said. It was a firm reminder to him and to herself that it was just a matter of time before she'd be gone.

"And speaking of leaving—" She checked her wristwatch. It was almost four. "I need to get home and check in with Kelsey. She's babysitting Finn's kids this evening."

They both got up from the sofa. She grabbed her purse and he walked her to the front door. "I meant it, you know," he said. "The next time I want to seduce you slowly and give you some romance."

She gazed up at him teasingly. "Are you complaining about what happened in your kitchen?"

"God, no." He drew in a tremulous breath, as if just the memory of what had occurred between them shook him to his very core. "That was amazing, magnificent, incredible—want me to go on?"

She laughed. "No, you've been quite eloquent on the matter." She pulled her keys from her purse. "Thank you for the lovely meal and everything else." She started to open the door, but he stopped her by once again pulling her into his arms.

He kissed her with a tenderness that found every dark place inside her and lit it up. "You know I'm not finished with you yet," he said as he released her.

She laughed. "You make me sound like a project of some kind."

"Not a project, just a woman who not only excites me but intrigues me, a woman I want to spend time with." He kissed her on the tip of her nose. "Now, get home to your daughter."

Minutes later as she headed home, she realized that she had to take care, that it would be easy to allow Jack into her heart, a place where no other man had been. Ultimately that would be a huge mistake.

She had no intention of staying in Plains Point and he didn't strike her as the kind of man who would simply pick up his established practice and move to Chicago, nor would she expect him to do such a thing.

It would probably be wise to cool things between them, but with the warmth that filled her heart at the moment, it was difficult for her to consider denying herself the pleasure of seeing him.

The warm fuzzies stayed with her all the way home until she pulled into the driveway and saw a strange car parked there. Nobody was in it, which meant whoever had driven it was inside with Kelsey.

Fear rocked through her. Who was inside her home with her daughter? She was out of her car before the engine had completely shut off. She raced to the front door, her heart pounding as a million worst-case scenarios filled her head.

She reached the front door and found it locked and realized she'd left her keys in her car. "Kelsey," she screamed, and pounded on the door with her fists.

The only thought that thundered again and again in her head was, what if it was he? Kelsey looked so much like Mariah had looked when she'd been seventeen.

What if he'd waited and watched until a time when Kelsey was alone, maybe confusing in his sick twisted mind mother and daughter? What if the man who had raped Mariah was now alone in the house with her daughter?

Chapter 17

Jack grabbed his cell phone and left the house as soon as Mariah had gone. He walked the short distance to the clinic's back door, unlocked it and stepped inside.

He was greeted by a cacophony of barks and meows. At the moment he had six animals in residence: two cats recuperating from neutering the day before and four dogs all being boarded while their families vacationed out of town.

He paid a teenage kid to clean cages and walk the dogs, but he liked to come in and check things out himself on a daily basis.

As he filled each of the animals' water bowls and put down fresh food, his thoughts were filled with Mariah. She'd stunned him. The sex had been explosive and intense and better than anything he'd ever had before.

He'd been crazy about her as a teenager and he was surprised to realize that nothing had changed. He liked her. He liked her a lot and even knowing that it was probably going to end badly, he was helpless to halt things with her.

Even now with the scent of her lingering on his skin and the taste of her still in his mouth, he was figuring out when and where he could see her again.

His fingers tingled as he remembered the feel of those welts on the backs of her upper thighs. He knew the kind of force it took to leave scars like those and it sickened him to think that a father had done that to his child.

Who knew what went on behind closed doors? It was only years after the fact that Jack had learned that Finn's father had walked out and left Finn in charge of his little sisters when Finn had been a teenager.

Behind closed doors Finn had shouldered the burden of being a man way before his time and Mariah had been beaten by her father. Joel had confessed one night that his father had been a wife beater, but nobody in town had known. Secrets. Jack had had his own with Rebecca. Nobody had known that he'd been married to a meth user until long after the divorce.

He opened the large cage where Rover lay on the floor and looked up at him with chiding, soulful eyes. "I know, I know, it wasn't fair of me to lock you up for the afternoon," Jack said to the schnauzer. "But I needed some time alone with my lady and you would have been too much competition for her attention." He slapped his leg and Rover rose, stretched, then ambled to Jack's side.

As Jack and Rover returned to the house, Jack was vaguely surprised to realize he was happy. Since his divorce from Rebecca he'd abandoned hope for any real, lasting happiness.

He'd been wary of getting involved with any

woman, especially any woman who had unresolved baggage from her past or emotional wounds that needed healing.

When Mariah had spoken of her father and his abuse, she'd remained calm, her gaze steady, and he'd gotten the definite feeling that she'd long ago resolved that issue in her mind.

Good, because even though he considered himself a healer at heart, it would be a cold day in hell before he took on a woman who needed more than he could give. He'd learned his lesson well with Rebecca.

Next time he got involved with a woman who had baggage from her past, he'd cut his losses and run.

Chapter 18

"What are you trying to do, break down the door?" Kelsey exclaimed as she let Mariah inside. Mariah grabbed her by the shoulders and pulled her into an embrace as her heart continued to pound the rhythm of terror.

"Mom? What's wrong with you?" Kelsey extricated herself from Mariah's arms and stepped back.

Now that the fear had passed, anger took its place as Mariah faced her daughter. "You know the rules. Nobody in the house when I'm not home. Who is here? I told you never to open the door to anyone while you were here alone."

"Surprise."

Mariah whirled around at the sound of the familiar voice. Janice stepped out of the kitchen and smiled ruefully. "Am I interrupting a tantrum?"

"Janice!" Mariah rushed forward to hug her friend. "What on earth are you doing here?"

"I told you I had some vacation time coming and I couldn't think of anyplace I'd rather spend it than here. You know, I've never experienced small-town living before. I thought it would be fun to spend a couple of days here with you." Janice smiled.

She was a small woman with elfish features. Petite upturned nose, oversized, slightly pointed ears and a large mouth made many people not take her seriously. But Janice was bright, intuitive and one of the most competent people Mariah had ever met in her life.

She now hugged her friend once again as they returned to the kitchen. "Why didn't you tell me you were coming?"

"Then it wouldn't have been a surprise," Janice replied.

It was obvious by the food and drinks on the table that Kelsey had done the hostess thing. Mariah smiled at her. "Sorry I yelled at you."

"It's okay," Kelsey replied. "But you should know I don't break the rules."

"If you've forgiven me for yelling at you, would you do me a favor?" Mariah asked. "I left my keys in the car. Would you mind getting them for me?"

"No problem," Kelsey agreed easily. When she returned from the car, the three of them sat at the table and chatted until Finn arrived to pick up Kelsey for her babysitting job. It was only after Kelsey left that the conversation grew more personal.

"Kelsey told me you had a date with your vet friend today," Janice said as she reached for a cracker and a cube of cheese that were on a platter in the center of the table.

"Hmm, that's right." Mariah couldn't help the smile that curved her lips.

"You're seeing him pretty regularly. Is this getting serious?" Janice raised a salt-and-pepper eyebrow.

"Not at all, I'm just taking your advice and having fun." Mariah hoped her friend didn't notice the flush of heat that had to be coloring her cheeks.

"Good, that's good," Janice said. "Has your old friend Clay figured out who spray-painted your house?"

"No, and I doubt that he will. If it was some kid, odds are we'll never know." Mariah reached for a piece of cheese. "What are all your clients doing while you're out of town?"

"I've set them all up with my partner, who will call me if there are any crises, but I'm not expecting any." She narrowed her eyes slightly. "To be honest, I've been more worried about you than any of my teenage clients."

"Worried about me? Why?"

"Gee, let me think about it. You've come back to a house where you only had bad memories, back to a town you ran from after you were brutally raped and found yourself pregnant. You've confessed to me that your nightmares have been coming far too frequently and are more intense than usual. And what worries me most of all is that you seem to be handling everything just fine."

Mariah laughed. "You'd feel better if I was falling apart?"

"Honestly? Yes." Janice eyed her intently. "That would be more normal."

"I'm fine, really." There was no way she intended to confess to her friend that there were odd moments of the days when the sense of impending doom was nearly overwhelming. No way she wanted Janice to know just how hard she worked to control her emotions each time she stood at her bedroom window and looked out at that grove of trees or that she often felt the presence of somebody watching her.

"I'll tell you what we're going to do," she said, wanting to change the subject. "That's a rental car in the driveway? First thing in the morning we'll take it back. There's no reason for you to pay for a rental car when I have a perfectly good vehicle at your disposal. I'm assuming it goes back to Kansas City."

Janice nodded. "Yes, but that's not necessary."

"Nonsense, we'll make a day of it," Mariah replied. "Joel, my handyman, is going to be varnishing the living room floors. It's the perfect time for us to spend some time away from here. We'll leave in the morning, have lunch in the city and do a little shopping."

"Sounds good to me," Janice agreed.

It was just after ten when Kelsey returned home, raving about how cute Finn's kids were and pleased by the money she'd been paid. She was even more pleased when she heard the plans for the next day.

By eleven they called it a night. Janice was settled in Mariah's parents' room and the house grew silent. Mariah intentionally got into bed without peering out her window. She wanted nothing to dispel the warm glow that filled her heart, the glow of her lovemaking with Jack capped off by the company of her most beloved friend.

She slept without dreams and awoke the next morning to the sound of Janice's and Kelsey's laughter drifting up the stairs.

Joel arrived to begin on the floors, Roger dropped off a painting estimate and then Mariah got into her car to follow Janice and Kelsey to Kansas City.

Mariah didn't mind the alone time in her car. She

found a soft-rock music station and thought about Jack. It still amazed her how she'd responded to him almost from the moment she'd seen him again. Even more incredible was that she'd reacted to him on such a sexual level.

If nothing else came from this trip back home, she would leave with the knowledge that she was open to a relationship with somebody special.

The day was one of fun and laughter. They window-shopped on the Plaza, an upscale shopping area, then found the nearest Wal-Mart, where Kelsey bought two new CDs and Janice bought a nightshirt in a grass green that would only increase her likeness to an elf.

They got back to the house at five that afternoon. Joel had left instructions not to walk on the gleaming living room floor until the next day. Thankfully they could go through the dining room to get from the kitchen to the staircase leading upstairs to the bed-rooms.

After a dinner of sandwiches, Janice and Kelsey made plans to go to the eight o'clock movie. "Come on, Mom. It will be fun," Kelsey said. "It's the new horror film that all my friends have been talking about."

Mariah laughed. "No thanks. You know the Hall-mark Channel is more my speed. But you two go ahead, knock yourselves out. I'm tired anyway. I'll probably just curl up in bed with that new book I bought."

"Are you sure you don't mind me deserting you tonight?" Janice asked when Kelsey had run upstairs to change for the evening.

"Of course not. I love it when you and Kelsey spend time together. She adores you, you know."

Janice smiled. "No more than I adore her."

By seven thirty Mariah was alone. When the phone rang, she knew it would be Jack. "I'd like to tell you I haven't thought of anything but you all day, but that would be a lie," he said.

"Oh? Bad day?" She could hear it in his voice and it surprised her that in such a brief time she knew him well enough to recognize his mood.

"Could have been better. I had to put down one of my clients' dogs today."

"I'm so sorry," she said.

"It had to be done. The dog was old and sick, but that never makes it any easier. How was your day?"

She told him about Janice's unexpected visit and their day of shopping and fun in Kansas City. "They've now gone to see some horror movie."

"Definitely not your cup of tea?"

"I don't like to be scared. I've never understood why people pay money to get frightened," she replied. "What about you?"

"I like roller coasters and mystery novels, but horror movies aren't my thing either. Now, when are we going to be able to get together again?"

"It's going to be a little more complicated while Janice is here," she said.

"Mariah, I don't want to see you just to have hot sex. I'd be perfectly satisfied to have dinner with you, your daughter and your friend," he replied.

God, this man was dangerous, she thought. He was the kind of man she'd once longed for, a good and kind man who would make her feel special, feel loved.

"Maybe we could all have dinner tomorrow or the next day." She had no idea what plans Kelsey and

Janice might be making at this very moment for the week. "Can I call you when I have a better idea of our schedule?"

"You can call me anytime on any day or night," he replied.

By the time they finished the conversation and hung up, Mariah was filled with a happiness she'd never known before. He was seducing not only her body but her mind, and for the first time in her life she found herself wondering what it would be like to share her life with a man, to share her life with Jack.

"Ridiculous," she told herself as she climbed the stairs. She wasn't about to share her life with anyone except Kelsey. She paused on the stairs to admire the living room floor. The warm golden oak gleamed in the soft light spilling in from the kitchen. This place could be wonderful with a little more money and time invested.

She'd even thought about wallpapering the old office, transforming it completely from what it had once been to a beautiful formal dining area. It was easy to imagine Kelsey serving one of her gourmet meals in the new, improved dining room.

Even though it was just eight o'clock, a cloudy night created early darkness. She turned on the lamp next to her bed, changed into her nightgown and then got into bed with the new book she'd bought that morning.

By eight thirty her eyelids were so heavy she could hardly hold them open. Finally giving up, knowing that Kelsey was in good hands with Janice, Mariah turned off her lamp and snuggled down in the bed.

*   *   *

She was alone!

He stood beneath the trees and stared at the old farmhouse. He'd been watching when Kelsey and the other woman had climbed into Mariah's car and taken off, leaving Mariah in the big house all alone.

He clenched and unclenched his fists at his sides, fighting for control. He hated himself for what he was about to do, but he needed her. He needed her to assuage the pain inside him.

When he saw the lamp go on in the upstairs bedroom, he knew she was there and thirty minutes later when the window went dark, he knew she was still there.

Alone.

Vulnerable.

Before he realized what he was doing, he stood in front of her back door. He didn't remember leaving the cover of the trees or walking around the house. He reached out and tried to twist the knob, but it was locked.

That didn't bother him. He had a key. He'd found it in the week following old man Sayers's death when the house had been empty and waiting for Mariah's return. The key had been hidden under a flowerpot on the front porch. Not exactly a brilliant hiding place.

He withdrew his key from his pocket and unlocked the door. It whispered open. His blood pumped hot and furious inside him as he stepped into the kitchen.

The first scent that greeted him was the smell of fresh varnish. The light over the stove was on, a night-light he assumed had been left on for Kelsey and the woman's return.

By the faint light he saw the gleam of the hardwood floor in the living room and detoured through the dining room to the bottom of the staircase.

The fury inside him, coupled with the anticipation of release, twisted in his stomach, a pain of such depth for a moment it made it difficult for him to move.

She was probably asleep. She wouldn't see him coming. She wouldn't know what was happening until he was on her. She'd scream and he'd let her.

He hadn't allowed any of the others to shriek or yell. But this time Mariah could scream and nobody would be able to hear her except him.

He closed his eyes as a shuddering excitement rocketed through him. His cock was rock hard and ready and already sheathed with a rubber. He was smart enough to know about sperm and DNA. He'd learned a lot since that first time so long ago.

Stepping on the first stair, he thought of her terror and her pain as he pounded into her. He'd be the one in control. He would have all the power. It was up to him if she lived or died.

For just that moment she'd be nothing. And he'd be God.

Chapter 19

Wasn't this the way it always was? Mariah thought with a touch of irritation. While her light had been on and she'd been trying to read, she'd grown so sleepy the words had blurred together and her eyelids had been too heavy to keep open. The minute she put the book down and turned off her lamp, her sleepiness disappeared.

She lay on her back in the darkness, her mind tumbling thoughts around and around. Janice's unexpected arrival had been a pleasant surprise and Mariah looked forward to showing her around the town where Mariah had been raised.

And then there was Jack. She felt like a teenager experiencing her first bloom of love and sexual awakening. He might have had a crush on her in high school, but she was developing a crush on him now. She smiled at the thought.

The smile fell and she froze as she thought she heard a noise from downstairs. She remained perfectly still as she listened.

Nothing.

Nothing except an overactive imagination and her

racing heartbeat, she thought. Her heartbeat slowed
and she yawned. Then she heard it. The distinctive
creak of the stair rung. She sat up as her heart
stopped.

The fourth stair.

Somebody had just stepped on the fourth stair
rung. Somebody was inside the house! Terror kept
her frozen. She bit the inside of her mouth to keep
from screaming, not wanting whoever it was to know
she'd heard.

The tangy taste of blood filled her mouth as a second creak sounded. The fifth stair. There was a total
of fourteen stairs leading from the downstairs to the
upstairs hallway. And somebody was on the fifth
stair, somebody who didn't belong.

Somebody creeping up the stairs in the darkness
of night.

The inertia that had gripped her broke as pungent
terror seized her. It was *him.* She knew it was *him.*
He'd come back for her. Once hadn't been enough.

Oh God. Oh God.

He'd be in the room within a matter of seconds.
She wouldn't survive it again. She couldn't survive
him again. Without thought, acting only on instinct,
on habits honed long ago, she rolled silently from the
bed and crept on her hands and knees to the closet.

Help me, she screamed inside her head. Somebody
please help me. She opened the closet door and got
inside, pulling the door closed behind her.

Scrambling to hide behind the hanging clothes, in
the darkest recess of the enclosure she curled into a
fetal ball, her heart pounding so loudly she could
hear nothing else.

Confusion muddied her thoughts, confusion bred

of terror. She was ten years old again and waiting for her father to find her, to punish her. She squeezed her eyes tightly closed. If you can't see the boogeyman, then he can't see you.

She was seventeen and on the ground beneath the trees, a bag over her head as she was brutalized. And now he was looking for her again. Not her father, but her rapist.

Holding her breath, she listened and waited for the closet door to be ripped open and his strong arms to yank her out of her hiding place. Seconds felt like an eternity as she waited for evil to find her for the second time in her life.

From outside she heard the sound of car doors, then the front door of the house open. "Mom!" Kelsey's voice rang out. "The movie sucked, so we left early."

Any fear Mariah might have felt for herself was superseded by her fear for her daughter. "Kelsey!" she screamed as she burst out of the closet. "Get out of the house."

She expected to encounter somebody in her bedroom, a person on the stairs as she stumbled down to where Janice and Kelsey stood at the front door, shock on their features.

"Somebody was here," she exclaimed with a half sob. "I heard them on the stairs. We have to get out. He could still be inside, hiding. We have to call Clay."

She grabbed them both by their arms and pulled them out to the front porch, the terror still clawing up her throat, burning in her stomach.

Janice pulled a small revolver from her purse. "No need to bother the sheriff. I'll check it out."

Before Mariah could protest, Janice disappeared back into the house. Working with troubled teens in some of the more dangerous areas of Chicago, Janice not only carried a gun on a regular basis but also knew how to use it.

Mariah shot glances around the area as she pulled Kelsey closer to her side. Was the person still in the house? Or had he left when he heard the car approach and realized Kelsey and Janice were home?

The darkness around the house was lit up as Janice turned on light after light inside and with each new glow of illumination some of Mariah's fear ebbed.

Kelsey remained quiet by Mariah's side, her gaze intent on the front door as if willing Janice back in the doorway safe and sound.

Finally Janice returned to the porch. "If somebody was in here, they aren't here now. I checked every room, every closet or cabinet big enough to hide somebody." She looked at Mariah with a hint of worry. "Why don't we all go back inside?"

Kelsey immediately ran upstairs to check on Tiny, who had been shut up in her bedroom, and Mariah and Janice sat at the kitchen table. Kelsey came back into the kitchen and announced that Tiny was fine.

They didn't speak about what had just happened until Kelsey went to bed and Mariah and Janice were once again alone at the kitchen table.

"The front door was locked when we got home," Janice said. "And when I checked out the house, the back door was locked as well. I can't imagine how anyone might have gotten inside." A worried frown tugged Janice's eyebrows together as she gazed at Mariah.

"I swear I heard somebody coming up the stairs.

The fourth and fifth step creak and that's what I heard." Mariah leaned back in the chair and wrapped her arms around herself, an icy chill deep inside her as she thought of those two ominous creaks. "I know I heard it. I know it," she said forcefully.

Janice continued to hold her gaze. "Is it possible you fell asleep and the noise you thought you heard was part of a dream?"

Mariah rubbed a hand across her forehead, where a fierce headache had blossomed. "I wasn't asleep. I hadn't fallen asleep yet." She frowned. "At least I didn't think I was asleep." God, was she losing her mind? Had coming back here created more internal stress than she'd realized?

She dropped her hand from her head and stared down at the table. "I thought it was him," she confessed.

"Him?"

She looked at her friend. "You know, him."

Janice's features all fell in dismay. "Oh, honey, why would you think such a thing? It's been so many years, you don't even know if he's around this area. You don't even know if he's alive."

"I know, I know. Rationally I understand all that." Mariah broke off and sighed in frustration. How could she explain to Janice the feelings of dread that overtook her, the feeling that her attacker wasn't dead or gone, but rather far too close? How could she make Janice understand the crazy feeling Mariah had that it wasn't done, that it would never be finished?

"When I heard those footsteps, all I could think about was to hide. I got into my closet and for a moment I got confused—I thought it was my father coming upstairs to beat me. Then I was certain it was my attacker returning."

Mariah's stomach was nothing but an icy center and she wondered if she'd ever be warm again, ever feel sane again.

"Look, maybe the best thing for you to do is to get out of here. You've made some nice progress on the house, but leave it for the new owners to complete. Put the For Sale sign in the yard, pack your bags and go home."

Mariah knew it was good advice, but her heart rebelled at the idea. "I don't want to do that. I need to see this through." Once again she raised a hand to her throbbing forehead. "I know it doesn't make any sense, but I need to see this place turned into something beautiful. I need to erase all the ugliness that's still in my head. I know it sounds stupid, but I know it's what I need to do."

Janice smiled. "It's not stupid. It's called closure. You had a crappy childhood with even crappier parents. If fixing up this place is what you need to do to put that behind you, then I'm all for it." She reached out and took Mariah's hand. "I just don't want you to be drawn back into the terror of that night."

"Maybe I did just imagine the footsteps on the stairs," Mariah conceded. "Maybe I only thought I was awake. And maybe that night that I thought I saw somebody in the woods, it was nothing more than my overactive imagination." She wasn't at all sure she believed it, but it was certainly easier to digest than the alternative.

"Kelsey told me about this boy Ryan Kent whose father hated your father. It's very possible one of them spray-painted the house," Janice said as she released Mariah's hand. "Do you remember Ryan's dad?"

"Vaguely. He was a couple of years older than me, but I do remember him glaring at me in the halls. I just thought he was a jerk. I haven't seen him since I've been back."

"Kelsey likes Ryan."

Mariah stared at Janice in dismay. "Isn't that a heartbreak waiting to happen? For all we know, his father blames me for my father's sins. Why do I suddenly have a scene from *Romeo and Juliet* flashing in my head?"

Janice laughed. "Trust me, Kelsey is far too level-headed and independent to do something like that over a guy. Besides, she just said she kind of liked him, not that she was madly, passionately in love with him."

"Thank God for small favors. I think I'll take some aspirin and get some sleep," Mariah said as she got up from the table. Janice stood as well and the two embraced.

"I'm so glad you're here," Mariah said. "I needed your calm tonight. I got just a little crazy."

Janice shot her an elfish grin. "You're the least crazy person I know." She leaned forward and kissed Mariah on the cheek. "Get a good night's sleep and I'll see you in the morning."

The night was long and sleepless as Mariah wondered if she was truly losing her mind. Was she being stalked by some unknown person or by her memories of a traumatic experience?

Certainly she knew all about post-traumatic stress syndrome. Janice had spoken to her at length about it. A scent that brings back the horror of a specific event, a sound that triggers an intense memory—yes, she knew all about it. But was that what was happening to her? Was she suffering some form of mental illness or was somebody after her?

Chapter 20

"Could you try to get a little less paint on me and a little bit more on the cabinets?" Mariah said with a laugh as Kelsey dripped white paint on her arm.

"Sorry," Kelsey exclaimed as Mariah grabbed a rag to clean up the spot.

It had been three days since the night Mariah had thought somebody had been in the house, three days of work and fun that had managed to send the horror of that night into the back reaches of her mind.

She, Kelsey and Janice had met Jack at the pizza place the night before, where he'd received her friend's official stamp of approval.

"There's no question he's hot," she said to Mariah when Kelsey and Jack went to play an arcade game. "But there's a strength of character in his eyes, a genuineness to his smile that is even more attractive than his hot exterior. And it's obvious he's crazy about you."

"Maybe just crazy about the seventeen-year-old girl he sat behind in English," Mariah had said.

Janice shook her head. "Don't count on it. It's not

the eyes of a high school boy that look at you now, and I have a feeling he's very clear on distinguishing between the girl you were and the woman you've become.''

Mariah was trying desperately to keep her heart from getting totally involved with the man who obviously wanted her. She kept reminding herself that there was no way her relationship with Jack could have a happy ending.

Roger had arrived the day before to begin the painting of the exterior of the house. He'd brought with him two young men from the football team, both of whom spent more time flexing their muscles for Kelsey's benefit than actually wielding a paintbrush.

She'd had Joel sand all the kitchen cabinets instead of starting work on replacing the tile floor. She'd decided a coat of white paint over the tired old wood would liven up the room.

She, Kelsey and Janice had been working for the past two hours, enjoying one another's company while making slow but steady progress. Tiny danced around the kitchen floor and barked occasionally to remind them of his presence.

They'd agreed that they'd work until four, then clean up and meet Jack for a meal at the Red Dragon. As always a buzz of excitement filled Mariah at the thought of seeing Jack again.

She would have thought that by now, after she'd seen him a half-dozen times, the fluttering of joy, the sizzle of sweet anticipation, would have waned. But it was just as intense as it had been when he'd first told her he intended to kiss her.

A knock on the back door pulled her from her

thoughts of Jack. Roger peeked into the window, his broad face gleaming with the sheen of sweat.

Mariah opened the door to allow him inside. "Whew, it's warm out there today," he said. His white T-shirt clung to the bulk of his big body and displayed sweat rings beneath his big arms. "I was wondering if I could get some ice so we can cool down our drinks." He nodded to Janice. "Don't believe we've met."

Janice raised her paintbrush in greeting. "I'm Janice Solomon, an old friend of Mariah's from Chicago."

"Nice to meet you," Roger said.

"I'll get you some ice." Mariah pulled out a large pitcher from one of the cabinets, then began to fill it with ice cubes.

"Hey, the cabinets are looking good," Roger said. "You've got a little drip going on there," he added to Kelsey.

"Thanks," Kelsey said, then giggled. "Mom keeps telling me I'm getting more paint on her and Aunt Janice than on the cabinets."

Roger rocked back on his heels and shook his head. "I can't believe how much you look like your mama looked the last time I saw her." He grinned at Mariah. "You were a looker, that's for sure. Half the guys in school were jealous of Clay, me included."

She thrust the pitcher of ice into his hands, uncomfortable with the glint in his eyes as his gaze lingered on her. "That reminds me, I've been meaning to call Marianne about getting together for lunch soon."

"I'm sure she'd like that," he replied as he backed toward the door. "Thanks for the ice."

"Now, that's the way to cool a man down," Janice said drily.

"What, with ice?" Kelsey asked.

"No, by reminding him that he has a wife," Janice replied.

As they got back to work, old memories of Roger flittered through Mariah's head. He had always been around in those high school days, sitting at the same lunch table as she, hanging around Clay whenever Clay was with her.

Roger had been a big guy then, big enough to pin down a girl, big enough to squash the breath out of her lungs and take by force what would never be offered. Or had Ryan Kent's father, Doug, punished her for her father's transgressions? Or had it maybe been Joel, who was undeniably strange?

She grabbed her paintbrush and attacked the cabinets with a new determination. These were exactly the kinds of thoughts that would make her insane and there were moments in the last two weeks when she thought she might be halfway there.

Instead of following the dark trail of thoughts of suspicion, she instead focused on the evening to come and Jack.

Jack leaned into the hot spray of shower water, rinsing out the shampoo that smelled like a fruit basket. It seemed like it was impossible anymore to buy shampoo that smelled like just shampoo. Coconut wasn't bad; it reminded him of the old days at the public pool, where the girls would slather themselves with coconut-scented tanning lotion.

With his hair squeaky clean, he shut off the water, opened the shower door and grabbed the big towel that awaited him. He knew what he was doing—he was focusing on shampoo because he didn't want to think about the phone calls.

For the past three days at exactly two thirty somebody had called his cell phone and even though nothing was said, he was a hundred percent certain it was Rebecca.

He'd begun to look for her on the streets of Plains Point, in the corner of the café and everyplace else he went. The calls portended another of her appearances in his life and he hated it. He hated that he was going to have to deal with her again, especially now with Mariah in his life.

Rebecca brought chaos whenever she showed up. He hated the chaos almost as much as the sense of failure he always felt when he talked to her or saw her.

He was a healer, but he hadn't been able to heal Rebecca. And now he didn't want a woman who needed more than he could give. He no longer suffered a rescue complex. Rebecca had cured him of that.

Drying off, he realized he was going to have to tell Mariah about Rebecca. Mariah meant too much to him to be blindsided by whatever chaos Rebecca blew into their lives.

He pulled on his jeans and allowed thoughts of Mariah to consume him. He was falling in love with her, falling in love in a way he'd never felt with Rebecca, never dreamed was possible.

The dark-haired girl with the bright blue eyes who had captured his passion in high school had grown into a woman who had taken his heart. At the moment he couldn't see a happy ending for them. He knew she had no intention of remaining in Plains Point and he had spent the four years since his divorce building a life and a practice here in the small town.

Still, even knowing that they were headed in different directions in their lives, he refused to stop seeing her and he couldn't stop himself from loving her more each time they were together.

He glanced at his clock on the nightstand. Five o'clock. He had fifteen minutes to finish getting ready and walk out the door so he wasn't late meeting Mariah, her friend and her daughter at five thirty.

And at some point in the evening he needed to arrange some private time with Mariah, time he'd rather use to make love to her but he would instead use to talk about his ex-wife. Jesus, he'd rather have a tooth pulled.

He had to park in the next block from the Red Dragon, as it looked like they had a crowd of diners already there. He should have made a reservation, he thought as he hurried toward the front door.

Thankfully Mariah, Janice and Kelsey had already arrived and were seated at a table for four toward the back of the restaurant.

His heartbeat bumped up a notch at the sight of Mariah. Wearing a pair of jeans and a summery blouse that dipped low enough to expose a bit of cleavage, she smiled at him and he realized he'd like to see that smile every day of his life. That smile made him happy, made him want to be the man who could bring it to her face.

Throughout dinner he fought against a simmering need to get Mariah alone, to kiss those sweet lips of hers. He hadn't lied to her when he'd told her that the next time they made love, he wanted slow and romantic.

But underlying his desire was the dread of knowing he needed to tell her the ugly details of his marriage and warn her that he had no idea what his ex-wife was capable of doing. And he knew that once he told Mariah, she could walk away from him. Who in their right mind would want to deal with a drug-crazed ex-wife?

And the thought of losing Mariah ached in his heart, just as her sudden absence from the desk in front of him had hurt all those years ago.

When he'd run his hands up the silky softness of the backs of her legs, then had encountered the raised welts of old scars, he'd wanted to kill somebody for hurting her.

"Dr. Taylor?"

He looked across the table at Kelsey, who had obviously asked him a question he hadn't heard. "I'm sorry, what did you say?"

"How much longer will Tiny need to wear the cast?" she asked.

"Another couple of weeks and we should be able to take it off." He smiled at the pretty teenager. "And I thought I told you to call me Jack."

"That dog follows Kelsey around like she gave birth to him," Janice said. "I've never seen anything like it."

"He loves me," Kelsey exclaimed. "And I love him."

"Until Katie calls," Mariah said with a warm smile to her daughter. "Then you're off and running."

"Tiny understands that a girl needs her friends as well as her pooches," Kelsey replied.

Jack couldn't help but feel the warmth and caring

that existed between the three women. It was obvious Janice and Mariah shared a deep, bonding friendship. Jack liked the elfish-looking woman who radiated a wealth of intelligence from her brown eyes.

When Janice and Kelsey left the table to go to the ladies' room, Jack reached over and covered Mariah's hand with his. "I need to talk to you," he said. "Is it possible Janice and Kelsey can go on home together and I can bring you home later?"

Her eyes glistened. "What exactly do you have in mind, Dr. Taylor?"

"Keep looking at me like that and I won't be able to get up from the table without embarrassing myself," he replied. "Actually I need to talk to you and I'd rather not get into it here."

She must have seen something in his eyes, something that made her realize whatever it was he wanted to talk to her about was serious. She pulled her hand from beneath his and held his gaze for a long moment. "All right, Janice can take Kelsey home and you and I will have a talk."

Thirty minutes later Jack ushered Mariah into his living room. "Would you like a drink?" he asked.

She sat on the sofa. "Am I going to need one?"

"I don't know, but I think I'd like one."

"Okay, then, a glass of wine?"

He nodded and went into the kitchen. He poured her a glass of wine, then made himself a stiff Scotch on the rocks. When he returned to the living room, she took the wine from him with a tentative smile. "I have to confess, you have me a little nervous."

"Don't be." He sat next to her and placed his glass on the coffee table. "I need to talk to you about my ex-wife."

She frowned. "Are you two getting back together? If so, you don't owe me anything, Jack."

"No, God no, it's nothing like that," he replied quickly. He reached out, grabbed his drink and took a deep swallow, the bite of the Scotch burning all the way down to the pit of his stomach.

"What is it, Jack?" Mariah leaned toward him and placed a hand on his forearm. "Just tell me."

Jack drew a deep breath and sent himself back in time, back to the beginning when he'd first met the pretty blonde who appeared to have it all, healthy ambition, intelligence and a sex-kittenish quality that Jack had found enchanting.

"She fooled me," he finally began. "When we got married, I thought she had it all together, that the two of us could take on the world and make a real success of our life."

"But that didn't happen." Mariah sat back and removed her hand from his arm.

He stood, unable to sit still while he spoke of his failure, the failure as a husband, his failure as a man. "Rebecca didn't have it as together as I thought she did. She was needy and in the beginning I didn't mind—I found it endearing. She was going to school for her nursing training and I was finishing up my schooling and preparing to open my clinic."

He walked over to the window and stared outside, where darkness had fallen. "We'd been married two years when one night I woke up and she wasn't in the bed next to me. I found her in the kitchen on her hands and knees, scrubbing the kitchen floor with a toothbrush."

He turned to look at Mariah. "She was going over the same spot again and again and I knew by her twitching and paranoia that she was high on drugs. She confessed that she'd tried crystal meth. She swore it was her first time and she'd never do it again and I believed her." He offered Mariah a rueful smile. "Never believe a drug user when they're high."

"She didn't quit?"

Jack shook his head and walked back to the sofa. He sank down in the cushion and once again reached for his drink. "I thought she had, or maybe I just wanted to believe it enough that I overlooked the signs of how bad it had become, and that was my failure as a husband, that and not understanding exactly what she needed of me."

He took a deep swallow of his drink and stared down at the top of the coffee table. "I refused to notice that she looked like a walking skeleton, that she'd become secretive and almost never slept. It wasn't until I wrote a check to cover some business expenses and it bounced that I realized she'd emptied our accounts to pay for the drugs. She begged me to forgive her, told me that she'd do anything to get better, so I sent her to rehab."

Once again Mariah's hand was on his arm, warming the cold places his memories had brought back into his heart. "But it didn't work," she said softly.

"The first time she stayed three days, then left. She insisted she was fine, could quit on her own and all I needed to do was trust her. Of course I didn't trust her and she didn't quit and so she tried rehab again. She stayed twenty days, just enough time to give me hope that we could pull it all back together again. On the twenty-first day she was kicked out for using. My bank account was empty, my charge cards were maxed out, but more than that, my love for her was gone. I knew I had to get out."

In frustration he looked at Mariah. "Maybe I should have loved her more—maybe I should have forgotten about my work and spent more time with her. I thought of myself as a healer, but all I wanted to do was get out."

Mariah squeezed his arm gently. "Why are you telling me this, Jack?"

"Our divorce four years ago wasn't exactly the end of things between us." He felt Mariah stiffen and quickly added, "It's not what you're thinking. Every three or four months she contacts me wanting money. The first couple of times I gave in, then realized I wasn't helping her that way. The last time she contacted me, I told her no, that I wasn't going to give her any more money and the next day my house was broken into and some things were stolen, things that could be easily pawned."

"I'm sorry, Jack, but I still don't understand why you think I need to hear about this."

"I've been getting some phone calls that lead me to believe Rebecca is about to make another appearance into my life." Jack took both of Mariah's hands in his. "I wanted to tell you this because I'm in love with you, Mariah." Emotion bubbled up in his chest. "Don't worry, I don't need to know how you feel about me. It's enough that you're here right now.

"I just felt the need to warn you that Rebecca may be someplace here in town. I have no idea what condition she might be in or what she's capable of. If you decide to walk out of here tonight and never see me again, I'll understand, but that won't stop me from loving you."

She pulled her hands away, her head tilted in the familiar way it did when she was thinking. "You talk like the problems Rebecca had with the drugs were your fault, somehow your personal failure," she said. "But surely you know that's a powerful drug and that ultimately you weren't capable of helping Rebecca if she didn't want to help herself."

"On an intellectual level I understand all that," he replied.

She smiled. "And you know that eventually I'm going back to Chicago."

"I know that and I don't have any expectations for what the future might bring. I just want to be with you, to spend time with you for as long as I can."

"I must be out of my mind, because that's what I want, too," Mariah confessed softly. He'd just given her a perfectly good reason to back away from him, no hard feelings. But she didn't want to. She wasn't ready to deny herself the pleasure of being with him.

There was no question that knowing he believed he loved her was empowering, and she was savvy enough to acknowledge that selfishly she wasn't ready to walk away from the way he looked at her as if she was something precious, the way he touched her as if she was something of value. She'd never had that before and hadn't realized until now how deep her hunger for that had been.

"So, we're here all alone and I don't have a curfew," she said. "You promised me slow and romantic."

His eyes flared with hunger. "And I always keep my promises."

He'd nearly been caught that night in her house. If he hadn't seen the flash of the car lights through the window, Kelsey and Mariah's friend would have found him in Mariah's bedroom.

Thankfully he'd managed to get out the back door before they realized what was going on. He'd watched the house for another hour, surprised when no law enforcement had been called.

She'd heard him on the stairs. He hadn't realized it at the time, but as he ran from the house her hysterical cries and the sound of her terror had filled him with an omnipotent power.

But it hadn't been enough. Her terror would never be enough. She'd begun it all and he had come to realize over the last two weeks that the only way he could be normal again, the only way he could completely rid himself of the rage that had transformed him into a monster, was to bury Mariah with all his other girls. She'd been the first and she'd be the last.

And if it took too long to get to her, if she proved to be difficult, there was always her daughter. Sweet young Kelsey looked just like her mother had looked sixteen years ago and the young ones were always so naive, so trusting.

Yes, Kelsey would make a good stand-in until Mariah was his once again.

Chapter 21

"Meth addiction is one of the worst," Janice said the next afternoon. Kelsey had left for the pool and Janice and Mariah were once again working on finishing painting the kitchen cabinets. "I've counseled a lot of teenagers and their families about it. The addiction to meth is as hard to break as an addiction to heroin. The deterioration of the body and of the soul is swift and horrible."

Mariah used the handle of her paintbrush to itch a spot on her cheek. "It must be terrible, to see somebody you love destroying themselves and be unable to help them."

Janice lowered her brush and turned to look at Mariah. "He must care about you a lot to confess to that kind of baggage in his background. Did you tell him about your baggage?"

"I certainly haven't bared my soul to him, but he knows my father was abusive and that my childhood was pretty miserable."

"That's not what I was talking about," Janice said. She put her brush in the paint pan and eased into a kitchen chair. "I think you've pretty well resolved that particular issue while you've been back here. I was talking about your rape."

"Of course I haven't told him about that and I don't intend to tell him about it," Mariah exclaimed. She glanced toward the window to make sure Roger wasn't lurking outside, listening to their conversation. She set her paintbrush down and joined Janice at the table.

"If anything, my time with Jack has given me the assurance that I can have a normal, healthy relationship with a man. There is no baggage to worry about."

Janice shoved a strand of her salt-and-pepper hair behind one pointy ear, her thin eyebrows pulling into a unibrow in the center of her forehead. "You hide in closets. You have terrible nightmares that wake you up screaming. You're paranoid. I'd call that baggage."

"I'm fine," Mariah replied, heat filling her cheeks. "Once I get back to Chicago, I'll be okay. It's just being here that's brought some of that up again. Besides, I can't tell anyone." Her voice vibrated with the depth of her feelings. "I have too much to lose."

"Like what?"

A wealth of emotion filled Mariah's chest, constricting painfully tight and momentarily taking away her breath. A vision of her daughter filled her head. "Kelsey," she managed to whisper.

"Kelsey loves you. You wouldn't lose her."

The constricting band around Mariah's heart grew tighter as she thought of her daughter and the potential consequences of Mariah's secret. If the truth came out, it would be like opening Pandora's box and only darkness and heartache would flow out of it.

"The most important value I instilled in Kelsey was truthfulness," she finally said. "How could I ever explain to her that everything I told her about her father and our life and her birth was nothing but a lie? How would I ever make that right for her?" Mariah shook her head, the very thought of Kelsey finding out the truth making her want to throw up. "She'd hate me."

Janice clucked her tongue. "You not only don't give her enough credit—you don't give yourself enough credit. The bond you've built with Kelsey is strong."

"It's a moot point," Mariah said with more than a touch of stubbornness. "Within a matter of weeks we'll all be back in Chicago and life will go on without any secrets needing to be told." She got up and grabbed her paintbrush. "Now, let's get these cabinets done so Joel can start work on the kitchen floor."

There were only four people who knew about that night beneath the trees: Mariah, Janice, Mariah's mother and the rapist. One of those people was dead, one was sworn to secrecy and neither Mariah nor her attacker would tell. Mariah intended to do everything in her power to keep it that way.

For the rest of the afternoon Mariah refused to allow herself to think about the conversation she'd had with Janice. Instead she focused on the night before with Jack.

True to his promise, he'd taken her into his bedroom and made love to her slowly and sweetly. His feelings for her were evident in his every touch, in the way he kissed her so soulfully, so passionately.

And as he made love to her, gazing into her eyes, she'd felt a raw, aching love for him. But as he drove her home, she dismissed that crazy emotion and told herself it had been nothing more than the intense physical release of the moment.

Over the next couple of days the house began to really take shape. Roger and his crew finished the outside paint. The house now sported a creamy beige color with burgundy shutters and front door. Joel laid the new yellow and white patterned tiles in the kitchen and Mariah picked out a wallpaper border for the dining room.

Thursday evening Mariah was in the kitchen hanging cheerful yellow curtains at the window when Janice came into the room. "Pretty," she said.

"Thanks, I feel like the room is filled with sunshine. In fact, I'm starting to feel like the whole house is filled with sunshine."

Janice smiled. "I have a favor to ask you. Do you mind if I borrow your car for a little while this evening?"

Mariah turned from the window to look at her friend. "Of course I don't mind. Is there something you need? Someplace I need to take you?"

"No, nothing like that. I'd just like to wander a little bit down Main Street of this quaint little town before I head back to Chicago tomorrow."

"You want company?"

"No, I'm a big girl. I know you wanted to get started on that wallpaper in the dining room and I won't be too long. I know Kelsey is spending the night with Katie. I could drop her off there on my way out."

"Okay," Mariah agreed. Although she and Janice were as close as sisters, Mariah knew Janice enjoyed her time alone. They had been together for nearly every minute of the week and a half Janice had been in Plains Point and it was no wonder Janice might feel the need for some time alone.

At seven thirty Mariah stood on the front porch and waved as Janice and Kelsey drove away. "It's just you and me, Tiny," she said to the little dog who clumped around at her feet.

She bent down and scooped him up in her arms. She'd grown ridiculously attached to the dog. She scratched him behind his ears, then laughed as he closed his eyes in pleasure, his mouth appearing to smile at her.

"You're a mess," she exclaimed as she put him back on the floor. "Come on, let's go see if I can manage to put up that wallpaper border without destroying the entire dining room."

She'd barely gotten started when there was a knock on the front door. A peek outside let her know it was Hannah. She opened the door and greeted her neighbor, who carried in one hand a tray of chocolate cupcakes. "I come bearing gifts." She held the tray out to Mariah.

"What's all this?" Mariah asked.

"I baked them this afternoon and didn't realize the recipe I had was already doubled. I doubled it and wound up with enough cupcakes to fatten up the entire population of Plains Point. I knew you had a friend here, so I thought you all might enjoy some."

"That's so nice," Mariah said. "Come on into the kitchen. I'll put on a pot of coffee and we'll sample your wares."

"I can't stay but for just a minute," Hannah said as she followed Mariah. "Finn is meeting some of the guys in town for a few beers. I promised him I'd be home quickly. Wow," she exclaimed as she entered the kitchen. "This room looks awesome. You've really been busy."

An unexpected burst of pride roared through Mariah as she set the cupcakes on the table. The kitchen did look awesome, but more importantly it looked warm, like a place where laughter occurred and people were welcome. It looked like a home, the home that Mariah had longed for when she'd been growing up.

"I can't imagine doing all this work and making everything so nice, then putting it up for sale so somebody else can live in it," Hannah said. "That's kind of like healing a man's wounds so he can fall in love with somebody else."

Mariah laughed. "But that's the plan," she replied, surprised to feel just the faintest stir of bittersweet regret. She was turning this place into the house of her dreams and it felt somehow wrong to just walk away from it.

"Well, I'd better get back home. It's time to get the kids in bed and if I leave Finn in charge, he'll have them so wound up they'll never get to sleep."

Mariah smiled. "He's a good daddy."

Hannah beamed. "The best, but he'll be a bear if he is late for his beer with the boys." She rolled her eyes as the two walked back to the front door.

"Thanks, Hannah, for the cupcakes. It was really nice of you to think of us."

"That's what we do in small towns. Don't you remember? We take care of each other. Have a good night," she said as she stepped out into the evening shadows.

Mariah watched from the porch as she got into her

car and drove down the lane toward the house next door. Thoughts of Finn filled her head. Of course he was a good daddy. He'd had plenty of practice raising his two little sisters.

Funny, as close as she and Finn had been, it had never crossed their minds to be a couple. Their relationship had always been that of friends and confidants. Never once had he given her an indication that he wanted anything different from her, nor had she wanted anything different from him.

She smiled as she returned to the kitchen. Maybe it was because Finn had been the first boy to see her puke after they'd tried to smoke a cigar. He'd been one of the few people who had seen her cry and she'd guess that she was probably the only person on earth who had seen him cry. Or maybe it was because from the time he'd been thirteen, he'd had a crush on Hot Pants Hannah. It was nice that they'd ended up together. It was always nice when the good guy won.

She poured herself a glass of milk and grabbed one of the cupcakes, then sat at the table. She expected Janice back soon and had a feeling this last night with her would involve a lot of talk and too many cupcakes.

The park in the town square was dark, but Janice wasn't afraid of the deep shadows of the night in this small town. In Chicago she wouldn't be foolish enough to enter any of the parks at night, but Plains Point was a different animal altogether.

She walked to the gazebo and entered. As she leaned against one of the wooden sides, she remembered that this was where Mariah and Clay Matheson had professed undying love for each other. Of course few seventeen-year-olds really understood the true meaning of love. How many other young lovers had stood here over the years? Janice tried to imagine what it would have been like to be raised in a town like Plains Point.

Janice was born and raised on the dangerous west side of Chicago. Her mother had been an alcoholic and her father an over-the-road truck driver who was mostly absent from her life. Being small for her age had made her vulnerable, but it also made her street smart. At an early age she knew the only way out for her was education.

She'd studied hard, graduated from high school early, earned a full ride to college and had chosen the nursing profession. She'd left the west side behind, but had never considered leaving the Windy City.

She'd been a nurse for a year when she began doing charity work, making the rounds of shelters to check for children and women in need of medical attention, and she'd never forget the night she met Mariah.

Despite being eight months pregnant, Mariah had been beautiful and scared to death. Initially she'd insisted that she was eighteen years old, that her parents were dead and she'd been kicked out of her boyfriend's house.

She'd been slightly belligerent with a tough-guy exterior belied by the abject terror that shone from her eyes. Janice would never know what forces pushed her to take Mariah on as a personal project, to invite the pregnant teenager into her home, into her life, but it had been the best thing she'd ever done.

Mariah and Kelsey had become the family Janice never had, and Janice had needed somebody to love, somebody to worry and care about.

Now, taking a deep breath of the clean-scented night air, she stepped out of the gazebo and instead walked to a nearby bench and sat down.

She was losing them.

The minute she'd walked into the house and had seen all the work that Mariah was doing, she'd sensed that a change was about to occur. Mariah was nesting as she'd never done in her high-rise Chicago apartment.

There was a part of Janice that was happy for her friend, that finally Mariah was making peace with a part of her past that had been so tragic. In renovating the house, she was healing the inner child who had longed for parents who were loving and kind.

But there was also a little piece of Janice that mourned the potential loss of Mariah and Kelsey in her life, that feared that once the house was ready to be put on the market, Mariah would change her mind and see her future here.

And Janice wouldn't blame her. She leaned her head back and stared up at the stars. She never saw stars in Chicago. And the silence was amazing. She closed her eyes and listened. Okay, it wasn't completely silent, but she wasn't accustomed to the sounds the night held in Plains Point.

Instead of blaring horns and sirens, there was the click and whir of insects. Instead of police whistles and the squeal of brakes, a dog barked in the distance and a light wind rustled the leaves of a nearby tree.

Life would be slower here, but that wasn't necessarily a bad thing. She told herself her melancholy was silly, that if Mariah and Kelsey decided to stay here, Chicago was only an hour and a half plane ride away and another forty minutes in a car. Just a little over two hours. There was no reason why they couldn't visit each other often.

She frowned, her eyes still closed, as she realized the night had truly become silent. It was a silence as if everything held its breath, a heavy potent quiet that shot uneasiness through her.

Time to head back to Mariah's. If it grew any later, Mariah might worry. Janice opened her eyes and prepared to rise.

A gasp escaped her as something dark and slick was yanked over her head and she was slammed backward, up and over the top of the bench.

She hit the ground on her back, the air whooshing out of her lungs as a heavy weight fell on top of her. When she caught her breath, her hands automatically rose in an attempt to rip off whatever covered her face, whatever pressed against her mouth and nose, threatening to suffocate her.

"Don't make a sound or I'll kill you." The guttural voice of a man iced her to the bone.

He moved against her and his erection stabbed her in the thigh. She gulped in a breath, drawing the plastic into her mouth and gagging. Terror like she'd never known twisted her bowels and stole any strength she might possess. She was about to be raped. God help her, she was about to be attacked just like Mariah had been.

As suddenly as the weight of him had fallen on top of her, it disappeared. She remained unmoving for a second, afraid to hope that he'd just gone away.

Once again she raised her hands to get rid of the

covering over her head. The kick connected with her ribs with such vicious power her hands fell and tiny spots of light flickered in front of her eyes.

A second kick followed the first and it was as if a beast had been unleashed. Fists pummeled her face and all she could do was writhe and curl up in a ball in an attempt to protect herself.

"I broke you," he hissed in her ear. "And now a piece of you belongs to me." He kicked her once again and the tiny lights inside her head exploded and she knew nothing more.

Chapter 22

The Tavern was one of the most popular drinking establishments in Plains Point. It certainly wasn't the atmosphere that made it a favorite watering hole. It had no atmosphere other than the smell of cheap beer, the noise of clacking pool balls and a jukebox that hadn't been updated since the 1970s.

Location, location, location, that's the only thing that kept the Tavern in business. Located on the town square, it was the easiest place to get to if you wanted to get your nose in the sauce, and it was the place Clay and his friends gathered for their weekly beer-drinking night.

"I'm heading out," Clay said to Henry, the bartender. He scooted back from the table. Finn and Roger and Charlie had left almost half an hour ago. Joel Clarkson had sat with them for a little while, but even he had called it a night.

Clay didn't want to be here anymore, but he was also reluctant to go home to another night of sleeping on the sofa.

He'd always known that Sherri was the jealous type, but who would have thought she'd be so nuts about a girl he hadn't seen for sixteen years? A girl he barely remembered on his best days.

As he thought of the charged silence that would greet him at his place, he sat down once again. "Ah, what the hell, bring me one more," he said to Henry.

Henry had just delivered the draft beer to the table when Sam Kincaid crashed open the door. "Sheriff! We need you in the park. I think there's a dead woman there."

Clay jumped up, spilling his beer as he raced for the door. His heartbeat ripped through him as he looked across the street where a small crowd of people had begun to gather near the gazebo.

"What happened?" he asked Sam.

"Some kid saw a man beating the hell out of somebody on the ground. He hollered and the man ran away." Sam hurried to keep up with Clay.

"Do me a favor—call the office and have Hazel call in all my deputies," Clay exclaimed.

"Hey, she's alive!" a voice cried out.

"Somebody call for an ambulance!"

"Everybody get back. Get back!" Clay yelled. Jesus, the crime scene would be compromised for sure. His blood turned cold as he saw the figure behind the bench. With the head covered by a garbage bag, it was impossible to know who it was, but Clay's mind quickly assessed other details.

It was obviously female and if he was to guess, it was somebody young. She was so small, so dainty, and she looked so broken.

At that moment her chest rose with a discernible breath and Clay fell to his knees beside her. As gently as possible he ripped the garbage bag to free her face and nearly gagged.

"Oh my God," somebody cried.

Her face looked like chewed-up meat. Blood oozed from her nose, which was obviously broken. Her eyes were swollen and already turning black and her bloody mouth was twice the size of what it had once been.

"Get back. Goddammit, everyone get the hell back," Clay shouted as he took her poor, pitiful hand in his. The sound of an approaching siren filled the air.

He knew who she was, that friend of Mariah's from Chicago. Why would anyone want to hurt her? Jesus, why would anyone want to beat the hell out of her?

Within minutes two of Clay's deputies had arrived and had moved the ever-growing crowd back from the scene. An ambulance arrived and Janice Solomon was loaded onto the gurney and carried away to the hospital, where Clay wouldn't bet she'd survive the night.

Sam pointed out the young man who had seen what had happened and had raised the initial alarm. Clay found him leaning against a tree, having just puked up his latest meal.

Clay knew most of the young people in Plains Point and recognized the slightly green-around-the-gills kid as Jess Cooper.

"You okay, boy?" he asked. A sheen of sweat lay on the young man's brow. Jess nodded and drew a breath as if to pull himself together. "Want to tell me what happened?" Clay asked.

Jess leaned back against the tree again, his legs still wobbly. "I was supposed to meet a few of my friends at the café and I was cutting through the park to get there when I saw a man beating somebody on the ground. Man, he was beating the hell out of her. He started to pick her up and I yelled. He dropped her and ran."

"Which way did he run?" Clay asked.

Jess pointed to the left, toward an alley between the post office and a dry-cleaning business. Clay knew whomever Jess had seen was long gone by now. "What did he look like, Jess?"

"Like a big, dark shadow." The young man swallowed hard, the bob of his Adam's apple visible in the faint illumination from a nearby streetlight. A sob suddenly escaped his lips. "You think she's gonna die?"

"I don't know, son. You didn't recognize the man?"

Jess shook his head feverishly from side to side. "I think I was in shock or something, but no. I can't tell you anything about what he looked like."

"Not even how he was dressed?" Clay asked.

Jess shrugged. "Sorry, it was just so dark."

"All right, stay here and I'll have somebody take an official statement from you." Within minutes Clay had delegated a variety of tasks to his men.

Two deputies were combing the area around the gazebo for evidence, one had taken Jess to the sheriff's office to get a written report from the traumatized young man, and Clay was on his way to the hospital to see if he was beginning an investigation into an assault or into a murder.

Chapter 23

Mariah didn't start worrying until it was nine o'clock. Most of the stores in Plains Point closed by eight thirty, and only the café, some fast-food joints and a few bars remained open later. So what was taking Janice so long?

Mariah couldn't imagine her friend going into any of the bars, nor could she see her stopping in for a late evening snack by herself.

"She's a grown woman," Mariah said to Tiny, who was in her lap. He raised his head and looked at Mariah with loving eyes. "There's no reason to worry about a grown woman."

Tiny lowered his head and snuggled back down. He certainly wasn't worried about Janice's absence. And you shouldn't be either, Mariah told herself.

But by nine thirty she was pacing in front of the window, watching the drive that led up to the house for familiar headlights.

When her phone rang, she raced to answer it, fully expecting the caller to be Janice apologizing for getting held up. Instead it was Jack.

"I was getting ready to call it a night and realized

the whole day had passed and we hadn't talked to each other," he said.

Despite her worry, she smiled and sank down on the sofa. "We've had a busy day. I'm thinking Janice will be glad to go home tomorrow, since I've been working her to death around here."

Jack laughed. "She's a neat lady."

"Yes, she is, but at the moment I'm a bit worried about her. She took off in my car earlier to go into town and when she left, I had the impression she'd be home soon. But here it is after nine thirty and she still isn't back."

"You sound like a worried mother," he teased. "Maybe she met somebody or decided to get a cup of coffee at the café."

"I'm sure you're right. I'm just being silly," she replied. But by the time she hung up with Jack, her worry hadn't decreased but rather had increased.

By ten thirty her mind began to play all kinds of scenarios and before she could make herself completely crazy, she called Jack back. "I'm sorry to bother you, but Janice isn't home yet and I'm worried sick. I've been calling her cell phone, but it's going right to voice mail. Would you mind coming to get me and taking me back into town to see if we can find her? I know I'm probably overreacting, but I just have a bad feeling."

"I'll be there in fifteen minutes," Jack promised.

True to his word, precisely fifteen minutes later he pulled up in her driveway. She met him at the car and jumped into his passenger seat. "I feel bad about getting you out, but I didn't know who else to call."

"You still haven't heard from her?" he asked as he backed down the drive.

"Nothing. I left a note at the house in case she gets home before us. She would have called me if she was going to be this late. I have visions of her in a ditch somewhere, unconscious and unable to call for help."

He drove slowly and together they looked on the sides of the road for Mariah's car but didn't find it. When they reached town, they spotted it parked in front of a gift shop. The shop had closed long ago and there was no sign of Janice anywhere in the area.

"Maybe she did decide to go into the Tavern and have a drink," Mariah said. "Although that's definitely not her usual style."

It was then Jack noticed the activity in the park and Mariah's dread nearly exploded in the pit of her stomach. He parked and she got out of his car and began to walk toward the deputies she saw working the area with large flashlights.

"Hello?" Her walk became a half run as the dread became a screeching alarm in her head.

"Stay back, ma'am. This is a crime scene," one of the deputies, a man Mariah didn't know, responded.

"A crime scene? What happened?" Jack stood beside Mariah and placed an arm around her, as if to steady her.

"A woman was attacked."

Oh God. Mariah's heart seemed to stop beating. "Who? What woman?" she asked urgently, a gasp escaping her as her heart pounded so hard, so fast, she felt light-headed.

"I don't know. The sheriff's with her over at the hospital," the deputy said.

Jack tightened his arm around Mariah and she welcomed the support, afraid that she might fall. "Come on, honey. We'll check there."

She felt as if she were in a nightmare as Jack led her back to his car and they headed toward the hospital. Maybe it wasn't her—please don't let it be Janice. The words were a mantra repeated over and over again in her brain.

Jack didn't try to ease her worry and she was grateful for that. She wasn't in the mood to hear any empty assurances. All her energy was focused on trying to make whatever woman was in the hospital not Janice.

However, when she and Jack raced through the emergency room doors, the first person she saw was Clay and in his sympathetic eyes she knew the truth. Her knees nearly buckled beneath her.

"Oh God, Clay, what happened?" Once again she was aware of Jack's comforting closeness, his arm around her waist as if to anchor her in a raging storm.

"Somebody attacked her, Mariah." Clay's eyes were somber, his expression grave enough to twist her insides into a million knots.

"Is she all right? Can I see her?"

Clay shook his head negatively. "The doctor isn't letting anyone in right now." His jaw tightened. "It's not good, Mariah. Somebody beat the holy hell out of her. Last report I got from the doctor is that she hasn't regained consciousness."

Mariah stumbled backward and might have fallen had Jack not caught her. Tears blurred her vision as she stared unseeing at Clay. "Who would have done this to her? Why would somebody do this?"

"I don't know, but I'll get to the bottom of it. I swear I will," Clay said grimly.

Jack led Mariah to the row of chairs in the waiting

room and she collapsed into one of the chairs. Burying her face in her hands, she couldn't stop the deep sobs that ripped through her.

Not Janice. Oh God, not Janice. Mariah couldn't imagine life without the spritelike woman with the heart of a giant and the wisdom of a sage.

She raised her face to look at Jack, whose expression mirrored her grief. "I don't understand," she said as she swiped at her tears. "I don't understand why this happened. Janice never hurt anyone. She doesn't know anyone here in town. Who would do this to her?"

Jack pulled her closer against his side. "We'll get some answers soon," he said. "Clay will find out who did it. Somebody had to have seen something in that park."

She leaned into him and buried her face in his shoulder, the familiar scent of him oddly comforting at a time when comfort was in short supply.

For the next hour she mentally said every prayer she'd ever learned in her life. She held tight to a foam cup of hot coffee that magically appeared in her hand, and wished the warmth could seek out and heat the cold block of ice inside her.

Each time the door to the emergency room swung open, she sat up, hoping the doctor would come out to let them know what was going on, to tell them that Janice was going to be fine.

Mariah was grateful that Kelsey was spending the night with Katie and had no idea what had happened to the woman Kelsey loved like an aunt. God, she didn't want to tell her daughter about this.

It was nearing midnight when a tall gray-haired

man came out to speak with them. "Brian," Jack said in greeting. "This is Mariah Sayers, Janice's closest friend. Mariah, this is Dr. Brian Walsh."

Dr. Walsh nodded to Mariah, the stress lines around his eyes indicating near exhaustion. "She's conscious and she's asking for you." Mariah closed her eyes in relief as Jack squeezed her shoulder. "In fact, she won't let me run tests or do anything else for her until she sees you. She's quite insistent."

"Where is she?" Mariah started to sweep past Dr. Walsh, who stopped her by grabbing her arm.

"She's in room three, but I have to warn you— she's banged up pretty badly. I don't want her upset. If you can't control your emotions, then I'd rather you not go back there. She doesn't need histrionics right now."

For a wild moment she wanted to run, away from this hospital, away from this horror. She didn't know if she had the strength to see Janice beaten and not lose it. She wasn't at all sure she could do as the doctor had instructed.

Then she thought of all that Janice had done for her. Janice had given her life, more than her own mother had ever done. Surely Mariah could suck it up for the woman she loved like a mother, like a sister.

She nodded. "I'll be right back," she said to Jack, then swept past Dr. Walsh and through the doors that led to the emergency room.

Plains Point Hospital was a small facility and there were only three examining rooms. Mariah kept her gaze focused on room three as she summoned every ounce of inner strength she possessed.

Still, she couldn't stop the gasp of shock that escaped her lips as she stepped into the room. The person on the bed was not her friend. Her mind rebelled at the very idea, and yet it was Janice, beaten so badly she was nearly unrecognizable. If it weren't for the point of her ears, Mariah wouldn't have been certain it was her.

It was like seeing somebody horribly deformed. You didn't want to stare yet couldn't seem to stop looking. Janice looked dead and as Mariah approached the side of the bed, she felt as if she were in a nightmare. The whole thing felt surreal and she wanted somebody to jump out from behind a curtain and squeal "April Fools!"

But it wasn't a nightmare and it wasn't a prank. It was real, as real as the oxygen tube that went into Janice's smashed nose, as real as the stench of blood and antiseptic that permeated the small room.

On wooden legs she walked to the edge of the bed. Janice's face was swollen and black-and-blue and her very stillness terrified Mariah.

Emotion surged up inside Mariah and tears burned at her eyes, but she squeezed them back and instead reached out and touched Janice's small, slender hand.

Cold. It was so cold it made Mariah ache. Janice sucked in a liquid breath and her eyes, mere slits in black pouches, gleamed overbright.

"I'm here, Janice. You're going to be all right," Mariah said fervently.

Janice's fingers tightened on Mariah's and her swollen lips parted. It was obvious she was in tremendous pain and despite all her efforts to the contrary, Mariah's eyes filled with tears.

"It's all right. Don't try to talk. I just wanted you to know that I'm here."

Janice squeezed her hand more tightly and her mouth worked feverishly as she tried to sit up. A monitor began to beep a frantic sound as Janice reached up and grabbed the back of Mariah's head and pulled her close.

She held Mariah next to her with a surprising strength. "He told me he broke me. He broke a piece of me. That's what he said."

For a moment everything seemed to stop. The sound of the monitor hushed and a roar took its place, a roar inside her brain as she stared into Janice's wounded eyes.

Mariah's head spun wildly as Janice released her and fell back on the bed. At that moment the doctor rushed in. "You need to go," he said to Mariah, who looked at him through a veil of shock.

As the doctor began to administer to Janice, Mariah stumbled backward, away from the bed. She bumped into a chair, nearly fell, then turned and ran from the room with Janice's words thundering in her head.

He broke a piece of me.

He broke a piece of me.

She didn't stop running until she collapsed in Jack's arms. "It's all right," he said as he held her tight and stroked her back. "Shh, it's going to be all right," he said. But she knew that was a lie. Nothing was going to be all right.

Because now she knew.

He was still out there.

The same man who had raped her sixteen years ago was still out there walking the streets of Plains Point, and as long as he was out there, no woman was safe.

Chapter 24

Jack left the driver's side of his car and opened the passenger door for Mariah.

The moment she'd come out of Janice's room, she'd crawled deep inside herself, not speaking to him, barely moving without his help.

He'd loaded her into the car, wondering if she was in a state of shock. As he grabbed her hand to help her out, the iciness of her skin worried him.

"Mariah, can you get the key out of your purse?" he asked when they reached her front door.

She lifted her face to look at him, her eyes empty and darker than he'd ever seen them. "Honey, you need to unlock the door," he said gently.

Like a robot she opened her purse and withdrew a ring of keys. He took them from her and opened the front door. Tiny greeted them, barking happily and dancing around their feet. Mariah didn't appear to notice. She stood inside the entry as if rooted in place.

He'd tried to get her to talk to him as they drove away from the hospital, but his efforts to bring her around had been fruitless. The only thing he knew to do for her was to get her warm and get her to bed.

He locked the front door, took her purse from her and led her up the stairs, all the while talking to her in soft, gentle tones.

"What you need is sleep. We'll get you warm and tucked into bed and things will be better tomorrow." He had no idea if that was true, but didn't know what else to say.

She walked up the stairs with him like a docile, obedient child and he wanted to wrap her up in his arms, keep her where nothing and nobody could ever touch her with pain again.

It was easy to tell which bedroom she'd been using, for the room smelled of her perfume and a blue silk nightgown was tossed across the back of a chair.

She didn't protest when he undressed her and pulled the nightgown over her head. If she'd been hysterical, he would have been less worried. But her silence coupled with the blankness in her eyes had him very worried.

It wasn't until he pulled down the covers on the bed that her eyes sparked with a hint of life. She stared at him for a long moment, an urgent plea in her eyes. "Don't go." She reached out and took his hand, squeezing painfully tight. "Please, don't go. Don't leave me here alone."

"I won't," he replied, and pulled her against him. She stood in his embrace, neither accepting nor rejecting it. His love for her nearly brought him to his knees.

He held her for several minutes and someplace in

the back of his mind recognized that the embrace wasn't so much for her but for him.

Finally he released her and got her into bed. He stripped down to his briefs and got in next to her and pulled her icy body against his.

Almost immediately she went to sleep, as if it was the only way she knew to cope with the horror the night had wrought.

Jack wasn't so lucky. He remained awake a long time, worried about the woman in his arms, praying for Janice and wondering who in the hell in his hometown was capable of such madness.

Chapter 25

It was the dream, no, the nightmare. Mariah stood beneath the trees outside her house and listened to the sounds of the storm approaching.

A rumble of thunder brought a breeze of cool air and was followed by a lighting of the sky in the southwest. She hoped her father went to bed before it rained. The last thing she wanted was to be stuck in the middle of a storm while Jed Sayers practiced his Sunday sermon.

A sound. A rustling noise. Something dark and slick slammed over her head at the same time she was shoved off her feet. She slammed into the ground and couldn't breathe.

"If you scream, I'll kill you."

Did she know that voice?

His weight fell on top of her. Hands pressed down on her, biting into the bare skin of her upper arms.

Did she know those hands?

He smelled of the approaching storm, of wind and rain and damp earth. Dear God, did she know that smell?

Who was this man?

Then he was taking her, hurting her. "I broke you and now I have a piece of you forever."

Mariah screamed.

"Mariah, honey."

Jack's deep voice pulled her from her dream and she opened her eyes and stared at him. His hair was charmingly bed tousled and his eyes were warm and sleepy. The light of dawn was just creeping into the bedroom window.

"Are you okay?" he asked.

"A nightmare." She snuggled closer to him and stifled a moan as she remembered that reality was almost as bad as her dreamscape.

He flung an arm around her and pulled her tight against his warm strong body. "It's early. Try to go back to sleep."

She tried to relax in his embrace, but images from the night before filtered through her brain. She was afraid to get up and face the day and afraid to fall asleep again and face her dreams.

At the moment life was an unrelenting nightmare. The boogeyman was alive and well and living in Plains Point. He'd nearly killed Janice last night. What was next? Who was next?

Jack, obviously feeling her tense muscles and unrest, began to stroke her thigh. It was not meant to be a sexual thing; rather the languid caress up and down her leg was meant to be soothing.

But in his touch her desire was born, the desire to banish the images from her nightmare, the need to be held and loved and to lose herself in him. She wanted to be mindless for just a little while because although Jack didn't know it yet, the time of her telling him good-bye was imminent.

She turned in his arms to face him and she leaned forward and kissed the warm skin of his neck at the same time her hand swept down his chest.

His eyes fluttered open and he groaned as she touched him through his briefs. The glow of his eyes told her he knew her intention.

As he took off his briefs and tossed them to the floor, Mariah pulled her nightgown over her head, then took off her panties.

Once again they moved together, a tangle of arms and legs, of hungry mouths and stroking hands. His mouth trekked down the side of her throat, down to capture one of her nipples, and as he suckled and intense sensations coursed through her, she shoved back thoughts of Janice, of evil, and focused only on Jack and the hot spark in his eyes and the pleasure of his touch.

He was her reality for now and she clung to him because she knew when they finished making love, when they got out of bed, she was going to pack her and her daughter's bags and prepare to leave, not only Jack behind, but also the evil that had touched her life sixteen years ago, the evil that still walked the streets of Plains Point.

Clay sat in his car in his driveway as the sun crested the horizon. He was sick and he was scared. He leaned back against the headrest. He was exhausted but reluctant to go inside.

Janice Solomon was going to live, but he had a feeling in the days and weeks to come there were going to be times when she wished she were dead.

She had four broken ribs, a swollen spleen, a punctured lung and enough facial damage that she was probably going to need some plastic surgery.

The attacker had meant for her to die. Clay tightened his hands on the steering wheel. Nobody did that kind of damage and not expect to kill a person.

It hadn't been an assault—it had been attempted murder and what worried Clay as much as anything was that Jess had said the man was about to pick her up when Jess had yelled.

Had he meant to carry her off and finish the job? Hide her body so nobody would find her? A pain pierced Clay's forehead as his brain worked overtime to make some sort of sense of everything.

He stared at the neat ranch house in front of him. He and Sherri had a good life here. He was respected as an officer of the law and Sherri had her group of friends that went to lunch and helped each other with babysitting.

He'd never wanted to live anyplace else. He liked the idea of his kids going to the same schools he'd gone to, that they'd play with the kids of his closest friends. Once again his head ached as he thought of what was going to happen next.

He tensed as his front door opened and Sherri looked out. The last thing he wanted or needed at the moment was another crazy argument with the woman he loved more than life itself.

She came outside wearing only the black spaghetti-strapped nightgown he'd bought her on their fifth anniversary. It was a little tighter on her than it had been when he'd first bought it, but as far as he was concerned, she was still the prettiest girl in the world.

She opened the passenger door of his car and slid

in. "Out all night like a tomcat," she said. "How's your girlfriend?"

He'd had enough. The stress of the night coupled with his exhaustion made him snap. "Don't start, Sherri Dawn," he warned her in a low, ominous voice. "Just don't go there."

Her full lower lip puffed out into one of her pouts. "They say you never forget your first love. I just can't stand the thought of you being with me but wishing you were with her."

Clay slammed his hands down on the steering wheel, losing the barely held control he'd maintained. "Let me tell you a little something about love because you don't seem to get it. Love isn't two teenagers standing in some dumb gazebo. Love is me holding back your hair while you puke with morning sickness. It's me cleaning up baby shit and playing with the kids so you can take a bubble bath. Love is wanting to be a better man for you and . . ." To his abject horror he began to weep. He hid his face in his hands as emotion spilled out of him in the form of deep, choking sobs.

"Oh, Big Dog," Sherri said softly, calling him by his old high school name. "I'm sorry. I know I've been silly and acting like a total bitch." She placed a loving hand on his forearm.

He shook his head and sucked in a breath as he dropped his hands from his face. "It's not just you," he said. "Last night somebody almost killed Mariah's friend Janice in the park. It was a brutal attack."

"Oh my God," Sherri exclaimed. "You have any idea who did it?"

He shook his head and stared at his wife. "I'm scared, Sherri." The words came from him as if released under enormous pressure, a hiss that steamed from a teapot.

She frowned. "Scared of what, Big Dog?"

His heart thundered in his chest, so painful that he wondered if maybe he was on the verge of a heart attack. "I'm scared that finally everyone in town is going to know the truth about me. I'm afraid that you'll realize I'm not the hero you think I am. I'm not a good sheriff for this town. I'm just a dumb ex-jock in way over my head."

Sherri's arms stretched to enfold him as she leaned across the console. "Come on, honey. Let's go inside. You need some of my biscuits and gravy, then sleep."

They got out of the car and when they reached the front door, Sherri raised up on her tiptoes and kissed him, a soul-stirring kiss meant to soothe, but it did nothing to warm the icy coldness of the fear that gripped Clay's bowels.

Chapter 26

The most difficult thing Mariah had ever done was tell her daughter what had happened to Janice. Jack was gone by the time Kelsey arrived home from Katie's just before noon.

By that time, Mariah had already called the hospital to check on Janice. According to the nurse she spoke to, Janice was listed in serious, but stable, condition.

Kelsey took the news as Mariah had thought she would, hard. She cried like a baby in Mariah's arms and Mariah cried with her.

Kelsey was now up in her room and Mariah stood at the front door watching for Jack, who was coming to take her and Kelsey to get Mariah's car, which was still parked on Main Street where Janice had left it.

What she wanted to do was get Janice transferred to a hospital in Chicago, place the house with a local Realtor and get the hell out of here.

She stepped out on the front porch, her gaze focused on the grove of trees. The air even smelled evil today, humid and thick. She wished she could get back the mental fog that had gripped her last night when she'd left the hospital.

But the morning had brought a clarity that was painful and sharp. The man who had raped her hadn't been a drifter on his way through town. He hadn't been caught and put in prison and he hadn't died.

Broken pieces.

How many other women had been broken by him over the past sixteen years? A razor edge of guilt sliced through her heart. If she'd told years ago, if she'd reported what had happened to her, would Janice have been attacked last night? And if she didn't tell now, how many more women would be brutalized?

There's nothing to tell, a small voice whispered inside her head. You don't know who attacked you. You can't describe him. You have no information that would help catch him.

And telling would destroy everything else in her life.

No, the best thing to do was run. Leave town. Wasn't that what had been painted across her house? *GO HOME*. It was time to obey that spray-painted command.

As Jack's car came up the drive, a new grief pierced her heart. She could have built a life with him. In the brief time they'd been together, he'd touched her on so many levels. In running from evil, she was also running from love and all the good things that Jack might have brought into her life.

"Kelsey, Jack is here," she called up the stairs.

"Can't I just stay here?" Kelsey asked as she came down the stairs. Her eyes were red and swollen and she held Tiny tightly in her arms.

"I'd rather you not," Mariah said. The last thing she wanted was for Kelsey to be home alone while a monster was loose. "Besides, I'm planning on stopping by the hospital. Don't you want to see Janice?"

Kelsey's face crumbled and tears streaked down her cheeks. "I don't know. I don't know if I can stand it."

Mariah placed an arm around her daughter's shoulder, her heart squeezing so tight it hurt her chest. "I'm not going to lie to you. She looks horrible, but I'm sure what she needs more than anything right now is to hear our voices, to know that we're close to her. She needs us both, Kelsey."

Mariah knew the strength her daughter possessed and Kelsey didn't disappoint her. "You're right," she said. She straightened as Mariah dropped her arm from around her. She placed Tiny on the floor, swiped at her tears with the backs of her hands, then marched out the front door like a soldier going to war.

Jack greeted Kelsey with a hug and as Mariah walked down the porch stairs, her heart ached at the sight of the man and the child she loved in a caring embrace. He would have made a good stepfather. He would have been a terrific male role model in her daughter's life.

He released Kelsey only to take Mariah into his arms. "You doing okay?" he asked when he released her. He held her gaze as if trying to see inside her, deep into her soul.

She nodded and the three of them got into the car. "I guess we'll need to stop by the sheriff's office to make sure I can get the car," she said once they were under way. She had no idea if it might have been impounded because of the crime.

"Have you talked to Clay to see if he's come up with anything to catch this guy?" Jack asked.

"I called earlier, but he wasn't in. The deputy I spoke to wouldn't give me any information. I'm hoping Janice saw enough to be able to identify him." That would certainly ease some of the guilt for me, Mariah thought.

If Clay caught the person who attacked Janice, then Mariah wouldn't have to feel so bad about keeping her silence and leaving town. She wouldn't have to think about how many others might suffer at the hands of this man.

But when they reached the sheriff's office, Clay quickly dashed Mariah's hopes. "She didn't see who it was," he said. "She was attacked from behind and whoever it was threw that bag over her head before she got even a glimpse of who it was."

"What about the witness?" Jack asked hopefully.

Clay grimaced. He looked exhausted, with bruise-like bags beneath his eyes. "A big dark shadow. That's the only description I've gotten so far. But my men are still questioning people and hopefully in the next day or two we'll get a break."

Please, let them find a clue. Give them a break, Mariah thought. "What about my car? Is it all right for me to take it?" she asked.

Clay nodded and pulled Janice's purse from the bottom drawer of his desk. "I took the liberty of taking this and bringing it here for safekeeping. The car isn't part of the crime scene, so I see no reason why you can't have it back." He handed her the purse. "The keys are inside."

Mariah realized there were other questions she wanted—no, needed—to ask him, but not now, not with Jack and Kelsey present. She'd have to figure out another time, another place, to ask him the questions that suddenly burned inside her.

Once they left the office, Jack walked them to her car. "You going on over to the hospital?" he asked. Mariah nodded. "You want company later this evening or would you prefer to be alone?"

She wanted him. Oh God, how she wanted him. She wanted to sit and have coffee with him and let him tell her silly animal stories. She wanted him to watch a sitcom with them and laugh together. She wanted anything but the piercing sadness she now felt as she looked at him.

"I think Kelsey and I need a night alone," she replied. She realized then that there had been a part of her that had entertained the idea of living here, of building a life in the house she'd transformed from something ugly into something beautiful.

Someplace in the magic of a barely realized fantasy, she'd begun to see Jack living with them here, sleeping beside her every night in a master bedroom transformed by love.

She'd even believed that Kelsey might embrace the idea. In the short time they'd been here, she'd made so many new friends and hadn't seemed eager to leave. She obviously liked Jack, and Mariah thought she would have welcomed him into their life.

But that was all changed now. Time to run. Time to run. Those were the words that echoed in Mariah's head as she and Kelsey entered the hospital.

Janice had been moved to room 112 and just before they entered the room, Mariah took Kelsey's hand. "Just remember no matter what she looks like on the outside, she's still the woman we love and she needs to know that now more than ever."

Kelsey's blue eyes misted, but she bit her lower lip and nodded. Together she and Mariah walked into the room. The lights were dim, the shades pulled tight against the late-afternoon sun.

But when Janice turned her head to look at them, a cry escaped Kelsey. "It's okay, baby," Janice said, the words half-garbled by both pain medication and the swollen condition of her face and mouth. "It looks much worse than it is."

She raised a hand to Kelsey, who had begun to weep. Mariah watched as her daughter grabbed Janice's hand and sat in the chair at her side. For the next few minutes it was Janice who offered comfort, whispering in low tones to Kelsey until the teenager's tears had dried.

"I'm going to need a new nose," Janice said. "I'm thinking of something long and elegant like Angelina Jolie's. Maybe then I'll give my man Brad a call and see if he wants a date."

A small giggle escaped Kelsey. "Aunt Janice, I think it will take more than a new nose to interest Brad." Kelsey's smile fell. "Are you sure you're going to be all right?"

"Right as rain, doll face," Janice replied. "Now stop looking so worried. I'm a tough old broad and I'm going to be just fine."

She might be a tough old broad, but it was obvious she was already growing tired. "Kelsey, why don't you run to the gift shop and see if there's a pretty flower arrangement to cheer up the room." Mariah pulled some bills out of her wallet.

Mariah sat in the chair Kelsey vacated and when her daughter left the room, she gazed at her friend. "Were you raped?"

Janice closed her eyes and shook her head. She looked at Mariah. "I thought that's what it was about. I thought that's what he was going to do. He had an erection. When he was laying on top of me, I felt him." She paused a moment, her face a grimace of pain. "But then he just went crazy and started kicking and punching me."

Mariah leaned closer. "And you're sure of what he said to you."

"It was him, Mariah. I'm positive of what he said, of what I heard." She turned on her side, releasing a gasp of pain.

"I want you transferred out of here as soon as it's possible," Mariah said. "We'll get you back to a hospital in Chicago, find the best doctors."

"I just need time to heal. Although I look and feel like hell, I'll probably be released from here in the next day or two."

"Then I'll get things ready for all of us to leave town then. We'll get back to Chicago and you can stay with us until you're healed up." A sickness rolled in the pit of Mariah's stomach as her friend stared at her with surprise.

"You're just going to leave? Just walk away from here? Mariah, he's escalated. He's not only a rapist anymore—he's something worse. He's become a killer."

"There's nothing I can do," Mariah exclaimed, a flush warming her face as her voice rose an octave. "There's no information I can give that will help find him." She drew a deep breath and lowered her voice. "Don't ask me to tell, Janice. Please, don't ask me."

"It's not my place to ask," she replied as Kelsey came back into the room carrying a vase filled with multicolored blooms.

A half hour later as Mariah drove home, Janice's words reverberated around and around in her head. *He's escalated. He's become a killer.* There was no question that he meant to kill Janice.

There was no doubt in Mariah's mind that if Jess Cooper hadn't decided to cut through the park at the time that he had, Janice would be dead.

By the time Mariah reached the house, she knew what she wanted to do was talk to Clay. She needed to ask some questions, to get some answers, before she made a final decision about leaving Plains Point.

"You think Katie's mom would let you spend the night again tonight?" Mariah asked her daughter as they came into the kitchen.

Kelsey looked at her in surprise. "I don't know, probably. Why? What are you going to do?"

"I just have some things I need to take care of and I know you'd be bored to tears and I don't think you should be here alone."

Kelsey's eyes widened. "Do you think he'll try to hurt you or me? Do you think that whoever attacked Aunt Janice might come here?"

"No, not at all," Mariah replied quickly. "There's no reason to think there was anything personal about Janice's attack. If I was to guess, maybe somebody tried to rob her, and you know Janice—she's spunky and maybe she fought back."

"Is that what Janice said happened?"

"She's still a little foggy on the details," Mariah replied.

"I'll go call Katie," Kelsey said. "But Mom, if you're out and around tonight, you will be careful, won't you?"

Mariah pulled her daughter into her arms and buried her face in the clean scent of Kelsey's hair. "Don't you worry about me. You just have fun with your friend." She held Kelsey for a moment longer, her intense love for her daughter nearly bringing her to tears.

She finally released her. "Now, go call Katie."

As Kelsey ran up the stairs, Mariah picked up Tiny, who'd been trying to get somebody's, anybody's, attention. She stood by the front window and stared outside. How many times would she look at those trees and feel as if there was something important in her head, something buried just beneath the surface of her memory?

Each time she had her nightmare and awakened, in those brief moments before full consciousness struck, she had the feeling that an important piece of information, a clue, was just within her reach, but before she could grasp it, it was gone.

"Katie's mom said yes." Kelsey came down the stairs. "She said you can drop me off anytime."

Mariah looked at her watch, then gave Tiny to Kelsey. "It's almost five. Why don't we eat some dinner, and then I'll drop you at Katie's."

Dinner consisted of sandwiches and chips, although neither Mariah nor Kelsey had much of an appetite. After eating, they cleaned up the kitchen, then got into the car to take Kelsey to her friend's house.

"Katie said that if we decided to stay here and not go back to Chicago, I could try out for cheerleader and I'd probably make the squad."

"Would you like that? I mean staying here, not making the cheerleader squad," Mariah asked.

"Yeah, kind of. I didn't think I'd like it here, but I've made some cool friends and I like our house. It's so much nicer than our apartment."

The nervous energy that had been with Mariah since the moment she'd talked to Janice after the attack twisted tightly in her stomach.

No, honey, we can't stay here because there's a madman walking the streets, and oh, by the way, I'm pretty sure he's your father.

"So, is there a possibility we might stay here?"

"Oh, honey, I don't know, but I wouldn't get my hopes up if I were you. It's complicated. Besides, that was really never in the plans." Mariah pulled up in front of Katie's house. "Call me when you're ready to come home in the morning and I'll come pick you up."

"Okay." Kelsey leaned over and gave Mariah a kiss on the cheek. "Love you, Mom." She grabbed her overnight bag from the backseat and then got out of the car.

Mariah watched as her daughter ran toward Katie's house, and an unexpected sense of impending danger crashed through Mariah. She wanted to jump out of the car and grab her daughter and keep her by her side until they left town. But she knew Kelsey would be safe at Katie's house. The Arrowoods were big on supervision and this was probably one of the safest places for Kelsey to be at the moment.

She pulled out of the driveway and headed into

town, a cold chunk inside her stomach. She thought of those times when she'd sensed somebody watching her, the night she'd seen the figure hiding among the trees.

Arctic air whipped through her as she thought about the night she'd believed that somebody had been in the house, coming up the stairs. Now that she knew that her rapist still walked these streets, those isolated incidents were all the more chilling.

He was after her. She felt it in her soul. She'd thought she was going crazy, but she wasn't. He was after her and she knew that if he managed to get her again, this time she wouldn't survive.

He was out of control. Crazy, heart-pounding, head-crashing out of control. As he sat in the café and sipped his coffee and listened to the latest gossip making the rounds, he realized just how lucky he'd been not to get caught.

He hadn't meant to attack her. He hadn't even realized he'd stuck a garbage bag into his back pocket when he'd left his house until it was over her head. And then the haze of rage was upon him and he couldn't have stopped himself if he'd wanted.

It was only the sound of somebody yelling that had brought him back into his own head. He'd wanted to pick her up and carry her to the others. So many pieces and still he wasn't whole.

He'd had to drop her and run. He'd thought for sure that she was dead, and he'd never known such fear as when he'd heard that she'd survived the attack. But this evening his fear was gone. The good old grapevine of Plains Point was as accurate as a personal report from the sheriff.

Janice Solomon had survived, but she'd been unable to identify her attacker. He was safe. He was fucking invincible.

And he was ready to end it the way it had begun—with Mariah.

Chapter 27

Clay wasn't at the office and one of the deputies told Mariah he had gone home for the day. She got his address from the deputy, who knew she was a friend of Clay's; then she headed there.

She knew she might be causing problems with his wife by showing up at his house, but she didn't care. The questions she had to ask Clay were too important to allow the petty jealousies of Sherri to stop her. In truth Mariah preferred to talk to him in the privacy of his home.

It wasn't difficult to find the neat little ranch house where he and Sherri lived. She pulled into the driveway next to Clay's official car but remained seated, hands tightly clutching the steering wheel.

Mariah thought back to the night in the gazebo with Clay. She had gained enough maturity through the years to realize that she would have felt the same euphoric joy if any boy in town had been there with her.

She'd been so hungry for something, for anybody to love her. She'd been starved for affection but not in love with Clay. Her feelings for Clay had never been real, unlike her feelings for Jack.

All she wanted from Clay now was some information. She wasn't about to make a big statement or confession about what had happened to her so long ago.

It was possible that the person who had attacked her years before had never attacked another woman until Janice. It was possible that it wasn't some crazed rapist/killer, but rather somebody who hated Mariah enough to hurt her and a woman he knew that Mariah loved. And that made her think of Doug Kent, the man who had hated her father.

There was a part of her that hoped it was personal, that prayed that throughout the years no other woman had been touched by this evil. That would certainly go a long way in alleviating her guilt, the guilt that if she'd only spoken up when it had happened to her, then perhaps this wouldn't have happened to Janice.

As a vision of Janice's face exploded into her mind, she tightened her grip on the steering wheel, her fingers aching beneath the pressure.

She would take a thousand licks of the willow switch if she could undo what had happened to Janice. It wasn't just the physical damage that was horrifying. Mariah knew the emotions her friend had felt in those moments before she'd lost consciousness.

Fear like that should be more than a four-letter word. There was no word in the English language that could describe the gut twisting, the utter horror of what you thought about when being raped, when believing you were going to die.

She jerked off her seat belt and got out of the car, desperately shoving that particular thought out of her mind. She couldn't go there or she'd go insane.

She knocked on the front door and Sherri answered. "Hi, Sherri. Look, I don't want any trouble from you, but I need to speak with Clay."

Sherri opened the door to let her inside. "He's in there." She pointed through the living room, where three kids were watching a video and a little one bounced in a playpen. "We were just cleaning up the dinner dishes."

Mariah walked in the room to see Clay standing at the sink, his arms buried up to the elbows in soapy water. "Mariah!" He grabbed a towel and dried his hands. "What are you doing here?" He cast a quick glance at his wife, who was standing just behind her.

"I'm sorry to bother you here at home and I don't want to cause any problems, but I needed to talk to you and it can't wait until morning."

"Why don't you have a seat?" Sherri said from behind her. "You want a cup of coffee or something?" There was a faint hint of apology in her gaze as she looked at Mariah.

Mariah sat at the large oak table and shook her head. "No, thanks, I'm fine."

"I was sorry to hear about your friend," Sherri said, and the amazing thing was that Mariah believed her. There was a genuine compassion radiating from Sherri's eyes. "I'm sorry about a lot of things," she added just beneath her breath.

"No hard feelings," Mariah replied. She had more important things to think about than Sherri being hateful to her.

"If you're here to ask about what I've found out

about the man who attacked your friend, I'm afraid you've wasted a trip here," Clay said as he sat at the opposite end of the table. He looked tired, lines of stress etched deep into his face.

"I'm sorry to hear that, but that's not why I'm here." She was surprised to realize that Sherri had gone, leaving the two of them alone at the table. "How long have you been sheriff, Clay?"

"Ten years. Why?"

Mariah drew a deep breath for strength. This was what she'd spent the last sixteen years dreading. This was her worst fear come true. "Have there been reports of rapes in that time?"

Clay's frown deepened. "Your friend wasn't raped. Why are you asking about that?"

"Please, Clay. It's important." Her nerves thrummed inside her. "Have there been any reported rapes in the last ten years?"

"None," he answered without hesitation.

Relief would have buckled her knees had she not been sitting. "You're sure?"

He nodded. "I'm positive. I only remember one rape in all my time living here. It was a couple of years after I graduated and I can't even remember her name, but she and her family moved away soon after that. What's going on, Mariah?"

Tell him.

The inner voice screamed in her head, but a vision of Kelsey filled her mind. Kelsey, who believed that her father was a soldier, a man who had loved Mariah, who would have loved Kelsey.

"I was just wondering, you know, about small-town crime." Her answer sounded stupid even to her own ears.

Clay leaned back in the chair, his shirt sporting a spot of what appeared to be spaghetti sauce. "Now, if you'd asked me about runaways, I would tell you we have more than our share here in Plains Point." Sherri came back into the room and sat next to her husband.

"What do you mean?" Mariah asked.

Once again Clay frowned and he stared at her for a long moment as if assessing whether he should tell her whatever was on his mind.

"Tell her," Sherri said softly, and reached out to take her husband's hand in hers. "Tell her what you're thinking."

Clay smiled at his wife, then looked back at Mariah, his expression stone-cold somber. "When the eyewitness told me about the attack on your friend, there was something that bothered me, I mean, something other than the obvious."

"What?" Once again tension twisted Mariah's insides.

"The kid said that he thought the perp was about to pick her up in his arms when he shouted." Clay disengaged his hand from his wife's and got up from the table. He went over to get a cup of coffee, then sat back down again. He twisted the cup between his hands, around and around, nearly spilling the contents before he finally stopped.

"I kept thinking, why would the attacker want to pick her up? Why not just leave her there? Then I got to thinking about all the supposed runaways there have been while I've been sheriff. I spent most of today going through my records and making a list."

The tension that had momentarily fled from Mariah came back with a vengeance, constricting her insides so tight she could scarcely breathe.

"A list?"

He took a sip of his coffee and grimaced as if he found the brew too bitter to bear. "Over the last ten years there have been seventeen young women who have disappeared from Plains Point."

Mariah couldn't help the gasp that escaped her. "Seventeen? That sounds like a lot for such a small town."

"I hadn't really put it together until this afternoon." Clay suddenly looked haggard. "I still don't know if it means anything or not."

"You never followed up to find these women?"

"Of course I did," Clay replied tersely. "At the time of each disappearance I did everything I could, given my budget and the tools and manpower at my disposal. Seven of the women were over eighteen and as adults had every right to take off. There were no signs of foul play, nothing to indicate any kind of a crime had taken place."

"And now what do you think?" Mariah asked, her heartbeat thrumming an irregular rhythm of incredible dread. She didn't want to know, yet she needed him to tell her, to confirm the horrible possibility boiling around in her head.

"I just keep thinking about him trying to pick up Janice as if to carry her off, and that makes me wonder if other women were picked up and taken someplace where they would never be found." Clay's eyes were dark and more than a little bit haunted. "Is it possible that a monster has been loose on the streets right under my nose?"

"If that is true, then what are you going to do?"

Once again Sherri took Clay's hand in hers, as if to give her husband the strength he needed to get through whatever lay ahead. "He's already called a friend of his, a detective on the Kansas City police force."

Clay nodded. "He's coming in first thing in the morning. He's going to go over all the old files, talk to your friend and help me decide if I need to call in the FBI. I hope you will keep this information to yourself for the time being. I don't want the whole town in a panic over all this."

"You don't have to worry about me talking," she said. The dread that had begun as a small knot in her stomach had now snowballed into a large brick. The horror of Clay's speculation made it impossible for her to remain silent any longer.

She knew what she had to do. She knew she could never live with herself if she didn't tell. "I need to tell you something, Clay, but I'd like to ask you and Sherri to keep it to yourselves long enough for me to tell my family first." She drew a deep breath as she realized it was possible she was about to destroy everything she'd built with the person she loved most in her life.

"I'd like to report a crime," she began. "Sixteen years ago I was raped."

Chapter 28

Jack paced his living room floor, nervous tension eating his insides like a vicious cancer. As if worrying about Mariah all day hadn't been enough, Rebecca had finally made contact. Thirty minutes ago she'd called him and insisted she needed to speak to him. She'd given him no chance to protest, saying only that she'd be at his house in an hour.

Two days ago he'd thought he was one of the happiest men on earth. Just goes to show how elusive happiness can be, he thought as he plopped onto the sofa and leaned over to scratch Rover behind the ears.

Even though Mariah had continued to insist that she would soon be leaving Plains Point, he'd hoped that wasn't going to happen.

He'd seen the way those blue eyes of hers sparkled when she talked about the renovations on the house. When she spoke of the town, there was real affection in her voice. He'd begun to hope that they might have a future together, here in Plains Point.

But there had also been something in her eyes when he'd taken her to get her car, a distance that had frightened him. And when she'd told him that she thought it best that she and Kelsey be alone that night, he'd gotten the distinct impression that she was intentionally pulling away from him, beginning the process of saying good-bye.

God, but he didn't want her to say good-bye.

And now Rebecca was about to arrive and happiness had never seemed such a distant dream. "Maybe it's just supposed to be you and me, Rover," he said to the faithful companion at his feet. Rover wagged his stub of a tail and looked up at him with adoring eyes. Maybe he was meant to live alone with a dog who was smarter than a lot of people he knew.

Even though Rover could warm his feet on a cold wintry night and would happily share a steak dinner, it certainly wasn't enough.

There had been other women between the time he and Rebecca had parted and Mariah, but none of them had stirred him as she had.

It was more than physical. His feelings for her were a complex mix of protectiveness, lust and respect. He loved her. He loved her with a force that humbled him, with a depth that was all-encompassing.

He leaned back and rubbed his temple, where a headache was trying to take hold. His dread at having to face his ex-wife again was equally all-encompassing. He had nothing to offer her, except what little compassion was left in his soul for her.

It was difficult to focus on Rebecca when he was so worried about Mariah. He didn't want her to leave. He hoped he could convince her to stay and build a life with him here.

What he didn't want was for Mariah to run from here because of an isolated incident of violence. Jack

had lived in Plains Point for most of his life and
never had anything like this happened before. The
attack on Janice had been a shocking anomaly in a
town that saw little crime.

Spending time with Mariah had shown him what
it would be like to be with a strong woman, a woman
who had no inner demons, who made good choices
for herself and her daughter.

God help him from women with inner demons.

Rover growled low in his throat and Jack sat up
as he heard the sound of a car door slam. A moment
later a knock fell on the door. His feet felt leaden as
he walked to the door and opened it to see Rebecca.

"Hello, Jack." A nervous smile lifted her lips as
she fidgeted with the chain strap on her purse. "May
I come in?"

"Please." He opened the door wider to allow her
entry. The first thing he noticed was that she was
wearing her hair different. It was short and curly
rather than how he remembered it.

"You want something to drink?" It felt so awkward. He didn't know what to say, how to feel.

"No thanks, I won't be staying."

"At least have a seat," he said, and gestured
toward the sofa. Rover eyed her suspiciously and
moved to stand next to Jack's legs. "It's all right,
buddy," he said.

Rebecca sat on the edge of the sofa, as if poised to
run. "It's taken me a couple of days to get up enough
nerve to do this," she said.

Jack sank into the chair opposite the sofa. "Rebecca, you can't keep doing this." A deep weariness
laced his words.

"I'm not here for money, Jack. And I'm not going

to leave here and sneak back later and rob you. I've been in treatment."

"I've heard that before," he said gently.

She nodded and offered him a tight smile. "I know, but this time it was the right time and the right place. I checked myself into a ninety-day program. I finished the ninety days two weeks ago and I'm now living in a clean and sober apartment complex."

It was then he really looked at her and realized her eyes were clear, her skin was luminous and she'd put on weight. She looked good. "So, why are you here?"

"Closure." She smiled and in that full, open gesture he saw a glimmer of the woman he'd fallen in love with years before. "And forgiveness." She leaned forward. "Jack, part of my recovery is recognizing the havoc I created in other people's lives. I needed to come here and tell you that I'm sorry for so many things. I'm sorry for lying to you, for stealing from you and for destroying what we might have had once upon a time."

A knot of tension that had sat in his chest loosened. "Rebecca, I'm not the one you need to forgive you," he said.

She smiled again and nodded. "Yes, I'm working on forgiving myself, but it was important to me that I come here and see you, to tell you I'm sorry and to say a final good-bye."

He didn't love her anymore, had lost that loving feeling years ago, but a bittersweet pang touched his heart at her words. "What are your plans?" he asked.

"Right now I'm working part-time as a cashier in a grocery store. It's a good job without too much stress and I'm just taking it one day at a time." She stood, as if her mission had been accomplished and now she just wanted to get on with her life.

"I'm glad for you," he said, also rising from his chair.

He walked with her to the front door, where she paused and reached up and placed her palm on the side of his face. "You're a nice man, Jack, and you would have been a wonderful husband. The problems were all mine and they had nothing to do with you."

She dropped her hand to her side, the imprint of it still warming his face. "You won't be hearing from me again. I think it's important to put the past behind us and move on. That's what I'm doing, but I wanted to thank you for trying to help me. I wanted to tell you that there was nothing you could do to help me."

He leaned forward and kissed her on the cheek and then she was gone. This time he was relatively certain she was gone forever. There had been a shining strength in her eyes that he'd never seen before, a welcomed peace that made him believe he would never see her again.

He closed the front door, then went into his bedroom and changed into a pair of running shorts, suddenly feeling the need to be outside in the evening air.

Minutes later he and Rover hit the sidewalk. "Only strong, well-adjusted women from now on," he told his furry companion. "If you see me even looking at a woman who has issues, you bite my ass, you hear me?" Rover barked with enthusiastic agreement.

Jack felt ten years younger as he ran. He hadn't

realized the weight of Rebecca that had hung around his neck for so long. Now that it was gone, he felt like a new man. A new man in love.

Thoughts of Mariah chased him all the way back home. After a long hot shower he pulled on a pair of sweats, grabbed a beer from the fridge and returned to the sofa to think about how he could turn the girl of his teenage fantasy into the woman who would be his happily ever after.

Chapter 29

It was almost ten when Mariah left Clay's house, and the light of a nearly full moon spilled down as she ran to her car. She got inside, locked the doors, then leaned her head down on the steering wheel, fighting back the tears that had threatened to over-whelm her for the last couple of hours.

She felt like she could throw up and if she did, she knew it would be nothing but the remnants of trauma. Going back to that night and consciously try-ing to remember every detail had nearly ripped her guts out.

This was the second-hardest thing she'd probably ever do in her life. The first hardest would come in the morning when she had to tell Kelsey the truth about the man who was her father.

Wearily she raised her head and started the engine but remained parked in Clay's driveway. She felt empty, hollowed out by the scalpel of the past.

Clay had been relentless in his questions of her, probing her memories, demanding answers that were beyond her reach. It had been grueling and disheartening because she didn't have anything concrete to give him.

Sherri had surprised her with her compassion. She'd held Mariah's hand during much of Clay's interrogation, offering a strength that Mariah had desperately needed. It had been hell, going back there, consciously returning to the scene of the crime that had changed the course of her life and haunted her ever since.

By tomorrow evening everyone in Plains Point would know what had happened to her, what force had driven her away from home sixteen years ago. News traveled fast in a small town. Not only would her friends and neighbors know, but also the man who had raped her would know that she'd finally told.

And if the gossipmongers got it right, he would know that even though she told, he was still safe, that he still remained unidentified. God, if she could just remember one thing to help identify him, a sound, a smell, anything that would point a finger to the guilty.

She finally put the car in reverse and pulled out of the driveway. It was too late to visit Janice in the hospital, but the last place she wanted to be was at the house alone in the dark.

She knew where she wanted to go. She knew where she wanted to be. She ached with the need for Jack's quiet strength, his steady hand and loving heart. She wanted to be wrapped in his arms and held tight until this nightmare was over. Besides, she owed it to him to be the one to tell him. She didn't want him to hear the story tomorrow from somebody else.

Would it ever be over?

Tears spilled down her cheeks as she drove toward the animal clinic and the little ranch house of Jack's. Tomorrow she'd have to rip her daughter's world apart. Was there anything more painful? She swiped the tears from her eyes in an attempt to clear her vision.

If she'd seen this coming sixteen years ago, would she have told the lies she had to her daughter? She honestly didn't know. Even though she hadn't been able to give Kelsey an actual, living and loving father, she'd wanted to give her daughter the illusion of such a man.

Had that been so wrong?

It didn't matter what she thought; it was more important what Kelsey would think and that's what she feared most of all. She and Kelsey had always had an open and honest relationship. What would her daughter think of her when she found out about all the lies?

By the time she got to Jack's, she was crying once again, the tears coming from a place so deep inside her she had no control.

Thank God illumination spilled out his front window, letting her know he was still awake. She turned off her car lights and shut off the engine, her hands clasping and unclasping the steering wheel. What would he think when she told him? How would he react?

He must have heard her car, for his front door opened and he stood silhouetted against the living room lights. Just the sight of him, so tall, so broad-shouldered, calmed her a bit.

He stepped out on the porch. "Mariah?"

The sound of his familiar deep voice brought a new burst of tears to her eyes. She got out of the car, took two faltering steps and then ran to him as a deep sob wrenched from her.

He asked no questions. He merely opened his arms to her and wrapped her up. There was welcome warmth and a sense of safety. He held her there on the porch as she wept.

She didn't know how long they remained that way, with the warm night air embracing them and his strong arms warming her as nothing else had done for the past twenty-four hours.

Finally her tears slowed and he led her inside the house, where a small schnauzer growled at her. "Rover, no," Jack said as he led her to the sofa.

She sank down with him and he captured her face between the palms of his hands, those green eyes of his filled with concern. "Is it Janice?" he asked.

"No, no. It's me." She'd thought the tears were gone, but they came again, spilling down her cheeks. "I . . . I was raped."

Every muscle in his body tensed and in an instant his green eyes turned black. "We need to call Clay." He was half off the sofa before she stopped him.

"No! Jack, wait. I just came from Clay's house. It happened—I was raped sixteen years ago."

He stared at her and slowly sank back down beside her. The lean angles of his face remained taut with tension. "Tell me what's going on, Mariah."

And she did. She told him in detail about the night of the rape, going over the same things she'd just told Clay. He didn't interrupt her and spoke only with his changing facial expressions. Anger, grief, compassion—they were all there on his handsome face as she spilled her secret of the past. When she was finished, she felt depleted, emptied of every emotion and every ounce of energy.

"What happened afterward?" he asked as he took one of her hands in his. She had come to love the feel of his hands with their square clean fingernails and strong grasp. "Was that the night you ran away?"

"No, not that night. Afterward I crept back into my bedroom window. I was bleeding and scared and didn't know what to do. I finally called to my mother and told her what had happened." She closed her eyes for a moment, remembering the utter betrayal, the pain that had hurt almost more than anything else that had happened that night.

"She blamed me, told me I got what I deserved because I was bad and had sneaked out of the house. Bad things happen to bad girls. She asked me if she should wake up my father or if I just wanted to get into bed, where I belonged. I took a shower and got into bed."

She'd thought there was no more emotion left inside her, but she'd been wrong. She'd never needed her mother's love more than she had that night with terror shaking her insides and blood on her thighs. But her mother had offered her nothing but another beating by her father.

A shudder raced through her. "The next morning I went to school, like nothing had happened, like it had all just been a bad dream." Jack's hand tightened around hers and she continued. "I barely remember those days after. I was like in a daze, moving like I was in a play. I laughed and did my homework and ate lunch, but nothing seemed real. Then almost a month later I missed my period and realized I was pregnant. That's when I left. That's when I ran.''

"And you didn't tell anyone?''

She shook her head. "The only person who knew the truth was Janice. I told her right before Kelsey was born.''

He pulled her into his arms and she went willingly. As he held her, she told him about Clay's suspicions concerning the runaways and the fact that it had been Mariah's rapist who had attacked Janice.

"Clay thinks maybe those runaway girls didn't run away at all, that it's possible they were victims of this man, that he killed them and hid their bodies. He intended to beat Janice to death. He's escalated over the years. He's not content with raping anymore.''

"And Clay has no idea who it might be? You don't remember anything about that night that could help him catch this madman?''

She sat up and shook her head. "I have nightmares and sometimes when I first wake up from one, I think I know something that's important, something that could help identify him, but before it gets fully formed in my head, before I can really grab on to it, it's gone.'' Even now a deep frustration edged through her. If she could just remember exactly what it was, what small detail haunted her.

"So what's Clay doing about all this?''

She sank back into his arms. "He has a friend, a cop from Kansas City, coming into town in the morning to look over the files of the missing women and see if Clay needs to call in some help.''

"What kind of help can he get?'' Jack asked. "I mean, he doesn't have crime scenes. He doesn't even know if any crimes took place as far as these missing women are concerned."

"I know." She squeezed her eyes closed. "If I could just remember what it is in my dreams."

He stroked a hand down her back and she wanted to remain in his strong arms forever. At this moment she felt more safe than she'd ever felt in her life.

She didn't want to face the morning when she'd rip apart Kelsey's world. She didn't want to face the time when Janice was able to leave the hospital, because she knew when that time came, they'd all be leaving here.

She'd done what she needed to do. She'd told her secret. And as much as she'd love to stay here in Plains Point, she couldn't remain as long as a killer walked the streets, a killer she somehow knew would eventually come looking for her again.

Jack lay in the bed next to Mariah, the moonlight spilling in to bathe her face as she slept. There had been no question of her going home. She'd been emotionally and physically exhausted by the time they'd finished talking.

As they'd gotten into bed, he'd told her about Rebecca's visit, hoping that a little bit of good news before she closed her eyes to sleep might help to relax her.

Now, as he listened to the soft, steady sound of her breathing, he thought that Rover should be biting his ass big-time. He'd believed he'd fallen in love with a woman who had no secrets, no issues. What a laugh.

If he was smart, he'd cut his losses and run, put her back in the category of a teenage fantasy and leave it at that. But he'd never been particularly smart when it came to matters of the heart.

And his heart was so involved with Mariah it ached. His love for her was almost painful as he thought of all that she'd been through, all that she'd survived.

She'd been asleep for only an hour when he realized she was having a dream. It began with a small moan and a thrashing of her legs beneath the sheets. In the moonlight he could see her features, no longer relaxed in sleep, but a frown wrinkling her forehead as her breathing came in short, quick gasps.

He wasn't sure what to do. He didn't want to wake her, but also didn't want her to suffer a nightmare. It wasn't until a scream released itself from her that he pulled her tight into his arms and whispered her name over and over again until she awoke with a jerk.

Immediately she began to cry and he held her tight as she told him her dream, of hands pressing into her upper arms, of the plastic bag making her feel as if she was suffocating and the thick bulk of her attacker's body pressing her deep into the ground beneath her.

"I'm sorry," she finally managed to say. "I didn't mean to wake you."

"Shh, it's all right. Are you okay?" She nodded and relaxed in his arms. He looked into her tear-stained face and love for her swelled his chest, making it difficult for him to draw a deep breath.

"Mariah, I love you." The words slipped out of him before he knew he was going to say them. He knew the timing sucked. He'd wanted to tell her with flowers and candy. He'd hoped to tell her with candlelight and wine.

She rose up and looked at him, her blue eyes filled with a new kind of pain. "I love you, too, Jack," she whispered.

Her words should have filled him with incredible joy, but the expression on her face when she said them broke his heart. "But I'm not staying here. As soon as Janice is capable, we're leaving here and we'll never be back again."

She placed a slender hand on his chest, where his heart beat like a galloping horse. "This has been a fantasy for both of us. You got a second chance with your high school crush and I got my first taste of real love, but that's all it was supposed to be. I don't belong here and you do. Tomorrow my whole world is going to explode apart and the last thing that's going to be on my mind is building a relationship with anyone other than my daughter."

Each and every word pierced his heart in a way he hadn't thought possible. "Chicago isn't that far away," he said, unwilling to give up all hope.

"It's a lifetime away," she replied, and in those words his last piece of hope slipped away. "But we do have the rest of tonight," she said, and leaned forward to kiss him.

Even knowing that making love to her again would only deepen the inevitable pain of losing her, he was helpless to stop it.

There was a touch of frantic urgency in their lovemaking because they both knew this was really good-bye.

Chapter 30

"I don't want to talk to you anymore!" Kelsey screamed, her tearstained face twisted with anger, with a pain that tore Mariah's heart. "You lied to me about everything. You're nothing but a big liar and you've totally ruined my life."

"Kelsey." Mariah tried to take hold of her daughter's arm, but Kelsey jerked it away from her. "Can't we just talk about this?"

"We've talked. I don't want to hear anything else you have to say." Kelsey whirled around and raced up the stairs, then slammed her bedroom door.

Mariah stood in the living room and stared after her. It had gone even worse than she'd expected. The minute Kelsey had come home from Katie's, Mariah had undertaken the difficult task of telling her the truth.

She wanted to run up the stairs and into her daughter's room. She needed to make it right, but she didn't know any words that would make it right.

Maybe if she gave Kelsey a little time, she'd calm down and the hatred that had shone from her eyes as she'd screamed at Mariah would disappear. Mariah desperately hoped that was the case.

She went into the kitchen and sank down at the table. She stared out the window where the bright sunshine felt like a personal affront. It should be gray and cloudy. It should be raining buckets when your life fell apart.

She'd spoken with Janice that morning but hadn't mentioned that she was finally going to tell Kelsey the truth. She wanted Janice to focus on recovering and though Mariah longed to have her friend to confide in, she also needed to give Janice her strength, not her burden, right now. Soon Janice would be well enough that they could all go home to Chicago and put Plains Point and its horrors behind them.

She'd also called a real estate agent that morning. Wilburta Moore from the Plains Point Realty was coming over at four to take a look at the house. That was still two hours away. Two hours of silence with a daughter whose heart was broken just up the stairs.

She stared over at the phone. Jack had called twice, leaving messages that she hadn't returned. Although she'd love to talk to him now, to hear his voice, to tell him about the aftermath of her conversation with Kelsey, she wouldn't call him. She'd told him good-bye last night when they'd made love and again this morning when she'd driven away from his house.

There was no way she could just sit here with Kelsey upstairs and alone. She got up from the table and climbed the stairs, the fourth and fifth rungs creaking beneath her weight. She walked to Kelsey's closed bedroom door and paused. Leave her alone or try to make her understand? Give her space or smother her with love?

Smother, she decided, and knocked on the door. She didn't wait for Kelsey to invite her in but rather pushed open the door to see her daughter lying on the bed, her face burrowed in her pillow as Tiny sat by her side.

Mariah picked up the dog and placed him on the floor, then sat on the edge of the bed. She wanted to pull Kelsey into her arms, to hold tight until the world righted itself for her daughter, but she didn't. She knew by the tenseness of Kelsey's body that she wouldn't welcome any touch at this moment.

"Maybe it was wrong," Mariah said softly. "Perhaps it was wrong of me to make up the story of a wonderful loving father for you. But I wanted you to have that—I needed you to have what I never had, the love of a father. I wanted that legacy for you instead of the truth."

Kelsey rolled over on her back and looked at Mariah. "Why didn't you just have an abortion?"

Mariah straightened her back and looked at her daughter in surprise. "That never entered my mind. The moment I realized I was pregnant, I loved you. And the decision I made to keep the truth from you was made from love." She fought the impulse just to touch Kelsey, to make a physical connection with the child of her heart. "It was always easy for me to separate the act that conceived you and you."

Kelsey raised her hands to her eyes and began to cry. "Just let me be alone for a while, okay? I need to be alone and think."

Mariah leaned forward and kissed her forehead. "I'll give you as much time as you need, but know this. There has never been a day that went by that I haven't thanked God for you. When I look at you, all I see is the baby I wanted, the child I adored and the young woman I love with all my heart."

She got up from the bed, knowing there was nothing more she could say. She'd just have to hope that her years of parenting, her years of loving Kelsey would be enough.

As she went back down the stairs, her thoughts turned to Jack. Telling him good-bye that morning had been difficult. For the first time in her life she'd realized what love was supposed to be, how it could be, and she was leaving it behind.

She told herself it hadn't been real, that Jack had simply been playing a game of make-believe, fulfilling an old fantasy from his high school days. She was actually doing him a favor by getting out of town, out of his life. Eventually Jack would have discovered she was just a woman, not a fantasy.

Wilburta Moore was punctual. At precisely four o'clock she knocked on the door and introduced herself to Mariah. "I was so pleased when I drove up and saw all the exterior work that's been done. The place looks beautiful."

"Thank you. Please come in." Mariah led her through the living room, where Wilburta praised the beautiful wood flooring, and as they entered the kitchen, she crowed about the warmth and welcome the room contained.

Mariah showed her the entire house except for Kelsey's room, where the door remained closed, and Mariah said her daughter wasn't feeling well.

"I shouldn't have any problems selling the property," Wilburta said as Mariah walked her to the front door. "It's a lovely house and will make a nice home for some family. I'll call you tomorrow when I have a contract ready for you to sign that will give me the power to show it while you're out of town."

"That will be fine," Mariah said. As she watched the woman get into her car and drive away, she leaned against the porch railing and looked out at the trees in the distance.

If what Clay believed was true, that there may have been more victims who just hadn't been found, then at least she knew it hadn't been personal. It was possible she'd been followed home that night from the gazebo. It was probable that somebody saw her alone and vulnerable, making her an easy target.

How many other easy targets had there been over the years in a place where people still felt the illusion of small-town safety?

Maybe Clay's dark fear would result in nothing. Maybe all those women did run away, leave town to seek something better than what their parents had built here.

She went back into the house, carefully locking the door behind her. She paused at the bottom of the stairs, looking up, hoping to see Kelsey coming down for dinner.

She fixed herself a salad, knowing that eventually Kelsey would come downstairs, to feed Tiny if nothing else. She'd just finished picking at her dinner when a knock sounded on the front door.

Maybe Wilburta had forgotten something, or maybe it was Jack coming to check on her even though she'd told him that morning that she'd be fine.

A peek outside the window showed her that it was

neither of those two people. Marianne Francis stood on the porch. You were supposed to call her to have lunch, a little voice whispered in Mariah's head as she opened the door.

"Marianne, come on in."

"Hi, Mariah. I'm sorry to bother you. Is this a bad time?"

A bad time? Mariah wanted to laugh. In the past twenty-four hours she'd made the decision to walk away from love, reported a heinous crime and ripped apart her daughter's sense of security and truth. A bad time? Yeah, right.

"Please, come in. I just finished up eating a little dinner. I'm sorry I haven't called you about lunch, but things have been crazy." She led the way to the kitchen.

"I was sorry to hear about your friend."

Mariah gestured to a chair at the table and Marianne sat. "Thanks. Can I get you something to drink?"

"No thanks, I'm fine." But she didn't look fine. She clasped her hands together in her lap, but not before Mariah saw the tremble of her fingers.

"Did you notice the paint job when you drove up?" Mariah asked. "Your husband and his team did a great job."

"Yes, it looks really nice." Marianne looked out the window and Mariah saw that her hands were clasped so tightly she was white-knuckled.

"Marianne? Is something wrong?"

Marianne looked at her, her hazel eyes wide. "I heard something today about you."

So it was out. She knew Clay wouldn't be able to

keep it to himself forever. At least he'd given her enough time to tell Jack and Kelsey before the rest of the town knew what had happened to her.

"Yeah, I figured it would be the talk of the town at some point today," she replied.

"So it's true?" Marianne's gaze held hers intently. "You were raped?

Mariah nodded.

"Where did it happen?"

Mariah got up and went to the kitchen cabinet beneath the sink. "You sure you don't want something to drink?" She pulled out a bottle of Scotch. "My father kept this for medicinal purposes. I'm not much of a drinker, but I suddenly feel like having a little medicine."

Marianne shook her head. "No, thanks."

Mariah got a glass and filled it with ice, then splashed a healthy shot of the booze on top. "It happened outside this house, in that grove of trees down by the street."

She returned to the chair next to Marianne and took a sip of the biting liquor, relishing the warmth that stole down her throat and into her stomach. "I was coming home from town. I'd sneaked out and met Clay. I was standing outside waiting for the light in my father's study to go off when he came up behind me, pulled a bag over my head and threw me to the ground."

As she told her story once again, she realized it was getting easier with each telling, as if shining a light on a secret made the memory not quite as painful.

When she was finished, Marianne unclasped her

hands and leaned forward. "That's why you ran away? Because you'd been raped?"

"I ran away to protect the baby I was carrying. I wanted to make sure the man who raped me never had a claim to her and I sure as hell didn't want my parents having any part of her upbringing."

Marianne's eyes widened. "Oh, I didn't know Kelsey . . . I mean everyone I talked to thinks you ran the night of the rape and that Kelsey is the daughter of the man you married after you left here."

So Clay and Sherri weren't telling everything they knew, Mariah thought. They obviously were attempting to protect Kelsey and for that, Mariah would forever be grateful, but Mariah was finished indulging in lies.

"Kelsey's the daughter of whoever raped me that night." And right now she's up in her room hating me for the life I created for her, she thought.

Marianne's lower lip trembled and she raced a hand through her short, pixie-cut hair. "How do you live with it?"

Marianne was always home before dark. Roger had said his wife thought there was a boogeyman in every shadow. It was at that moment Mariah knew. Marianne was a victim, too.

She reached out and grabbed Marianne's icy-cold hand. "When did it happen? When did he rape you?"

Tears spilled down Marianne's cheeks as she squeezed Mariah's hand with a death grip. "It was a year after we graduated from high school. Roger and I had been at the café and time got away from us and he had to get the car home." She frowned. "I don't remember why—maybe his dad needed it for something. Anyway, I insisted he drive on home, that I could walk the two blocks to my house. I was halfway home when I heard something behind me. But before I could turn around, a bag went over my head and he threw me off the sidewalk and on the ground."

She pulled her hand from Mariah's and leaned back against the chair, her gaze going to the window as if she was checking the position of the sun in the sky.

"Did he say anything to you?" Mariah asked.

Marianne swiped the tears from her face and looked at Mariah once again. "He said something about taking a piece of me or something like that."

It was the same man, Mariah thought in horror. "Did you report it?" It would have been at a time before Clay became sheriff.

"No." The word whispered out of her as tears once again formed. "I was so scared and so ashamed and there was nothing I could tell anyone about who did it."

Even though it was crazy and Mariah knew that the feeling of shame was totally irrational, she understood. Long after her rape she'd done some research and had learned that sexual assault was one of the most underreported of crimes. More than half went unreported. It was a dirty, ugly secret that festered inside victims.

"Have you told Roger?" Mariah asked.

Marianne's eyes widened. "No, and I don't want him to know."

"He's your husband. He loves you and could be a huge support," Mariah replied, remembering Jack's tenderness, his caring, when she'd told him.

Marianne stared down at the surface of the oak table and her hands found each other and once again clasped tightly. "I heard that Clay thinks there might be other victims, and Roger, he's out a lot. At night. I'm not sure where he goes or what he does." The words came haltingly, as if dredged from the darkest place in her soul.

"He brought me flowers the next morning. I'd forgotten about that until today. He said they were because I had to walk home the night before."

"Don't do this, Marianne," Mariah said. "Don't make yourself crazy. Roger is your husband. He's a good man."

Marianne offered a weak smile. "I guess every wife in Plains Point is going to wonder about the man lying next to them in bed tonight." She pushed back her chair and stood. "I've got to get home."

Mariah didn't have to ask her why. Even though it was a good hour before sunset, she knew Marianne's need to get home, where she believed she would be safe. She walked with her to the front door and there Marianne paused. "I can't even take out the garbage. Since that night, I can't touch one of those plastic trash bags."

"I'm sorry," Mariah replied, unsure what else to say.

Marianne stepped closer to her and embraced her. "Thank you," she whispered into Mariah's ear. "Thank you for being brave enough to tell." She stepped back and Mariah took her hands.

"You should talk to Clay," Mariah said. "He needs to know all he can about these crimes."

"I'll think about it," she said. "I'm not as brave as you, Mariah. Besides, you'll be leaving here soon and

I have to live here long after this is all over. I'm not sure I want people to know."

They hugged again. Then Mariah watched as Marianne hurried down the porch and to her car. She closed the door and locked it, then turned to go back into the kitchen.

"Mom?" Kelsey sat on the stairs, her eyes red and swollen.

"Hi, baby. You want some dinner?" Mariah moved to the staircase. Dinner, what a lame question when what she really wanted to know was whether Kelsey still loved her, whether things were going to be okay.

"I'm not really hungry," Kelsey replied, and she scooted over so Mariah could sit next to her. Although what Mariah wanted to do more than anything was put her arm around Kelsey and pull her tight against her, she didn't. It was all up to Kelsey. She'd let Mariah know what she needed from her and what she was ready to accept.

"I was listening to you and Mrs. Francis."

"I'm sorry you had to hear that. If I could, I'd protect you from all the ugliness in the world. If I could, I'd put you in a bubble where only happy things could happen in your life."

Kelsey frowned. "Do you think he did that to other women who didn't tell?"

"I think he probably has," Mariah replied, and breathed a sigh of sweet relief as Kelsey leaned into her.

"Then he's evil and bad."

Wrapping an arm around Kelsey's slender shoulders, Mariah was grateful when her daughter didn't pull away, but rather leaned closer. "I don't know what kind of a man he is. But I do know what kind of a person you are. You're kind and gentle and have a loving, caring spirit. You're my daughter, Kelsey, and I love you more anything else on earth."

"I don't hate you, Mom. I love you," Kelsey cried, and burrowed closer to Mariah.

"I know that, honey."

"Is it true what you said, that you ran away from here to protect me?"

"I ran away from here for a lot of reasons, but yes, one of them was to protect you. I was afraid that somehow the man who had raped me would find out about you, and then he'd somehow twist the facts and make it that we'd had consensual sex and he'd want to be a part of your life. I didn't want him in your life—that's why I created a fantasy for us both."

Kelsey heaved a tremulous sigh and sat up. "I think this deserves a cell phone."

Mariah laughed, for in her daughter's words, in the shine of love from Kelsey's eyes, she knew it was going to be okay. She knew the bond of mother and daughter had withstood this tremendous test.

"I'll tell you what." She stood and pulled Kelsey to her feet. "When we get back to Chicago, we'll get you a cell phone and in the meantime if you come into the kitchen, I'll make your favorite, a box of macaroni and cheese."

"So, we're really going back to Chicago," Kelsey said later as she ate a bowl of the macaroni. Tiny sat at her feet, having finished his bowl of dog food and hoping for a tidbit dropped to the floor.

"Aunt Janice is going to be released from the hospital in the next day or two and then we'll head back."

Kelsey obviously had the same ambivalent feelings

about leaving as Mariah did. She frowned down at her bowl. "I liked it here," she said softly.

"So did I," Mariah agreed. "But I think it's best if we get back to our lives in Chicago and put this summer and this place far behind us."

"What about you and Dr. Hot?" Kelsey looked at her. "I thought you two were, you know, really getting together."

A spasm of pain shot through Mariah at thoughts of Jack. "I guess some things just aren't meant to be," she said.

"That's sad 'cause I liked him and I like you with him."

"I know. So did I," Mariah replied.

It was after ten when Mariah stood in the doorway of Kelsey's bedroom and watched her daughter sleep. Even from her distance from the bed, she could hear the faint tinny sound of the music that played in the earphones her daughter wore. Someday all the kids of this generation would probably need hearing aids, Mariah thought.

She turned away and went to the bathroom, where she changed into her nightgown, then went into her own bedroom. With the lights off she stared out the window at the trees, as she had several nights before.

The light of a full moon spilled down, painting the tops of the trees in a shimmery silvery light. It would be difficult for somebody to hide there tonight with the moon like a spotlight from the sky.

He's out a lot. At night. Marianne's words played and replayed in her mind. *He brought me flowers the next morning.* Flowers because she'd had to walk home or because he'd lost control and raped her?

Roger, who had always seemed to be hanging

around in high school. Roger, who coached during the school year and painted homes in the summers. Was he capable of such a thing?

He was a husband and a father. He was respected and well liked by his peers. Beneath the surface was he a monster?

How many times in the news had she read the stories of serial killers who, on the surface, were fine, upstanding men, men whom neighbors never suspected, men who when discovered shocked friends and family members?

She turned away and got into bed and reached out to touch the cold metal of Janice's gun on her nightstand. Clay hadn't mentioned its presence when he'd given her Janice's purse. He'd probably found the license in Janice's wallet and knew it was legal.

Whether it was legal or not, there was no question that Mariah felt better knowing it was within easy grasp. She'd never shot a gun before, but that wouldn't stop her from doing so if it was to save her life or the life of her daughter. How hard could it be? Point and pull the trigger.

She rolled over on her back and stared up at the ceiling where the moonlight through the tree danced intricate shadows.

A couple more days and this town would be nothing more than a distant memory. She'd come back one more time to close on the house; then she'd look ahead and never look back again.

She'd faced her biggest fear, that somehow Kelsey would find out the truth, and she'd survived. Her friend had lived to tell the tale of her vicious attack and even the pain of leaving Jack would eventually heal.

Marianne had told her she was brave, but she wasn't brave. She was running from a place she'd grown to love, running away from a man she loved, because she was afraid, afraid that somehow the man who had raped her, the man who had fathered Kelsey, had been waiting here for her all along.

Chapter 31

He was going to explode. The pain no longer went away but was an unrelenting dagger inside him. The rage was like a beast within him, clawing and biting to get out.

He walked the deserted street, fighting for control but feeling the resignation of a battle lost. There was a certain euphoric joy in just giving in to the madness, allowing it to carry him down the path to damnation. It was so much easier to give in to it than to fight it.

Like a predatory animal, he shot his narrowed gaze left and then right, seeking vulnerability, eager to release the boiling emotions that burned in his gut.

He stayed away from the town park, unsure if one of Clay's men would be watching the area after the attack on Mariah's friend.

There had to be somebody out and about, some teenager walking home alone, a young housewife out for a little night air. He needed somebody. God, he was in so much pain.

But after an hour his frustration level was at a fever pitch. He knew from the gossip he'd heard that day that Mariah had told. She'd gone to Clay and told him about the attack she'd suffered years ago. He also knew from the gossip that she hadn't been able to give Clay anything that might identify him.

What she had managed to do was ruin his hunting ground. Dammit, she'd ruined things. Tonight there were no young girls hanging out on the corners, no single women on the streets at all. The only place there were people was at the Tavern and a peek inside the window showed them all to be of the male variety.

There was no relief for him here and the demons inside him were screaming for release. But he knew where to go. He knew who would calm the shriek inside his head, still the banging drum of need.

Mariah.

Was she the final piece? Was she the one who would finally make him whole? Stop the relentless madness inside his soul? God, he wanted it to stop.

Sometimes in the deepest darkness of the night he wept, for in rare moments of clarity he knew what he was, what he'd become. A monster.

But tonight the monster was loose and he needed her.

Mariah.

Chapter 32

Mariah's eyes snapped open and she was instantly awake. She remained unmoving, holding her breath as she stared up at the ceiling, muscles tensed in fight-or-flight readiness.

What?

What had pulled her from her sleep?

What had interrupted her sweet dreams of Jack and love? She released a slow, steady breath, muscles relaxing bit by bit. Maybe she'd gotten too warm. Certainly the nights in this house without air-conditioning were getting a bit less pleasant, especially since she kept the windows on the lower level locked up tight at night.

She pushed the sheet off her body and closed her eyes once again, wishing she could reclaim the pleasant dream she'd been having.

Creak.

Her heart stopped beating as her breath caught painfully in her chest. Every muscle in her body tensed once again. The fourth stair. Somebody had stepped on the fourth stair. She turned her head toward the bedroom doorway.

It wasn't Kelsey, for no lights had gone on. Kelsey would never have gone downstairs without flipping on a light. Somebody's in the house. Panic seared through her, momentarily immobilizing her as she froze with terror.

Creak.

The fifth stair! Oh God, somebody was coming up the stairs, somebody hiding in the darkness of the night, moving with an intruder's stealth.

It was him! He was in the house. On the stairs. He'd come back for her.

Get in the closet. Hide! Hide! She choked back a sob as she slid from the bed to the floor, her heartbeat crashing erratically, making her short of breath.

The moment her knees made contact with the floor, a vision of Kelsey exploded in her head. Kelsey, who was in her room. Kelsey, who was vulnerable. The music playing in her ears as she slept would make her even more vulnerable. She'd never hear him coming.

Mariah couldn't hide. She had to protect her daughter. She had to keep Kelsey safe and to do that, she had to face the monster on the stairs.

In that instant of awareness she remembered the gun. Janice's gun. Her hand scrambled on the top of the nightstand and she gasped in frantic relief as her fingers curled tightly around the cool metal of the handle.

Gun clutched in hand, she quietly rose to her feet, hoping she had the element of surprise. She hurried toward her bedroom doorway. No matter what, she couldn't allow him to get past her. She'd shoot and ask questions later.

Drawing a deep breath, she stepped out of the bedroom and into the hall. A dark shadow came up the stairs toward her.

It was too dark to see who it was. She knew only that he was big and didn't belong. "Stop," she exclaimed. Instead of stopping, he rushed her and with a sob she pulled the trigger.

And nothing happened.

He hit her with the force of a freight train, his shoulder barreling into her stomach. She fell backward and her head banged into the floor with a sickening thud.

She knew nothing more as darkness swallowed her.

It was almost midnight when Jack got out of his car in front of the Tavern. He should be in bed with Rover snoring soundly on the floor nearby. He should be in bed with Mariah, her warm body snuggled against his and the scent of her lingering in his head.

But Mariah hadn't answered any of the phone messages he'd left for her that day, and by the time night had fallen, a fierce depression had settled over him.

It was over. It was done. She obviously didn't intend to have anything else to do with him. She'd told him good-bye, but he just hadn't realized it was so final.

Officially the Tavern closed at two, but when Jack walked through the door, it looked as if the place was already closed for the night.

Henry, the bartender, sat at one of the tables talking to the only other person in the place, Clay Matheson.

Clay looked like a dead man walking. His broad face was haggard, his eyes red and strained-looking. "You're out late, Dr. Taylor."

"I could say the same for you, Sheriff," Jack replied as he joined the two men.

"What are you drinking, Jack?" Henry asked.

Jack noticed Clay had what appeared to be a soda in front of him. "I'll take a bottle of Bud." As Henry got up to get the beer, Jack looked at Clay. "Long day?"

He nodded. "I have a feeling they're all going to be long from now on."

"Mariah told me you had somebody coming in today from Kansas City to look at some of the old missing-persons cases."

"Scott Haynes. He's a homicide detective on the Kansas City police force. We spent the day going over all the reports and trying to follow up with friends and family members of those missing."

Henry returned to the table with the bottled beer. "Clay's friend thinks we have a big problem here in town," Henry said.

"Unfortunately, it's just his gut feeling and nothing based in fact or evidence," Clay added. "I'm taking the cases one at a time and reinvestigating them all, hoping we'll come up with something concrete."

"And you definitely think these missing persons are tied to the rapist?" Jack asked.

"Hell, man, I don't know what to think. All I know is that it's time for me to step up my game. As far as I'm concerned, the only three men I know for certain aren't guilty are sitting right here at this table. Henry here because he just moved to town two years ago. And you because Mariah was positive you were too skinny to be her attacker years ago, and on the night of her friend's attack, she told me, she talked to you on the phone and you were home. Then later you picked her up to search for her friend."

Jack took a swig of his beer, then set the bottle back on the table. "That leaves a lot of men in this town who might be guilty."

Clay leaned back in his chair and his eyes narrowed. "You know, I've spent the last ten years afraid that if something bad happened in this town, I wasn't good enough to fix it. Now something bad has happened and I'm not afraid—I'm just plain pissed off. I'm going to catch this creep. I won't stop until he's behind bars. This is still my town and I'll be damned if I'll allow this to continue."

"I'll drink to that," Jack said, and once again lifted his bottle. If and when Clay got the man who had raped Mariah all those years ago, Jack wouldn't mind having a few minutes alone with the man. Kicking animals and hurting women—there was a special place in hell for men who shattered innocence, who preyed on the vulnerable.

As thoughts of Mariah filled his head once again, a new wave of depression settled over his shoulders. He felt the same way he had when he'd been seventeen years old and found out the girl of his heart had left town. It was happening all over again and he was helpless to stop it.

Marianne Francis awoke with a start. She'd been having a nightmare. It wasn't unusual for a nightmare to wake her up in the middle of the night. She never remembered the dreams when she awakened, but she knew they were about the night she'd been raped.

The bedroom was pitch-black, although she could see a faint outline of gray around the edges of the light-blocking shades that hung at the windows.

She faced the wall and the luminous face of the clock on her nightstand told her it was just after midnight. Cold. She was always cold when she woke up from a bad dream.

She moved closer to the middle of the bed, seeking Roger's warmth. He was like having her very own furnace. He radiated heat when he slept. She inched over and over, but didn't feel her husband's warmth, didn't hear the familiar sound of his breathing.

They'd gone to bed together at ten. He'd told her he was exhausted. Of course that was because he was out late almost every night. She'd taken one of her sleeping pills and had almost immediately fallen into a deep sleep.

She swept her hand out but encountered only the yawn of cold sheets and emptiness beside her. Turning on the lamp on her nightstand, she confirmed what she'd thought. She was alone in the bed.

There was no sound coming from the bathroom or anyplace else in the house. "Roger?" she called, but there was no answer. She hadn't really expected one.

She slid from the bed and went to the window and peeked out behind the shade. His car was gone. She quickly got back into bed and pulled the covers up around her. Cold. So cold.

Where are you, Roger? Oh God, she was afraid to know. She huddled beneath the blankets and prayed her husband wasn't a monster.

Chapter 33

She was back in the dream with Jack. They were having a picnic on a blanket spread out beneath a majestic oak tree. Tiny ran in circles, barking with excitement at every squirrel that jumped from limb to limb, rustling the bright green foliage overhead.

Sunshine filtered through the leaves and shone on Jack's face, emphasizing the lines and angles she loved to see. He reached out a hand and caressed her face, the warmth and love in his touch swelling her heart.

"You have to go," he said, and there was a wealth of sadness in his green eyes.

"No, I want to stay," she replied. "I want to stay here with you."

"You must go." He dropped his hand from her face and wind began to buffet the branches of the trees overhead. "There's a storm coming." He got to his feet as the skies turned dark, boiling with black, angry clouds. "There's a terrible storm coming."

A flash of lightning nearly blinded her. Thunder roared and Tiny's yips intensified, no longer happy but instead frantic and afraid. Mariah suddenly realized where she *was, in the grove of trees outside her house. Where he'd once found her and hurt her.*

She scrambled to her feet, suddenly afraid. She reached out for Jack's hand, but he backed away from her. "You have to go." He yelled to be heard above the din of the storm.

"Please. I'm afraid. Don't make me go," she cried. Again lightning rent the skies, followed by a tremendous boom. Tiny barked and ran in circles.

"You have to go," Jack repeated as he was swallowed up by the storm. "You have to find Kelsey."

Kelsey.

Consciousness came in bits and pieces. The first conscious thought was pain. The back of her head felt as if it had been split open like an overripe plum. To make matters worse, Tiny barked and barked, the incessant noise only making her head ache more.

"Tiny, enough," she murmured.

She twisted her head and frowned as she realized she wasn't in bed. In that instant, total recall smashed into her brain.

Kelsey!

She shot up and nearly stumbled over Tiny. She ran to Kelsey's room and flipped on the light. She fell to her knees and screamed at the sight of Kelsey's empty bed. The covers were strewn on the floor and the lamp on the nightstand was overturned.

He had Kelsey! Oh God. Oh God. She dry-heaved as she got to her feet. How long had she been unconscious, how long? Minutes? Hours?

As she stumbled backward out of the room, she stepped on the gun, the gun that hadn't fired when she'd tried to pull the trigger.

Urgency screamed through her. Do something.

Call somebody. She picked up the gun and realized she'd never taken off the safety. That's why it hadn't fired. She did so now as Tiny clumped down the stairs, barking all the way.

Mariah followed, feet flying as she ran downstairs and to the front door. Maybe she'd see him. Maybe she had been unconscious for only a few seconds and he was now loading Kelsey into the back of a car or the bed of a pickup.

She gripped the gun firmly and opened the door, nearly sobbing in despair as she saw nothing . . . nobody. Where was her baby? Where was Kelsey?

Tiny barked once again and she looked down at the little dog who Kelsey loved, the dog who loved Kelsey. He followed her everywhere.

"Tiny, where's Kelsey?" she said. "Where's Kelsey?" To her surprise Tiny danced off the front porch and took off running.

Toward Finn's place.

Mariah froze.

All she could hear was the thunder of her heart in her head. All she felt was the cold grip of memory. And she smelled the fires of sudden, burning knowledge.

Hands pressing into her upper arms. Fingers biting into her skin. Fingers. Nine fingers, not ten. No thumb. No thumb!

Finn!

She took off running after Tiny, the gun held tightly in her hand. Her brain shut down. She didn't feel the rough ground beneath her bare feet, or the cool night air that blew over her half-naked body.

The full moon illuminated her way as she raced toward her neighbor's house. Finn. He'd been her best friend. Finn. She couldn't think about it or she'd go mad.

She couldn't think about Kelsey and what might have already happened. If she did, she'd fall to the ground, too incapacitated with grief, with despair, to do anything.

Just run, her brain commanded. Legs pumped and lungs burned as she raced, afraid she was too late. Not too late. Please, God, don't make it be too late.

Kelsey. Kelsey. The name screamed inside her head and ripped apart her heart. What if she was wrong? What if it wasn't Finn at all? What if Tiny was just chasing a rabbit through the woods?

She should have called Clay. The minute she'd regained consciousness, she should have called for help instead of following a dog who might be leading her farther away from Kelsey rather than closer.

As she reached Finn's property, she came to a stop behind a tree. The house was directly in front of her. Dark and silent. Finn's truck was parked in the driveway and nothing appeared amiss.

Had she just wasted precious minutes? Had this just been a wild-goose chase that led to nothing? Kelsey! Where was her baby? Once again the urge to vomit welled up inside her.

Tiny growled from someplace nearby and Mariah heard a low mutter. A man's voice. Finn's voice. She followed the sound and saw him coming out of the old smokehouse.

As he turned to secure the door, she ran toward him. "Finn!"

He whirled around to face her as she held the gun leveled at his chest. "Mariah! What in the hell are you doing out here in the middle of the night in your nightgown?'' He shoved a key ring in his pocket and smiled, that beautiful open grin that had always imbued her with warmth. "And I don't even want to ask about the gun."

With a whine Tiny scratched at the smokehouse door. "Open it," Mariah said with steely determination. "Open the door, Finn."

"What's wrong with you, Mariah?" He looked at her as if she'd lost her mind. "It's the middle of the night. I can't believe you're out here pointing a gun at me." He took a step toward her. "I heard what happened to you. Honey, I'm so sorry. But I think you're having some sort of a breakdown."

"I am," she agreed, and tightened her grip on the gun. "I am having a breakdown and if you don't open that door, I'm going to shoot. This time I won't make the mistake of pulling the trigger with the safety on. And when I shoot, the noise will wake up your wife and your children. You don't want that, Finn."

"Hannah and the kids are gone for a couple of days." He took another step toward her. "Mariah, put the gun down and let's talk. Remember how we used to talk?" His voice was soft. The moonlight bathed his face and for just a moment it was the face of the boy she'd known, the boy she'd loved like a brother.

Emotion rose up inside her and brought tears to her eyes. "How could you, Finn?" Emotion made her voice tremble. "How could you hurt me like that?"

For a moment he stood perfectly still, like a moonbathed statue. Then his features transformed into something unrecognizable, something dark and ugly. "Hurt you? Hurt you?" He screamed the words as his hands tightened into fists at his sides. "What about me? What about my pain?"

"Just open the damn door," she exclaimed.

"No. Not until you listen to me." Once again his features softened. "You have to understand, Mariah. I need to make you understand. The pain. Oh God, the pain." He brought his hands up to either side of his head and squeezed so hard his hands whitened in the bleach of the moon.

"That night . . . I didn't want to hurt you. But the pain was so bad I couldn't stand it anymore." He dropped his hands to his sides once again. "I had to hold it together. I had to do it all. I was nothing but a kid, but I had to take care of them, do everything for them. My old man was useless. He cut off my thumb, for Christ's sake." Once again he was screaming with such venom even Tiny was silent and huddled against the door of the smokehouse as if waiting for a kick.

"I love my sisters. I do. But I was trapped. I didn't get to hang out—I couldn't go to college. I had to be a man and take care of things. I didn't do anything but take care of everyone else and if I had a moment to rest, my old man took that moment to beat the hell out of me."

His body vibrated with the force of the storm inside him. "The night before, he came back, like he did every once in a while. He took what money I had put away, and went out and got stinking drunk. Stumbled back home and puked in the hallway, pissed on the sofa and just made a mess, such a mess. The next morning he was gone and I had to clean it up. I had to clean up everything. That night I got the girls into bed, then left the house, and I had such a pain inside me. And I saw you and you were so good and I thought if I could just get a piece of you, a piece of your goodness, then maybe my pain would go away. And it did for a while."

Mariah hadn't noticed the coolness of the night until that moment. Staring into the eyes of the man who had held her when her father had beaten her, the man who had lain in the sweet-smelling grass beside her and made clover chains, she saw his madness.

"And there were others besides me," she whispered as an arctic wind blew through her.

He seemed to calm then as he nodded. "Pieces. Pieces of good. They took away the pain and the rage for a little while, but it always came back." He pointed to the smokehouse. "They're in there. All my pieces, but you were my first." He smiled, an almost dreamy expression on his face. "She looks just like you did that night, Mariah."

He rushed her then and before she could pull the trigger, his hand was on the gun. She struggled to hang on to it, but he was bigger, stronger. As he gained possession, he stood over her.

Sobs ripped through her. It was over. In an instant, thoughts flew through her head. Kelsey would never get her cell phone. Mariah would never see her daughter graduate, go to culinary school and get her own television show.

And now it seemed so foolish that she'd intended to run from Jack and the love that he held out to her like a shining trophy. It hadn't been fear of a monster that had been going to chase her out of town. It had been her own fear of not living up to his fantasy, her fear that he would discover that she was just a woman who couldn't cook and had bad dreams.

She raised her head to look at Finn. In the moonlight and with the shimmer of her tears, he didn't look quite real, but the gun he pointed at her was very real. Nobody would hear the shot that ended it all. Nobody would hear her screams.

One last plea. If Kelsey was still alive, then she had to do something, try one final time to save her daughter's life. "For God's sake, Finn. She's your daughter."

The gun boomed.

Chapter 34

"I've got to get going," Clay said, and rose slowly from the table. "I want to take a drive by the Sayers place before I call it a night."

"Why? You expect trouble there?" Jack asked.

Clay shrugged. "Not really, but I can't stop thinking about how she called me out there because she thought she saw somebody lurking around her property. The whole town knows she came to me about what happened to her. I'm just trying to be safe rather than sorry. I had one of my deputies drive by earlier this evening and everything looked fine, but I just want to take a final run by before heading home."

"Mind if I ride along?"

Clay stifled a yawn with the back of his hand. "I suppose not. You can talk to me on the way and keep me awake. I'll bring you back here for your car."

"Thanks." Minutes later Jack was in the passenger seat of Clay's patrol car and heading toward Mariah's. "You don't think he'd go after her again, do you?"

Apparently Clay knew exactly whom Jack was asking about. "Who knows? I can't begin to get into the head of somebody like this guy."

"I'm in love with her." Jack winced. He hadn't intended to speak the words out loud. They just spurted out of him like he was some kind of damned fool.

Clay shot him a glance and grinned. "Yeah, I know. She was a nice girl as a teenager and she's still a nice lady. And you're a stand-up kind of guy."

"She plans on leaving town as soon as Janice is well enough to travel."

"You gonna let her go?"

Jack smiled ruefully. "She strikes me as the kind of woman who makes her own decisions." He gazed out the window, where the moonlight bathed the landscape in pale light. "Plains Point is a nice place to live in, but I imagine there are sick dogs and cats in Chicago."

"Every single woman in town will mourn your leaving," Clay said with a touch of humor. "Although it would be nice if you could talk her into staying here."

"Yeah, well, I've always been a one-woman kind of man and I've found the woman I want to spend the rest of my life with. I don't care if it's here or in the city." He straightened in his seat as they came to the turn that led to Mariah's house.

He wasn't sure when he'd made the decision that he'd go to Chicago if that was what it took to have Mariah in his life. But the decision was made. He was not going to lose her again.

Clay's car crept up the driveway, and in the splash of his headlights on the front of the house, Jack saw

that the front door was ajar. Why would it be standing open at this time of night?

"Shit," Clay muttered as he jammed on the brakes,
threw the gear into park and opened his car door.
Jack was already out of the car and racing toward
the house.

He burst into the entry, heart pounding in frantic
rhythm. "Mariah!" There were no lights on in the
lower level, but a light spilled down the stairway
and he raced up the stairs.

Mariah's room was empty, as was Kelsey's, but
Kelsey's bedcovers were half on the floor and the
lamp next to her bed was on its side. "Mariah!
Kelsey?" he cried. He looked in the bathroom and
the other bedroom, then raced back down the stairs
and crashed into Clay on his way up.

"They aren't up there," he said.

"I'll check the kitchen," Clay said, leading with his
gun. Jack followed right behind him, terror crawling
up the back of his throat, making him feel half-sick.

It was the middle of the night. Why weren't Mariah and Kelsey in bed where they belonged? And
where was Tiny? Why wasn't he barking?

Clay flipped on the kitchen light and both men
expelled sighs of relief. At least there weren't any
bodies on the floor. "It looked like there might have
been a struggle in Kelsey's room," Jack said, surprised by the tremble in his voice. "Jesus, Clay,
where can they be?" With hollow eyes he stared at
the lawman.

"Let's take a look outside," Clay replied.

They had just stepped out on the front porch when
they heard it. The unmistakable sound of a gun report.

"That sounded like it came from Finn's place," Clay exclaimed.

Jack took off running. He didn't wait to see whether Clay was following. His heart thundered in his chest. He had no idea if the gunshot was related to Mariah and Kelsey's disappearance, but terror chased him across the ground.

The only sound he heard was his own breathing. Who had shot a gun? Where were Mariah and Kelsey? As he got closer to Finn's place, he heard a dog bark. Tiny. Rather than fill him with relief, the sound of Tiny's barking amplified the terror that roared through him. If Tiny was someplace out here in the night, then that meant Kelsey and Mariah had to be out here, too.

He broke out of the woods and into the clearing in front of Finn's house and saw nothing. Then Tiny barked and he whirled toward the pasture and saw the smokehouse.

Relief crashed through him as he saw Mariah standing at the door. He called her name and she turned to look at him and in the moonlight he saw her eyes widened with horror. He also realized somebody was lying prone on the ground near her.

"Jack! I can't get it open. We have to get it open." She began to babble as he ran toward her. "It can't be too late. It can't. She has to be all right."

He realized she had a key ring and she was attempting to unfasten the padlock on the door, but her hands were shaking so badly she couldn't get the key into the slot.

The scent of death hung in the air along with the acrid smell of gunfire. As he took the key ring from her trembling hands, he shot a glance to the figure on the ground. Finn. He was obviously dead. Half his head appeared to be missing.

"Jack, for God's sake, hurry. Kelsey's inside and I don't know if she's dead or alive." Mariah's voice held all the despair of a mother on the edge. Her fingernails bit into his arm as she urged him to unlock the door.

Clay came huffing up, gun still drawn. At that moment Jack managed to get the key into the padlock and remove it. He said a silent prayer for Kelsey, for Mariah, then opened the smokehouse door.

The stench that wafted out the door forced Jack back a step, but not Mariah. She ran into the dark building and cried Kelsey's name.

Clay pulled a high-powered flashlight from his belt and shone it through the door. A graveyard. That's what was inside. There was no floor, only earth that had been overturned. The first body the flashlight beam caught was Missy Temple's.

Mariah screamed at the sight and that scream cut Jack to his core. She sagged against him even as she whispered Kelsey's name.

The beam of light moved to a pile of purses and items in the corner, and in the other corner it shone on Kelsey's unmoving form. Jack's heart plummeted to his feet.

Mariah shot straight up and ran for her daughter. "Kelsey!" As she fell to her knees next to Kelsey, a deep moan came from the very depths of her, a moan filled with such despair it brought a raw anguish to Jack.

"She's alive!" Mariah grabbed her daughter into her arms. "She's breathing."

The next few minutes were a blur to Jack. In those

heart-stopping seconds immediately following the sound of the gunshot, both men had taken off running, leaving the patrol car back at Mariah's.

Clay threw him the keys to the car and Jack ran as he'd never run before, cursing himself and Clay for not having the forethought to drive to Finn's, and praying that the extra time didn't make the difference between life and death.

He had no idea what condition Kelsey was in, had no idea what Finn might have done to her. All he knew was that seconds counted and so he ran like his life was at stake, and it was, for he knew if Kelsey died, all would be lost.

By the time he got the car back to the smokehouse, Kelsey's condition hadn't changed. She remained unconscious, but breathing.

They loaded her into the backseat with Mariah, and Jack held Tiny on his lap; then Clay drove like a madman to the hospital, where she was immediately taken into the emergency room. A nurse stopped Mariah from following and Jack led her to the chairs, where she collapsed.

Somebody from the hospital took Tiny from Jack, promising to see that he got food and water. Clay was on his phone, calling in men and directing them to get lights and get over to Finn's smokehouse. It was going to be a long night for everyone.

Somebody gave Mariah a hospital gown and she pulled it on over her silky nightgown. She had never been so cold in her life. Her body trembled with it, and her heart shivered inside her as she prayed for her daughter.

Thankfully Jack asked no questions. He simply sat beside her, his hand tightly enfolded around hers.

She felt his strength through his warm skin, knew he prayed with her.

She didn't want to talk, didn't want to use the energy it would take. She needed all her energy, all her thoughts, on Kelsey. Be okay. Please, be okay, she cried inside.

Time passed, but it had no meaning. She had no idea if they sat there for two hours or two minutes. Clay disappeared and still she and Jack sat waiting.

What had Finn done to her? Thankfully Kelsey hadn't been beaten like Janice. Her face had been unmarked, her body without bruises. So why wouldn't she wake up?

"Mariah?" She looked up at Clay. "Can I ask you a few questions?"

Jack's hand tightened around hers as she nodded. "Okay."

"You want to tell me what happened tonight?"

She told him everything, about Finn sneaking into the house, about her being knocked unconscious and waking up to find Kelsey gone. She told him how Tiny had led her to Finn's and about the final confrontation.

"He grabbed the gun from me. I thought he was going to kill me." She leaned into Jack as he placed an arm around her shoulder. "I didn't care about me, but if there was a chance he hadn't hurt Kelsey yet, I wanted him to leave her alone. I yelled at him that Kelsey was his daughter."

Mariah squeezed her eyes closed, her head filled with the look on Finn's face. For just a moment she'd seen the raging beast, the agonizing pain that lived inside him shining from his eyes.

Then he'd smiled at her and in that single, heartbreaking moment he'd been the boy of her child-hood, her best friend and her confidant. He'd still been smiling when he put the gun to his head and pulled the trigger.

She opened her eyes and gazed at Clay. "He shot himself. He could have killed both Kelsey and me out there. He could have buried our bodies in the smokehouse and nobody would have known, but there was still something good at the core of him. He knew he'd become a monster."

At that moment the doctor came out and all other thoughts fled her mind. "She's fine," he said before she could ask. "We ran some blood tests and found that she's been given a shot of a tranquilizer. She's still asleep, but her vitals are good and we expect her to start coming around in the next couple of hours."

"Thank God," Jack murmured.

The relief that flooded through Mariah was inde-scribable. "Can I see her?"

"I've transferred her to room 106. Give it a few minutes and you can go on in." With a reassuring smile the doctor turned on his heels and went back through the swinging doors and into the inner sanc-tum of the emergency room.

"Between Janice and Kelsey I think you're going to be seeing a lot of this place in the next few days," Jack said.

She nodded and leaned against the wall. "It's over, isn't it?"

Jack nodded. "It's over."

All the feelings that she'd been holding in since awakening to the sound of the stair creak cascaded through her and she began to weep.

The tears came from a place so deep inside her

they nearly crumpled her to the floor and would have if Jack hadn't grabbed her and wrapped her up in his arms.

He didn't try to stop her from crying. He simply held her while the emotion crashed through her. Fear slowly fell away. She grieved for a friend lost but found relief in the monster found and destroyed.

Finally there was nothing left except Jack's embrace. The scent of his skin was sweetly familiar as she burrowed her face in the hollow of his neck. She raised her face to look at him and he smiled. "Come on, let's go wait for Kelsey to wake up."

She nodded and together they walked down the hall to the hospital room where Kelsey was already in the bed. Mariah sat in a chair and took her daughter's hand in hers. Jack sat in a chair nearby.

"You don't have to stay," she said to him.

"I'll stay."

"It really isn't necessary." There was no point in both of them spending the rest of the night in the hospital.

He smiled. "I'll stay."

He did.

Eventually he fell asleep in the chair. Mariah didn't sleep. She sat next to Kelsey and breathed her scent and thought of all the wonderful things her daughter would accomplish in her lifetime. She stared at her daughter's beautiful face for much of the night.

She prayed that Kelsey hadn't seen the carnage in the smokehouse, that Finn had knocked her out with the drug before he'd carried her there. She hoped her daughter remembered nothing of the night of terror.

She must have finally fallen asleep, for when she opened her eyes, dawn's light was creeping into the window. Kelsey looked peaceful in sleep, a faint snore rumbling from her with each breath.

"Good morning," Jack said softly as Mariah stretched with her arms overhead. He walked to where she sat and handed her a foam cup of coffee.

"Oh, thank you. What would I do without you?"

"Actually, we need to talk about that." He pulled his chair up next to hers. "I know this might not be the time or the place, but I'm afraid if I don't say a few things now, I might never get the chance again." He drew a deep breath. "I love you, Mariah Sayers. I love you like I've never loved a woman in my life. If I have to pack my bags and follow you to Chicago, then that's what I'll do. I lost you when we were kids and I don't want to lose you again."

"I'm not a fantasy, Jack. I can't cook. I have nightmares. I'm a real grouch before my first cup of coffee in the morning," she said.

"Jeez, Mom, you never tell a guy all the bad things about you," Kelsey said groggily as she opened her eyes.

"Honey!" Mariah jumped up and grabbed Kelsey's hand in hers. "How do you feel?"

"Good. Hungry." Kelsey looked over Mariah's shoulder at Jack. "She doesn't get cranky that often and she makes a great boxed macaroni and cheese."

"You don't have to sell me, Kelsey. I was sold on your mom a long time ago and nothing that's happened has changed my mind. I'd like to ask her to marry me if it's all right with you."

"I think it would be awesome," Kelsey replied. "What do you think, Mom?"

Mariah gazed at the two people she loved more than anyone else on the face of the earth. Did life get any better than this? What a miracle it was that love could heal old wounds, fill up a soul so completely. "I think it's a wonderful idea."

Jack drew her into his arms. "Really?" His gaze held hers intently. She saw her future there, in the glorious green depths.

"Really," she replied half breathlessly.

"Go ahead and kiss," Kelsey said. "You both know you want to. This is so cool. Mom gets a husband and maybe now I can finally get a cell phone."

Jack laughed and lowered his mouth to Mariah's. He tasted of passion and love, of laughter and, more than anything, her future.

Epilogue

"**M**om, hurry up. People are going to start arriving and you aren't even dressed yet," Kelsey exclaimed. Tiny barked as if to punctuate Kelsey's sentence.

Mariah turned from the window and smiled at her daughter. "I'll be right down. I just have to slip on my dress."

"Okay, but hurry." As Kelsey ran down the stairs, Mariah turned back to look out the window and saw Jack sweeping off the sidewalk with a broom.

She smiled as a gust of September air lifted his hair off his forehead and blew the pile of leaves he'd just swept back to the sidewalk. How she loved him.

She tapped on the glass and he looked up at her, his features forming the smile that warmed her from her head to her toes. She waved, blew him a kiss and watched as he went back to work.

Her gaze went beyond him to the grove of trees in the distance, the place where once she'd been a young girl and something bad had happened. That was no longer a place of nightmares. It was just part of the yard.

The leaves on the trees were just beginning to change colors, hinting at the glorious fall colors to come. Mariah loved autumn.

She paused at the window only a moment longer to catch the sparkle of the sun shining on her diamond ring. She and Jack had gotten married two weeks before in a quiet ceremony with just Kelsey and Janice in attendance.

"Mom!" Kelsey called up the stairs with all the impatience of a teenager.

"Coming!" She hurriedly shrugged out of the robe she'd had on and pulled on the red dress that was laid out on the bed.

The housewarming party was set to begin at one. Kelsey had catered all the food and had been cooking for days with both Katie and Ryan Kent as her assistants.

It was obvious Ryan was more interested in making Kelsey laugh than learning to cook, but that was fine with Mariah. She couldn't get enough of the sound of her daughter's laughter.

They'd decided to stay in Plains Point. Together she and Jack had made the final renovations on the house they now called home.

Kelsey had no memories of the night of her attack and for that, Mariah would always be grateful. Initially Mariah had worried about them staying here in town, afraid the gossip would be too much for Kelsey to handle, but the town had rallied behind them.

Clay had been busy piecing together the total picture of Finn's madness and bringing closure to the families of his victims. The ex-jock turned sheriff had handled the entire situation with strength and a quiet confidence that had gained him even more respect from the people he served.

One of the biggest surprises was that Marianne Francis had divorced Roger, who had been having an affair with the mother of one of his football players. Marianne would be one of the guests attending today. Roger hadn't been invited.

As Mariah walked down the stairs to the lower level, she heard the familiar creak of the fourth and fifth stairs. Although the stairs could have been fixed, the creaking silenced, she'd insisted nothing be done. The noise was a reminder of how close death had come and a squeaky nudge to her to remember her blessings.

She was taking this year off, but planned on seeking a teaching position next fall. Life was good, although there were occasional moments when thoughts of a red-haired boy with a sunshine smile intruded.

Finn.

Hannah and her children had moved. The grapevine said they had gone to Oklahoma City to live with Hannah's parents. Mariah hoped they found peace.

When the news got out, everyone was stunned. Finn had been a great father, a loving husband and a friend to many. Nobody had seen a hint of the demons inside him. The rapes had been his desperate need to control, to dominate and release the rage inside.

"Hey, you." Jack came up behind her and wrapped his arms around her.

She turned in his embrace. "Hey, yourself." She smiled, casting away thoughts of Finn and instead falling into the loving eyes of her husband.

"You look ravishing in red," he exclaimed. "You look ravishing naked. How about we blow this joint and head to the nearest motel for a couple of hours of mind-blowing sex?"

"Oh, Dr. Hot, you do make a woman blush," she said with a laugh.

"I'll make you do more than blush later," he replied.

"Is that a promise or a threat?"

His eyes flamed with heat. "That's definitely a promise."

Kelsey poked her head out of the kitchen. "Okay, you two, knock off the mushy stuff. I just saw two cars pulling up the driveway." She disappeared once again into the kitchen.

"You heard her. We have to knock off the mushy stuff," Mariah said as she molded her body closer to him.

"Okay, right after I do this." He bent his head and took her mouth with his in a kiss that held the promise of her happiness.

Within minutes the house rang with laughter as friends arrived. The house that had once held so little love and joy now burst at the seams with it.

The ghosts of the past were silent. There were no more whispers of terror, only the shouts of love. They were building new memories, Mariah and Jack and Kelsey.

She was home. Mariah was truly home.

Read on for a sneak preview of Carla Cassidy's

LAST GASP

Coming in April 2009

The minute Allison and Sam stepped out on the porch to leave the old farmhouse and return home, she saw it—the ominous, rolling black wall of a dust storm. It filled the sky in the distance, like dark billowing smoke driven by a tremendous force beyond the horizon. Allison had seen the natural phenomenon only once before in her life, and that had been on that terrible day fifteen years ago.

"Wow!" Sam exclaimed. "Awesome."

She touched her son's shoulder. "Come on, let's get back in the house. We'll have to wait it out inside," she said. The last thing she wanted was for the two of them to be in the car when the storm struck.

They moved off the porch and back into the house, where Sam ran to the window with a southwest view. "It's getting closer," he said, a hint of fear deepening his voice. What had initially appeared awesome to the twelve-year-old obviously no longer seemed so cool.

Allison moved to stand behind him and placed her hands on his slender shoulders. "I know it looks kind of scary, but it's just wind and dust."

She stared beyond Sam to the approaching mael-strom and, almost hypnotized by the boiling, swirl-ing sight, went back in time, back to when she'd been sixteen years old and on her way home from school.

It had been Ellie Walker who had seen it first. Ellie had squealed in horror as she stared out the window, but nobody had paid much attention to her because Ellie was always squealing about something.

It was only when Jennifer Landers, Ellie's seat mate on the bus, had screamed as well that everyone looked out the window and saw the boiling brown mass descending upon them.

Chaos ensued. The girls screamed and the boys darted from window to window as the bus driver, Mrs. Johnson, yelled for all of them to calm down, to sit down. As the dark cloud approached, the bus began to rock from the force of the wind, and the sky darkened, turning the sunny day into night.

Mrs. Johnson pulled the vehicle off the road and parked as the brunt of the storm hit them. Tumble-weeds and other debris struck the side of the bus as the wind screeched like a banshee.

"It's the end of the world," Ellie screamed, tears coursing down her face. "God's wrath is coming down on us all. Oh, sweet Jesus, forgive me for my sins and deliver me from evil."

"Shut up, Ellie," one of the boys shouted.

"Yeah, it's just a dust storm," somebody else added.

Mary Jacobs, who was seated next to Allison on the bus and was one of her best friends, laughed and grabbed Allison's hand. "Everyone knows the last time Ellie prayed was when she thought she was pregnant and prayed for a period."

Allison laughed, too, but she squeezed tight to Mary's hand until the storm passed and the sun once again began to shine.

"Show's over," the bus driver said, and started the engine to finish delivering the students to their bus stops.

Ellie got off the bus at her stop; then it was time for Allison to do the same. She climbed off the bus and waved to her classmates as she noticed that the black cloud of dirt had moved northward.

The first thing she was going to do when she got inside was take a shower. Even though the bus windows had been up, the dust had seeped in through the minute cracks and crevices and swirled in the air. She felt grimy with it. She smiled as she thought of her little sister and brother in the house with her mom.

She'd bet her mother had spun a story to ease the fears of the two young kids, and, knowing her mother, it would have been a story about a princess saved from the evil dust monster by a handsome prince. If there was one thing Joleen Donovan loved, it was telling fairy tales where dragons were slain and princesses and princes lived happily ever after.

The porch was covered with a layer of dirt as she climbed the stairs to the front door. She couldn't wait to get inside and tell her mom that she'd aced her English test, that Bobby had asked her to go to the prom and that silly Ellie had thought the dust storm was the end of the world.

She'd had no warning of what was to come, no sense of foreboding about the horror that awaited her.

"Mom?" she called as she flung open the door. She

took three steps into the room and saw her mother seated on the sofa. Joleen wore her favorite pink flowered duster and was sitting where she always sat to watch *General Hospital*.

Her head. For a moment Allison couldn't make sense of it. Joleen's head wasn't where it belonged. Rather than being on her neck, on her shoulders, it was in her lap. It was only then that Allison smelled it, the rich copper scent of blood, the raw, ugly scent of death. She opened her mouth to scream, but never released the sound of her horror as she was struck over the head from behind and knew no more.

"Mom! You're hurting me!"

She slammed back to the present with Sam wiggling to escape the biting imprints of her fingernails in the top of his shoulders. She dropped her hands and backed away from the window. "I'm sorry, honey. Move back. I don't want you standing in front of the glass."

She tasted the tang of blood and realized she'd bitten the inside of her mouth as she'd remembered that day. What had happened to Mary Jacobs? Funny, Allison had never seen her again after that day on the bus when they had held hands and laughed, not knowing the nightmare that Allison would face.

The storm now fell upon the little farmhouse. The room darkened and the house began to creak and groan beneath the onslaught of the wind. A thud sounded against the outside wall. "What was that?" Sam asked, his eyes wide as they stood in the center of the living room area.

Probably a poor bird, disoriented from the storm,

she mused, but she didn't speak the thought aloud. Sam was so softhearted, he'd want to go outside to see if the bird could be saved. "Just trash or something picked up by the wind," she replied.

"How long will this last?" Sam asked, and shot a worried glance back toward the window, where it was almost as dark as night.

"Not long." At least that's what she hoped.

"Will we be safe in here?" His forehead furrowed with little lines of worry.

She offered him a reassuring smile. "We should be fine. This old place might look like a mess, but it was built strong. Why don't you show me some of those karate moves of yours?" she asked. "You have all this space." She gestured around the empty room, then forced a smile. "And you have me as a captive audience."

She needed something, anything, to take her mind off the dust storm. The memories it had evoked in her tried to take hold of her once again, to pull her back to that day when her entire world had exploded apart, when a killer had beaten her home and taken from her everything she loved.

As Sam began his first series of movements, her head filled with the vision of her mother's milky blue eyes, of that single moment when she'd tried to make sense of what had happened. In the single instant just before she'd been struck unconscious, she'd seen the blood everywhere, as if a crazed painter had tried to turn the room red. This room, right here where she and Sam stood. Her mother had been murdered here, along with her little brother and sister.

And she should have died as well. The killer had meant for her to die.

She smiled and nodded at her son as her mind filled with the horror and the wind shrieked around the farmhouse like a loosed wild beast. It will be over in a minute, she thought. The storm will pass and we'll go back to our house, back to our lives, and we won't ever come here again.

"That's great, Sam," she said as he finished a series of moves. She glanced toward the window and saw there was no change in the darkness of the sky. How long could it last? She already felt as if she'd been trapped in this house of death for an eternity.

She and Sam both jumped as the front door flew open and a swirl of thick dust entered like an unwelcomed guest. Allison had taken two steps toward the door to close it when he appeared in the doorway, a man in jeans and a T-shirt, wearing a ski mask. In his hands he held a hatchet.

For a moment she thought he was a horrifying phantom from her past, a specter of evil conjured up from her imagination. But as he took a step forward and his boot echoed on the wooden floor, as Sam gasped and ran to her side, she knew he wasn't from her imagination.

He was real.

He was death.

She'd escaped him fifteen years ago and now he was back to claim her.